To Exist

Ashley Boynes-Shuck

ISBN 978-0-6926-7404-8
ISBN 978-1-4958-0479-3 eBook
Library of Congress Catalog Card Number Pending

Published April 2016
Sick Idiot Imprint
Second Edition

Cover Design by Matthew Shuck
mattshuck.com

Dedication

My debut novel is dedicated to: my entire family, including my endlessly-supportive (and loving) parents and husband, to my amazing friends who have always encouraged me to be myself and follow my dreams, and to all of my teachers who always pushed me to pursue my passion for writing.

ACKNOWLEDGEMENTS

First and foremost, I want to acknowledge the NaNoWriMo (National Novel Writing Month) initiative that first inspired me to write this novel back in 2012. I must also thank my mother Sharon Boynes and husband Mike Shuck, who read the earliest versions of the book and provided helpful feedback, and also my dad, Rick Boynes, who, in addition to my mom and husband, has helped me to fund this journey.

A special thank-you goes out to Carol Killman Rosenberg who edited the first draft of my book, and literary agent Linda Langton who guided me in the early stages of this project.

Lastly, I'd like to give a shout-out to Mrs. Paula Johannes who was my Gifted and Talented Enrichment teacher at South Fayette Elementary School. Thank you, Mrs. J. for encouraging me to embrace my creativity, take pride in my uniqueness, cultivate my love of words, and to write, write, write!

Chapter 1

I awoke, alone, cold, and disoriented. The state of shock I was experiencing was not conducive to feeling much of anything, let alone fear. In my bewilderment and exhaustion, I didn't even have the wits to panic. Survival mode set in, and I had the urge to run. I didn't know why, or even where I would go, but I felt it deep in my bones that something was terribly wrong.

I stood up. Big mistake. My entire body ached, quivering as though I'd never stood before. I tried again, like a fawn gaining its legs for the first time. I knew I needed to ignore the dizziness, the mental cloud that set over me, the rapid pace of my heart. This was no time for frailty. Taking deep breaths, I steadied myself, and looked around. Where was I?

Rubble surrounded me. All I saw was gray. All I smelled was dust and death. My eyes burned, head pounded, throat ached. The feeling of urgency came again: I felt claustrophobic, and I needed to leave.

Now.

Fighting the desire to collapse, I listened to my gut and fled towards the expanse of nothingness. I just ran, my legs pumping under me, the parts of my body working in unison, a choir harmonizing to help me escape whatever it was that I was escaping.

Darkness seemed to part as a crack of light appeared, and I picked up my pace, sprinting towards it. Climbing through rock and destruction, I moved carefully through the crevice. Astounded, I surveyed the scene before me. It was unlike anything I'd ever seen before. It was unlike anything anyone had ever seen before.

Bodies lie sprawled about, everywhere. An eerie calm contrasted the chaos of the scene. Stray dogs devoured human flesh. A smattering of children lay dead near a daycare center, clinging to the teachers' lifeless, blood-soaked bosoms and their torn and tattered teddy bears. I felt the urge to vomit.

How long was I unconscious? Was I a lone survivor? I wasn't sure. I thought I heard a groan nearby, but I couldn't be certain. I wondered if I was hallucinating, but I nonetheless glanced at the pile of rock and wood to my left. There was a hand – complete with hot pink fingernails and a huge, glistening diamond upon it – sticking out of the debris, as though waving for help. While my instinct for survival and self-preservation was at an all-time high, I couldn't leave this woman behind. I grasped her hand in my own and pulled, saying a silent prayer that this newfound companion could help me to make sense of it all.

I struggled to hoist the well-manicured lady into her salvation, but was taken by surprise as I found myself holding an arm: a bodiless, ownerless, arm. An arm with no person. I flung the perfectly-pink, severed limb away from me, as though it had scorched my own skin.

So, this was my new normal, then? I let out a shriek, immediately realizing that this may be a deadly mistake. Quickly, I clasped my hands – the hands that just held a corpse appendage – over my mouth, willing the screams and the vomit to stay contained within me. I stood there for a moment in sheer bewilderment, choking back tears and beginning to hyperventilate before passing out to blackness.

"Hey there."

I heard the gentle words, and felt a cool, slightly damp cloth on my forehead. Once again, I woke up feeling disoriented, only this time, I wasn't alone. I had no idea how much time had passed.

I struggled to open my eyes, and when I did, I found myself staring into the face of a large black man who I'd never seen before. He had a friendly, round face, and caring, concerned eyes. It was hard to tell his age: his hair was gray from ashes and dust, leaving no hint as to its original hue.

"Hello," he said again.

"H-hi." I managed to stutter shyly, still in a state of vast confusion. It wouldn't be the first time I had questioned my sanity, and idly, I wondered if I was dreaming. Or dead.

I stared thoughtfully at the man. Many women would be unnerved to awake to a strange guy in a strange place, but he made me feel content and comfortable in a way that I could not explain.

"I'm Owen," he said, helping me to sit up and extending a beefy hand, which I left awkwardly hanging as it awaited a shake.

"Shelby," I said, introducing myself, arms crossed with a still-lingering uncertainty.

Looking around, I began to panic. Maybe I *should* be scared, after all. It looked like I was in a cave, and caves were not something with which I'd been familiar, prior to this new existence.

"I don't have much," Owen said, "but I do have some chicken broth and green tea. We have to be conservative, but let's get you warmed up and nourished."

I picked up on the "we" in that statement, and it made me feel safer, somehow. "We" meant that I wasn't in this alone.

While Owen prepared the food, I began to recall flashes of memory. I remembered preparing for the unprecedented storm with my roommate in Brooklyn. I remember fires and looting, flooding and damage. I remembered fleeing to my parents' comfortable basement. But, what happened next? How did we go from there to here? And where was my roomate? My mind felt cloudy, but I knew that I wasn't in Brooklyn. I remember going to my childhood home.

Beyond that, my memories seemed scattered, and out of order. I remembered running out of the structure earlier that day. What I saw was a town that was obliterated, littered with lives that were no more. I sifted through my memories: piles of ashes where there were once buildings, boats in the street, cars overturned, bridges destroyed, with woods in the distance, as nature looked on. I saw dead bodies. Everywhere I looked there was blood and heartache. I saw vast stretches of nothing and no one, where there used to be people and traffic and hustle and bustle in this upstate New York town center. Simply put, this was not the hometown I'd remembered.

Another flash of memory from before my awakening: an explosion. Running. A mob of people in hysterics. But why?

"What happened?" I asked Owen, awkwardly, because I knew it was going to be a loaded answer.

"Honey, let's eat. We have all the time in the world to talk."

Though I highly doubted that, it was a simpler response than I'd been anticipating, but surprisingly, a welcome one. I wanted to know, of course: how I'd gotten there, who he was, where I was, and what disastrous series of events had indeed taken place. But, my mind and body were exhausted, presumably from the constant fight-or-flight reactions taking place within me. My intuition said to just let this moment happen. Rest. Eat. At my core, I instinctively knew I was going to need strength and nourishment, and I sensed that food may be scarce.

While I finished my soup, Owen tended to the fire. I observed our meager surroundings more closely, taking stock. No furniture. A few blankets. A couple of pillows. A small kettle over a fledgling fire. Coals. Flashlights. A lantern. A backpack. A Bible. A whistle. A lighter. Some packs of Ramen noodles; a box of tea bags; some snack-sized boxes of raisins; and a large quantity of peanuts likely bought in bulk at a big box store. A bucket. A cloth. Bottles of water, that were undoubtedly dwindling in quantity. A First Aid kit. Knives. Crisco. Rope. A faded photograph of a woman – his wife, his daughter? I wasn't sure. What I was sure, of, though, is that Owen seemed prepared. Whatever had happened, and whatever would happen, we – yes, this was now a "we" situation – had provisions.

"So. The storm. You remember the storm?"

Owen snapped me out of my daze.

I cleared my throat, "Yes. I mean, mostly."

"Unprecedented. We thought it would be one for the record books, but we never thought it would lead to a practical apocalypse. The forecasters told us it would be of biblical proportions – so we did as best we knew how, following the guidelines of what we usually would do: sandbags, flashlights, batteries, canned goods, you know. The usual. Some people evacuated.

We didn't – and we luckily survived the storms. Even had a radio for a while. The news was depressing. The hurricane basically paralyzed the entire East Coast and parts of the Midwest. Last I heard, a separate storm was ravaging our West Coast. Quakes, and a record-breaker of a tsunami. Between both superstorms, and all of the climate changes over the past few years, Alaska is probably the U.S. state that had a chance of survival, to be honest. And who would have ever thought it? The folks on the news would cultivate their clever headlines, talkin' that Mother Nature was a terrorist. What no one could have expected, though, was that actual, real terrorists would take advantage of our weakness while all this was goin' on. From Sin City to the Big Apple … done, in one fell swoop."

I gasped a little. "The explosions," I interrupted, piecing that part of the puzzle together, vaguely rustling up some more faded memories. They had to have been bombs of some sort.

"All hell broke lose. It was literally like hell on earth. Just about our whole country, obliterated. No means of communication, all of our infrastructure, wiped out. Looked like those zombie apocalypse flicks or something from the sci-fi channel. Lotsa folks didn't even make it through the storms, then so many people died from the first bomb and its aftermath … it's been surreal. The rest of us who'd survived, we just fled. Utter chaos. Marta and me – Marta's my wife – we had emergency bags packed. Brought our dog Pippa along and just left. Left our home, left our neighborhood, left our friends – we just needed to get out. We were always prepared, nothing crazy, you know. Not outlandish, just practical and cautious. But still – we were always prepared, but nonetheless, nothing could prepare you for this. Not ever, in my opinion. People went nuts. Trying to rob us, trying to steal our water, our backpacks. Everyone screaming, crying, running to nothing and nowhere. Lots of violence. At one point, we got separated from our poor Pippa. She had become skittish and lil' girl got spooked by a noise. At that point we were so distraught and exhausted that it was not even a conscious decision. We had to look out for ourselves. So we just...we just left her. We looked briefly, and just couldn't find her ... but we could have tried harder, I guess. She was never a burden. She was scared and we should have done more to protect her but...we had to keep going."

His voice cracked at that point, and he took a shaky breath. He shook his head, with his chin quivering, and tears woefully glistening in his eyes, and reflected in my own. His guilt and the heartache, well ... it was palpable.

"We made it to this place before the second explosion, Marta and me, I mean. It seems to have been an old bomb shelter or some kind of hideaway from the prohibition days. At any rate, we hit the jackpot finding it. There aren't many secret underground rooms like this one, not in a boring ol' town like this, at least. Had to fight off some young men – teenagers – but we made it. Marta said God was looking out for us. But she...well...Marta was hysterical, worried about the dog. When I fell asleep, she must have gone out looking for her. When I woke up, she was nowhere to be found. I got up to go find them, just as there was another explosion. No Marta, no Pippa. Naturally, I presume they've perished. All you could hear was screams, and then silence. Just silence. Nothing. No one. Dead."

I let Owen cry. I cried with him. What response could be adequate, after that story? Too great was the loss of life; too real was the loss of his wife, his dog; and our former selves. The loss of our nation, of most of humanity. It was far too much loss to properly mourn. I didn't know how to act; I wasn't sure how to manage my emotions anymore. I felt overwhelmed with anxiety and grief, even as I shared these burdens with Owen. Though I didn't know him, I already felt a special bond with this man.

"I went to look for them every day, for a few days, you know. I heard you whimpering near the old bank building early this morning. Judging by the sun, probably 5am or so. I do not know the date. You were barely conscious. I rescued you and brought you back here. You, girly, are the only life I've seen since that second explosion."

We sat in silence punctuated by sadness. At some point, fatigue consumed me, and I helplessly, gratefully gave in to sleep.

CHAPTER 2

I squinted as I awoke with a start. It was hard to know what time it was, what day it was, or even if it was all real. I felt as though I was trapped inside a nightmare, or perhaps I was dead already and this was all fiction, my soul playing a trick on me before I settled into the fabled reward of a rumored Heaven. My thoughts felt scattered; I still couldn't piece together this puzzle, and it was all too much to absorb.

"Ouch," I thought, slowly stretching. Amongst other aches and pains, my forearm was throbbing. I glanced down and noticed a blackened bruise that spread from my palm right up to the crux of my elbow. The contusion puzzled me, at first, but a foggy cobwebbed memory from the week before the disaster came trickling into my mind: the clinical trial. Ah, yes. I sighed.

Owen sat like a guard watching over me as I rest. He took a swig of whiskey – a ration that I'd overlooked in my earlier surveillance of the scene. He held the bottle out to me, solemnly.

I took a drink, equally solemnly. He then handed me the cloth. I hadn't even been aware of the hot tears rolling in fat drops down my dirty face. Suddenly, I became racked with sobs – the violent, heaving kind that are bordering on painful, the kind that make you want to laugh because they feel good, in some twisted, tormented way.

Although I couldn't truly wrap my mind around what was going on, and even though I was certainly still in a state of shock, the unabsorbed reality had apparently become too much to bear. I didn't have to know all of the facts, or remember all of the details. I didn't need to grasp it just yet, but almost by sheer instinct, the enormity of the situation came washing over me, wave after wave, until I sank once again into the oblivion of sleep, and, for the moment, all was calm.

My dreams that night were beautiful. If I'd had the gift of hindsight, I'd venture to say that they were memories – my brain's way of piecing together my life before the catastrophe.

I dreamt of Tamra, my roommate. Davis and Daphne, my best friends. Ezra, my ex-fiancé. Jared, the proverbial boy next door and the unrequited love of my life. My parents, Tony and Estelle. My grandma Pat who had passed on years ago. My cat Biggie, who I had as a child. Old teachers, members of my yoga class, the pets I'd fostered, co-workers at jobs I'd since forgotten. They all showed up, here and there, in the Technicolor dreams of that night. I saw Audrey Hepburn, who I'd always idolized, and CS Lewis, whose works I'd loved to read.

Owen showed up in my dream. Owen was surrounded by an aura of color, but when he appeared, the world went dark. I didn't know what it meant, but my vivid dreams turned to black-and-white, tones of sepia, and gray. So much gray. I saw an old television, playing a video of an atomic bomb, over and over. And then I saw a little girl – was it me? – who whispered "hope."

Everything felt wet and sticky. I started to panic. Was the girl a symbol of the calm before another literal or figurative storm? Was this the actual end? In a state of utter panic, I awoke, staring into the eyes of a dog. A Corgi, to be precise. The dog fervently licked my face, which explained the wet, sticky atmosphere of my dream as I transitioned from a state of sleep to wake.

A tsunami of joy crashed upon me as I realized that this could be – no, it *had* to be – Pippa.

"Owen!" I yelled.

He awoke with urgency, and saw me grinning ear-to-ear, for the first time since he'd known me, as I pet the dog.

"Pippa!" he cried, with big, happy tears streaming down his face, and his grin matching mine.

As I watched the obliviously happy dog joyfully reuniting with her owner, I sensed that the little girl in the dream was right.

There was hope.

There had to be, right?

Chapter 3

The days to follow were laced with fear and uncertainty, but also ultimately boring, and long. They were hard, and I was hungry. Owen, Pippa, and I had settled into a routine. Our existence was just that: existing, and not much more. We were in survival-mode, with meager means to meager ends, and we certainly weren't living. Not really.

Owen and I didn't discuss our loved ones. We'd accepted what was almost inevitable: they were gone. From what we could tell, it could be days, weeks, or even months before we saw another human being. It could be an eternity before we'd see our family and friends. We both cried a lot, but didn't talk about it much. I knew Owen mourned Marta. He held her picture to his heart, any chance he got. Pippa would snuggle up close to Owen or me if one of us were feeling especially blue. Dogs sense these things.

My stomach hurt. The acidity born of emptiness was almost unbearable, but, I would survive. I made it this far — for some reason — so I had to survive. I just had to. That question, though: "why?"

It haunted me. "Why have I made it this far?" I know, "Why me?" sounded so cliché. "Why me?" was usually whiny — it was usually a complaint that cowards made in order to collect sympathy and cultivate pity. Those things certainly weren't my nature, and yet, here I was asking, "why me?" For me, though, it was more a question of bewilderment, and of fear. I didn't know what I was feeling. Why was I alive, when so many others were not? I wasn't complaining, but I was perplexed: why was I here, instead of, say, Marta? Tamra? My parents? Why me? Why did I get to breathe another breath, and see another day? Was it a privilege, or a punishment? Was this purgatory, or just a living hell? Why? Why? Why?

I felt conflicted. On one hand, I was, of course, thankful to be alive, especially given the battle I'd been fighting since before all of this began. It's a natural instinct for us as human beings: we strive to live, and, for most of us, we strive to live as best we can. So, there was that. I was here, I was alive.

But on the other hand, I didn't know if I wanted to be. Alive, that is. There just didn't seem to be much good in it, anymore. What was the point? What was the value in my life if I wasn't sharing it with my loved ones, and if no one was there to witness it?

If a tree falls in the forest, and no one is around to hear it, does it make a sound? If a person is alive, and no one is around to realize it, does their existence even matter? Was there any way for that life to be validated? Was there any way for my life to matter anymore?

I didn't know the answers. I also felt as though it was extremely unfair that I was still here. I was sick before the disaster, probably bound to die a young death, regardless, and yet, I somehow got to live, while perfectly healthy people perished? Me, an imperfect person. I got to live. Others who were far better people than me had died. I just didn't understand. It almost seemed to be some kind of vicious joke.

I was glad Owen was with me, though. At least he, and Pippa, could bear witness to my life, or what was left of it. Maybe they could make me matter. In this dark hour, I could support him, and he, me. I trusted him. We were becoming friends, or, perhaps more like family. So, I knew I wasn't truly alone, but I still wondered "why me?" and I suspected that Owen did, too. Why us?

"I have cancer." I said. I would say that I'd said it out of the clear blue sky, except we hadn't seen the sky for days — and when we had, it certainly wasn't blue. We rarely ventured out, and when we did, it was hard to see anything but dust. Everywhere.

Sharing this news with Owen was like a knife to my stomach. It was the first time I'd said the words out loud to anyone but my doctor, and I immediately regretted saying it to Owen. I felt almost guilty to add extra burden to this man who already had so many burdens to bear.

"What?" he asked, incredulously.

"Well, I knew for a while that I had the markers for breast cancer, and, even though I was young, my doctors kept an eye on it because it ran in my family. My last mammogram came back with some spots that appeared to show malignancy or, at the very least, pre-malignancy. We all thought that was the worst thing that would ever happen to us. To me. I was so scared. Now..."

My voice trailed off.

"I'm sorry," he said.

"No, I'm sorry," I said. "Sorry, it really isn't a big deal..." I trailed off, unconvincingly. He gave me a hug. It was a big deal. We both knew it. It used to be the most horrific part of my existence; now it almost seemed like an afterthought.

My words were appallingly insufficient. I didn't know what else to say – nothing could really make the situation okay. I was dealing with a potentially deadly illness, and he had every semblance of normal life swept away in a storm, and then, his wife was swept away by a storm of violence. Our families were dead. Our friends were dead. Food and water were scarce. Safety was far from a given. Neither one of us was doing so hot.

All he had was Pippa and me.

All I had was him and Pippa.

We looked at one another, and smiled our sad, sullen smiles. What else was there to do, after all?

–

Sleep came easy after our story-swapping night by the fire. During the course of the evening, I learned that Owen had taken up painting as a hobby; he learned that I took ballet. That night I dreamt of Pippa and us, frolicking in a field of ashes, under a gray sun. The only colors were those on his canvas. The only soundtrack was the Nutcracker ballet suite.

I awoke to a growl. Pippa was uncharacteristically on edge. It sent chills right through me, and sent my intuition into high gear. Owen was awake, too. What was it? What could be upsetting the dog?

"Shelby, stay here. Keep Pippa close. I'll be back."

He picked up a knife. I panicked. Owen wasn't elderly, by any means, but he was no young buck, either – and I could only speculate about his present state of health, given our circumstances.

"I'll come with you!" I urged.

He looked at me with stern, steely eyes. I knew the answer was a fatherly, resounding no.

Pippa and I waited. We heard nothing, but then again, we were very secluded and thankfully pretty protected where we were staying. I didn't expect to hear anything, really, but Pippa's ears were perked up, standing tall, listening to whatever it was that she was hearing out there in what was left of this world.

The moments passed. I couldn't tell you how long we were waiting; time wasn't something that I was re-acclimated to just yet, in our new environment which lacked phones and clocks and computers. It was beyond difficult to get used to our new lives, and it was taking a lot of adaptation. I didn't have a very good concept of time before the tragedy, and I certainly didn't now. Time seemed to be completely arbitrary in this new day and age, yet, on the other hand, it was all that mattered. It was all we had, all we fought for. It was what we measured our lives by, after all. Time: a precious gift and our worst enemy, all rolled into one.

Speaking of, Owen was taking too much time, out there all by himself. I couldn't wait any longer. My worry for Owen was outweighing any concern I had for myself. I wasn't as worried about Pippa – she'd been gone on her own out there, for God knows how long, and she made it, even if Marta hadn't. If Pippa made it, so could I. Together, we made our way out to find Owen. It took a minute for me to adjust: wind was foreign, and the night was cold, and crisp. I saw my breath. The darkness wasn't a problem. I was becoming used to having minimal light.

I could faintly make out voices; they sounded far away. We hid behind some rubble and I tiptoed closer. Pippa wouldn't leave my side, for which I was immensely grateful.

"Have you seen a girl?" a gruff voice demanded. It was a voice I'd never heard before, and one I wasn't very fond of.

"I told you, I ain't seen no girl. I'll keep an eye out for her. Tell me about her," Owen said, with a placating tone in his voice.

"My pal said he saw a young girl, 'round this area. Awhile back. Running. Dark hair. Pretty. White. Tall and fit. Said she was hot; looked to be in her 20s or 30s," the man told Owen.

I gasped. It could have been a descriptor for a number of women, but, it had to have been me. After all, we'd barely seen anyone else in the days since I'd been acquainted with Owen. I suddenly realized that we definitely had not seen any other young females. I wondered if I should be relieved that someone was looking for me, or alarmed. My instinct was that this wasn't a friendly inquiry. I didn't recognize the voice, and it somehow chilled me to the bone. At the same time, though, I clung to a glimmer of hope that he could be here to rescue me. Maybe my family was alive after all; maybe they'd sent someone. I doubted myself the moment I thought it. Owen seemed to share in my skepticism.

Owen laughed nervously, "I certainly have not seen any hot young girls around these parts, my friend. I wish!" he said with a guffaw. I could almost picture him forcing a wink.

"We haven't seen any women at all. But I can't see why he'd lie. So no girl?" said the gruff stranger, with an almost ravenous tone in his voice.

The general lascivious undercurrent in his words confirmed my sense that this was not someone with whom I'd want to become acquainted. I knew inherently that he was, in fact, asking about me. I hadn't seen any women, but, then again, I hadn't seen many men, either. I'd only seen Owen. I didn't know what to make of it. Just then, I heard a growl forming in Pippa's throat.

"No! No girl!" I frantically whispered.

She took off towards the direction of Owen and the man. I couldn't see what was going on from where I was hidden, but I could hear a struggle ensuing. I prayed to a God I hadn't prayed to in years, hoping that Owen and the dog would be okay.

Suddenly, there was silence. I couldn't stay put at my station any longer, and ran towards the scene. Before I could get there, Owen appeared before me, with Pippa trailing along. Owen held a mustard-colored canvas bag in one hand, his knife in the other, and he wore a blank expression on his face. I didn't ask questions, I just fell in line and we headed back to our abode.

"Owen..." I started, once we got settled in.

"I don't want to talk at the moment," he said, calmly.

I gave him his space, but watched as he removed items from the stranger's bag.

Band-aids, a canteen, a pocket knife, a bag of what appeared to be beef jerky, 2 cans of beer, a rotted apple, a pencil, some crumpled newspaper, two fingerless gloves, one mitten, some batteries, a slice of cheese, bullets, and – Hallelujah! – a handheld CB radio. I knew Owen didn't want to talk, but, with trepidation, I asked him if we could use any of the items, particularly, the radio.

"I sure hope so. Don't know if we'll be able to communicate with anyone, but, you never know. We can try to get this radio working. Another hobby of mine," he winked.

After Owen tinkered around with the radio for what seemed to be a couple of hours, we sat down to eat. The beef jerky was a treat. We ate very small pieces and shared a small bite with Pippa, who was barely eating more than the occasional tufts of grass or animal carcasses that we'd stumble upon here and there. As for Owen and I, we couldn't eat too much, as we had to conserve food as best we could. We picked apart the apple, which tasted rancid, and likely was, but, it was better than nothing. The cheese was also smelling foul, so we figured we'd better eat that before it was completely rotten, too. That half an apple, small bite of beef jerky, and half a rotting slice of cheese was the best meal I'd had in what seemed like a very, very long time.

"What happened to the guy?" I finally asked.

Owen sighed. "I stabbed him. He went after Pippa when she ran over, and then in the scuffle, tried to attack me, too. Plus, he was a little too interested in you. So, I stabbed him," he said matter-of-factly.

He shrugged. "He ran away. So he's not dead, at least he wasn't as of then."

That made me feel both pleased, as I didn't want to picture Owen as a murderer, and disturbed, as I wasn't sure I wanted the gruff stranger to be out there running around when he could be after me. I don't know why, but the more that I thought about it, his voice, and the way he talked about me like a commodity, gave me the heebie-jeebies.

"Did you hear what he was asking about, Shelby?" he asked me. He seemed uneasy. Whether it was about the stabbing, or what the man said, I did not know.

"I did. Should we be concerned?" I replied.

"I will tell you this, girlie. I haven't seen another female around. The last woman I saw was my wife. I don't know what this means, or what it means for you, or how it could even be logical, but you just have to consider the laws of supply and demand. Can't imagine romancin' is on anyone's mind right now, but when people get bored, and lonely, they get desperate. People can be crazy." I shuddered. He repeated, "People can be crazy..."

"Well. I am certainly not in the mood for romancin', either," I joked, trying to lighten the mood.

Owen laughed, to be polite, I assume, and then, as if struck with a revelation, asked me gently, "Shelby, did you leave anyone behind? Boyfriend, husband?" Then quickly added, "or girlfriend?"

I giggled at his attempted political correctness. It was endearing.

"No boyfriend. I was engaged once, but it was a toxic relationship. His name was Ezra. We were together for about 5 years. We brought each other down, though. We definitely weren't our best selves together. We were codependent. There was drama. I was stifled. Plus, even though I really did love Ezra, my heart always belonged to someone else."

"Oh?" Owen said, raising an eyebrow. "Go on."

"Well, his name was Jared. We'd grown up together. We were neighbors, like family, always close, you know? Most people thought we'd get married someday. I think on both our parts, there was always the wondering, 'what if?' We had little flings, if you will, but we never ended up dating. We were still close, though, until I met Ezra. Jared disappeared from my life. He stopped calling, and I guess he stopped caring.

I don't know if he had just moved on, but, he was suddenly gone. I, for one, felt like this great love was lost. I'll never know if he felt the same. I dreamt about him every night, even when I was with Ezra. I still do, sometimes. I always wished that Jared knew how I felt, and I don't know if he did. I wish he'd known, even though I suspect that he didn't feel the same. If he did, I wouldn't have known it. Put it this way – he wasn't vocal about feelings, he was a bit of a womanizer, and never really took anything seriously, let alone me. I don't know that he would have ever settled down, and if so, I don't know if I'd have been the one. But, man, did I love him, Owen. I really did. I loved him so much that it hurt sometimes. Even when I hated him, I loved him. And now, it's too late. It's just too late."

I was suddenly overcome with grief. Of course, I missed my old life, my parents, my family, and my friends, but I already cried over them more than I'd ever thought possible. And before this all happened, they all knew how much I had loved them. I made it a point to always let the people in my life know that I cared. I of course still thought about them all the time, and the grief was unbearable. But while I thought of Jared often, too, this was the first time I really let myself mourn the relationship – or lack thereof – that was long gone even before the catastrophe struck. They all knew I loved them; Jared never would. That was the difference and here we were. It was just too late.

Then a wave of anxiety hit me. The reality was blinding: it was too late for a lot of things. Life, as we knew it, was over. This was the first time I was able to truly realize that, and consider what it meant. This was not some temporary game that would soon be over. This wasn't a survival contest on reality television. This was real, very real, and this was it. This was all I had. So yes, it was too late.

It was too late to tell Jared I loved him. It was too late to get married, to have a baby, to buy a home, to build the career that I wanted, to travel the world, and to write a hit movie. It was too late to go to a ballet in Russia, or visit the oldest Chanel store in the world, or watch my kids graduate, go to college, and have spouses and kids of their own. I was likely never going to go to the beach again, or lazily roll out of my comfy, cozy bed late on a Sunday morning to head to Starbucks for a latte and a writing session. I was not going to have book club anymore. I was never going to eat another pizza, or drink another smoothie, or have another martini at a swanky and overpriced, fleetingly hip nightclub. I was probably never going to have new clothing, new underwear, or clean hair. Fresh breath was a thing of the past. Shaving was obsolete. A bubble bath was a distant memory. I was not going to be able to go to the movies and order the biggest popcorn possible and drool over my favorite movie stars. My favorite movie stars were probably dead, and so were my dreams. So, unless I was going to marry Owen and start a family with him, this was it. I was alone. Soon there would just be nothing. Soon I would be dead like everyone else. Was that good or bad? I didn't know, but it wasn't a pleasant or welcome thought, either way.

With each new realization of what I'd never have, the panic within me grew. There were no tears: I was all cried out.

I felt my pulse accelerate. I had trouble breathing. My palms were sweating, my entire body was shaking. Soon I was hyperventilating. My fists were clenched, my mouth was cottony, and my heart was pounding faster than any heart ever should. I thought my chest and my head were going to explode. I had goosebumps, and felt dizzy. I was nauseous. I felt hot and cold at the very same time. I was exhausted and antsy, simultaneously. Something and nothing hurt. Oh my God. Was this it? Was I dying? Were the exhaustion, malnutrition, and certain dehydration finally getting to me? Oh, God, was it the cancer? I tried to catch my breath. I tried to move, but I was frozen. I wanted to die, but at the same time, I didn't. I was overcome with fear. I glanced at a concerned Owen, and cried out for help.

CHAPTER 4

It became clear that I'd had a panic attack. Owen said he'd never seen one so intense, but, with a mother who suffered from severe anxiety, he knew what to look out for, and I'd had all of the classic signs. My own past was also spotted with anxiety. It was an undercurrent throughout my whole adult life, but it had never gotten to this point, and I wondered if this new existence, combined with my unstable state of health, was just far too much for me to handle, physically and emotionally. It was not something that I had bargained for – but then again, who had? If Owen could handle it, after all he'd been through, certainly I could, too, right?

Oddly enough, though, I felt like my anxiety stemmed from more than the current state of the world and all the events leading up to it – cancer included. It felt as though there were even more underlying feelings driving the panic. The weight of loss was crushing, and I was drowning in the feelings of inadequacy brought upon me by unfinished dreams and unmet goals. Had I wasted my life? My parents and my friends, who were once my rocks and my strongholds, were now presumably gone. They'd all vanished within a tick of the minute-hand on my mom's old grandfather clock, which was also now surely washed away or blown to pieces. The sense of incompletion was stifling. I had to get out. I was a runner in my "former life," and I'd be a runner now.

"Owen, I need to get out of here. I need to go for a run, to clear my mind. I quite literally feel like I am going crazy. I'm suffocating. Please, Owen. Please," I begged.

"Shelby, you're a grown woman, and I can't very well tell you what to do, but I'm going to ask you to stay put. Please, I implore you. It could be dangerous out there. We don't know what we're dealing with, who's where, what's going on...it's just not worth the risk. I let Marta out of my sight and ... and I just can't do the same with you."

Like a petulant little child, I pouted. Sure, I could have left...but I knew, in the deepest part of my heart and in the background of my busy mind, that Owen was right. The general "not-knowing" was adding to my anxiety even more, though. I had to get out. I was feeling claustrophobic, and to say I had cabin fever would be putting it mildly. I needed to explore my present world, and to clear my mind as best I could.

"Come with me?" I asked.

Owen sighed.

"I'm not a runner, but we can take a walk. We should see if there's any more resources available for us to take, anyway. I guess it is about time that we do a more thorough survey a little farther out, and see what's good for the taking. Pippa could use the exercise, too. Poor girl," he replied, petting the dog.

We gathered up some necessities: the knife and pocketknife, a bottle of water, and a few band-aids, just in case. Owen slathered his face with Crisco. I didn't even question it, and did the same.

"Owen, what are we doing?" I asked, trying to suppress a giggle. Nothing was funny these days, but buttering up my face was certainly something new.

"Old Army trick that my brother taught me. It'll help protect our face from the wind, will help our lips from drying out, will keep in some moisture and warmth."

I wasn't sure if this was fact, or just some old wives' tale, but, I wasn't in a position to question anything or anyone. This was about surviving, and preserving what we had. If preventing windburn or chapped lips was a part of it, great. At the very least, maybe my skin would thank me. I'm sure the events had aged me quite a bit.

I laughed out loud at that thought. The old me was still in there, somewhere, if I was thinking about stress-induced worry lines and wrinkles in the midst of all of this. Maybe there was hope for us, yet. Maybe, just maybe, life would return to a normalcy where worrying about aging skin or a "muffin top" hanging over my jeans would be my biggest problem in life. But then, I thought of the cancer. Perhaps, my life would never return to normal, after all.

"Let's go!" Owen hollered, shaking me out of my daze, and off we went, my shallow musings hanging in the air like a question mark.

As we stepped into the openness, I noticed that the dust was settling a bit. A terrestrial cloud no longer lingered in the air. The wind was bitter and cold, but not as strong as it was the last time I was outside. The town was surely not what it used to be. It was sad, so sad, but even sadder than the decrepit buildings were the ever-present rotting bodies. It looked like a horror film, and smelled unlike anything I'd ever smelled before. The putrid scent of decrepit flesh, coupled with the hunger of my growling tummy, was not a good combination. There wasn't much to throw up, yet I managed to do just that. Vomiting water and bile, I heaved violently, to the point where there were tears in my eyes, and a sharp ache in my head. Pippa appeared to be concerned. She stood by my side, whimpering, as she focused on me with unwavering loyalty. But Owen left me alone, offering me a seedling of dignity in a world that no longer provided it.

When I was finished, Owen asked, "you good?"

I nodded a lightheaded and wordless yes, and we started walking again. I had to focus on anything else but the death. I tried to get somewhat used to the smell of old flesh, dry blood, and stale smoke, and just concentrated on breathing. In, out, in, out. I tried yogic breathing, like a dragon or a lion, and remembered what my shrink told me once, before the end of life as we knew it. "Don't dwell," he'd said. I told myself that I wasn't going to dwell on any negative thoughts that entered my mind. I'd notice them, accept them, and then move on. The dwelling was what would feed my anxiety, and my anxiety surely could be my demise if I wasn't careful. I already felt my mental state entering fragile territory. I couldn't let myself crack.

Admittedly, the scenery was unpleasant, but it felt good to walk. I was a bit weak and dizzy from this newly-strenuous activity: when you were cooped up all day and barely eating, walking suddenly became a treacherous and challenging new feat. (And I'd wanted to go for a run? Who was I kidding?)

We heard footsteps and froze in place. Pippa was on high alert, and there I was once again praying to a God that I thought I'd long forgotten. Owen put a finger to his lips. "Shhh." He didn't have to tell me twice. I couldn't utter a peep if I'd wanted to.

An old man turned the corner, near the bank where Owen had first found me. He looked to be in his 80s, was dressed in a suit and bow tie, complete with once-shiny dress shoes, pocket square, and all. He had silvery hair, and kind eyes that in another life would have been dancing with laughter, and overflowing with happiness. Now his eyes had seen too much.

The old man was quite literally dragging his right leg along. Was he injured? Had he had a stroke? He looked friendly enough, and carried a leather bag with him; much like a doctor might have carried to a house call, back in the olden days.

"Hello, there." Owen said, hesitantly.

"Hello, hello!" replied the man, in a cheerful tone that unfittingly contrasted our environment.

Who was this guy? He broke into a smile, the kind that you see on Hallmark commercials, full of joy, pure of heart. It was truly infectious. He seemed to be pleased to see us, and it was refreshing.

We introduced ourselves. "I'm Owen. This is Shelby. And this here, is Pippa."

"Eugene McDougal." He tipped his hat, and extended a shaky, leathery hand.

His eyes were blue and crinkled at the corners. They now twinkled with every new syllable, and every new glance. He struck me as vivacious, sharp, and hungry for life. He seemed curious, and optimistic, in this time when optimism was hard to come by. I immediately liked him.

"Eugene was my grandfather's name, and a lovely name it is." I told him, adding a playful curtsy and a wink to lighten up the awkwardly morbid situation that surrounded us.

"A great name indeed!" he said, responding with a wink of his own. "Nice to meet you all. So, what are you up to on this fine day?" he joked. "As for me, I'm all dressed up with nowhere to go!"

We all laughed. This charming old man was a much-needed ray of sun.

"Do you need help?" I asked. I glanced sideways at Owen, who offered up,

"Come back with us. We can try to keep you safe, at least for the time being. Got any food?"

"I have some crackers in my bag, and some peanut butter, too. Also some peppermint candies. Not much else, I'm afraid. But awhile back, I spotted a cardboard box half-full of jars of baby food. And not so far from that, a paper bag with some cans of powdered milk," he replied. "And a box of fish food. I couldn't carry it all, but meant to go back at some point. I'd be happy to show you the way, and come stay with you all, if you'll have me." Eugene said.

"Well, you look to be in no condition for a walk. Shelby, help Mr. Eugene back to our place, and I'll take Pippa along to try to find the milk and the baby food. Guess I'll grab the fish food, too. Desperate times call for desperate measures." Eugene pointed and gestured, arms flailing, as he explained to Owen how to find the items, which I presumed were once in the perfectly-aligned aisles of the local family grocery store. I tuned them out.

It saddened me to think I'd have to succumb to eating fish food, and the realization that we truly were in desperate times wasn't lost on me, either. But what hurt my heart most was to think about babies who had perished. It hurt even more to think that now, I'd most likely never have a baby of my own. It was also odd to hear Owen refer to the dungeon where we stayed as "our place." It wasn't home. This wasn't home. This was once my hometown, but not anymore. It was nothing now. It was nowhere. It was just a lifeless place with nothing to offer besides fear and fish food.

Snapping out of my daze, I agreed with Owen, reminding myself that this place was offering up some friendships, too. Nonetheless, and despite Eugene's seemingly harmless nature, I had a knife with me, just in case — and I wasn't afraid to use it.

Eugene threw an arm around my neck and together, we hobbled back to the place that I couldn't yet call home. Before we climbed our way through the destruction, down into the depths of our humble little bomb-shelter-ish abode, Eugene stopped, lay a hand gently on my arm, and, looking directly in my eyes, simply uttered, "Shelby, it's going to be okay."

In that moment, I truly wanted to believe him. Eugene was like a guardian angel, sent to calm my nerves, ease my mind, and bring some hope to me and Owen, just like the little girl in my dream. Without another word, he started forward, and down we went into the depths of our nothing-home, which, because of Eugene, now felt a little more welcoming. I could sense that he brought an ease and a warmth to everyone around him, and I could imagine him being wildly popular in his heyday.

I helped him elevate his leg, and let him rest his eyes. The time for conversation would come, but I wanted to take care of Eugene in the way that Owen had taken care of me, so I let him simply rest. Words would come later. In the meantime, I just sat, and waited. I decided to try to meditate. I hadn't attempted yoga or meditation since this whole debacle happened — I mean, who would have? But, it seemed to me that I could use a little focusing. It was time to get myself centered, and try to relax. I sat, cross-legged on the floor, in a Sukhasana pose. I touched the tips of my fingers together and inhaled: in through my nose, out through my mouth. Strong, deep, steady breaths. It was relaxing, and truly freeing to have nothing on my mind. Breathe in, breathe out. I instantly felt better. After about 20 minutes of meditating, I heard Owen coming back down, and Pippa excitedly scampered in.

"Hey girl," I said, petting her stout little body and letting her give me kisses all over my face.

Owen was dragging along the box of baby and fish food, and with the crumbled bag of condensed milk cans thrown on top.

Yum.

"Quite a score you've got there, O!" I said with a smile.

"Someone's in a better mood!" was his reply.

"You know, Owen, something about Eugene cheered me up. I also needed that walk, and when I came back and meditated, everything just felt at peace. Now, with you and Pippa home, all seems right with the world… for the moment."

I took note of the fact that I used the word, "home," and I felt okay with it. Maybe I was getting past the stage of denial, and moving on to acceptance. This *was* home, now.

"Hungry?" Owen asked.

"Famished," I answered. After vomiting up the little bit that was in my stomach, it was definitely time to refuel.

I considered my options. Fish food? No thanks. However, the baby food actually seemed like a nice change, surprisingly. Peas, carrots, sweet potatoes, creamed corn, squash … hmm. I had no idea what I was in for, but I decided to give the mush a try. There was more squash than anything else. As an adult, I'd always been a fan of butternut squash, so, I figured I'd give it a whirl. It didn't taste too bad – a little on the bland side, and with the consistency of Cream of Wheat, but really, I wasn't sure why babies often made such a fuss over eating it. Babies always cried about bath time, bedtime, and mealtime: things that I relished in as a grown-up, and things that I particularly longed for now, more than ever.

"Who would have thought?" I mused. "From gourmet to Gerber's." I laughed. I tried to recall the last real meal I'd had before all this had occurred. The memory made me sad: it was sushi with Tamra, Davis, and Daphne. In fact, we ran into Ezra that night, too. It was the last time I'd seen him, and he told me to batten down the hatches, and not to get swept away to Oz. I would have preferred Oz to this. (And Dorothy's to-die-for ruby red slippers? Yes, please!) Tamra and I had seen Davis and Daphne the next morning for coffee. Davis was a fabulous gay stereotype: a fierce and flamboyant barista with bleached-blonde hair who was in fashion design school. Daphne was his twin sister, a conservative accountant and self-proclaimed "power-bitch." They were total opposites, but the best of friends, and super close, as most twins are. They joked that they had the ultimate Twintuition, and that their twin-ESP would make it impossible for them to ever be rid of one another. After all that had happened, I hoped this was true. Dead or alive, wherever they were, I hoped that Davis and Daphne were together. Tears formed in my eyes with the memory of them, and the last thing they said to Tamra and me.

"Keep your heads up, sistas! You'll survive without Facebook and hairdryers for a couple days!" said Davis.

Daphne, after rolling her eyes, gave us each a quick hug, and said, "Really, be safe."

In unison, as they always did, it was "Toodles! Love you!," as they left.

I would miss them. I'd miss Tamra too. That morning, after we parted from the twinsies, as we called them, we went and bought all the supplies we thought we'd need for the impending storm: extra blankets, some gloves and scarves, lots of canned goods, bottled water, Gatorade, extra flashlights and batteries, candles, a deck of cards, cleansing wipes, dry shampoo, mouthwash, and instant coffee. Some items were necessities, some not. We then bought a few bottles of wine. (That, in our minds, was most certainly a necessity.) When we got home, we each showered and then filled the tub with bathwater. We boarded the windows and put sandbags outside of our door, and just waited. I hadn't prayed in a while, I hadn't gone to church in a long time, either. With all of the awfulness, injustice, violence, and disease in the world, I found it hard to believe, and my faith was dwindling, especially since my diagnosis. But, I did make sure to find the rosary that my grandma had given me. It felt like I needed it, and I kept it close by. The storm was taking longer to hit than we'd thought. Even though it was midday, we both changed into PJs, popped some popcorn, and made peanut butter and jelly sandwiches, because, why not?

We flipped on the news and it was a lot of jibber-jabber about the usual uprisings in the Middle East and other parts of the world, that our ethnocentric, New York state of minds couldn't be bothered with. Threats on the United States were a dime a dozen as we made new enemies year after year, with the newest threat being a biochemical terror attack. The threats had become so frequent that we let it go in one ear, and out the other, so we could make room for the tabloid headlines and celebrity gossip to fill our brains. As Tamra often flippantly said, "Someone's always got some beef with the U.S." And that was true.

Once the storm coverage began, though, we started to pay attention. We popped open the wine. The feeling I'd had at that time was so odd. I remembered being calm, anxious, terrified, and, oddly enough, excited, all at once. It was the kind of excitement that occurs when a huge event is happening, but one that doesn't seem real. Like watching a hostage situation play out on TV – it's awful, but something about that television screen between you and the action makes you feel disconnected from it, so your adrenaline is pumping and it is almost like watching a really good, very realistic movie. It also felt like I was a third-grader again, waiting for the big blizzard to hit, so that I could have a "snow day" from school the next day.

At first, we scoffed at how the media was overreacting, like they always do. Ever the hipster, Tamra blogged about the catastrophist media and how they sensationalize everything; about how the American public are a bunch of sheep for blindly buying into whatever "emergency" the news is perpetuating to boost our economy. To her, everything was some capitalistic game, or some conspiracy, not to be taken seriously, and most of us were idiots for believing what the news and the government said. I, too, loved a good conspiracy theory, so, I sometimes admittedly got caught up in Tamra's mentality, and the more I drank, the funnier it became: the little old ladies on the local news, stocking up on enough toilet paper to last a lifetime and then some; the dentallychallenged hillbillies on the weather channel who were crying about the local bait shop being torn to pieces. It was definitely nothing to make fun of, and, inside, we both knew that, but it was easier to make jokes in this situation, rather than to acknowledge our fear. Our favorite clip of the day was the college guy who went streaking in the rain, right behind a reporter, live and on-air.

While we blogged and laughed and drank and waited, the entire East Coast braced for the worst. To say that we were oblivious to the enormity of the situation was probably an accurate assessment. A hurricane had already hit in the lower states, and it was making it up to us in New York. But, we'd had some bad weather before, and some major citywide power outages, we could handle this – New Yorkers could handle anything. I mean, what was the worst that could happen? Right?

A gust of wind howled outside of our Brooklyn window. The sky went from blue-gray to black, within moments. Our lights flickered, and the mayor on TV was urging us to evacuate NOW. It seemed sudden. He seemed serious. The situation no longer seemed funny, and I began to regret my wine decision. I was worried. I clutched grandma's rosary and tried to focus. I wondered what my parents would do in this situation. They lived upstate, and a part of me wondered if I should go home to them. I didn't want to leave Tamra, but her attitude wasn't the best. "Again, I urge you, if you are going to leave, do so now. I implore citizens to evacuate to higher ground. The evacuation routes are highlighted. Please, if you are able to leave, do so now. You are not going to want to ride this one out. People, this is a storm of biblical proportions, and nothing to take lightly. I am not asking, I am telling you to evacuate. We are in a state of emergency, and this is mandatory. Staying is not an option, so if you can leave, leave."

"Tam, what are we gonna do?"

She snorted. "Fuck that. I'm staying."

I knew she wouldn't leave. The home that we lived in was where she'd grown up. Her parents had passed away and left it to her, and I couldn't imagine her leaving anyway, but particularly for that reason alone.

"You can go, ya know." She said to me solemnly. I knew that she meant it.

I burst into tears, unsure where they came from.

"What is your problem?" she asked, in typical Tamra fashion.

"I don't want to leave you! But I want to leave..." I said between sobs.

"Shel, go. I can't hold you back here. In fact, I don't want you to stay. I don't expect you to say. Go home to Boonieville with your family." I had to laugh. She was always making fun of my hometown. "Honestly, Shelby. I can't leave, I'll never leave, but I'd never forgive myself if I forced you to stay here. So please, go, and be safe."

She grabbed the wine glass out of my hand. "Go. I'll help you pack. I'm not asking, I'm telling," she said, mocking the words of our mayor.

We hastily threw whatever we could into a suitcase, and packed some water and snacks for the road. I knew that I'd be sitting in an endless amount of traffic, with all of the other stubborn New Yorkers who didn't leave in the days before. As we said our goodbyes, I handed her my grandma's rosary. She wasn't religious, but I saw the gleam in her eye, so I know that she was touched by the gesture.

"I love you, Tam." I said, hugging her hard, tears rolling down my face.

"Stop it, Shelby. This isn't a forever goodbye. Dude…. it's just….weather. We'll be fine. I'll see you in a few days. Ok? Drive safely. I'll be fine here. I'm prepared!" she said, holding up a bottle of wine with one hand, and Pop Tarts in the other.

"Love you, Shelby," she added.

"I'll call you." I said.

"You'd better," was her reply...and that was goodbye.

I snapped back to the present, baby food in hand. Sigh. From sushi, to squash. From Tamra, Davis, and Daphne, to Pippa, Owen, and Eugene. It was all happening so fast, and everything was changing.

I said another prayer – something I found myself doing more and more often as of late. I prayed that all my old friends were safe: Davis, Daphne, Tamra, even Ezra. And if they weren't safe, I asked God to watch over them up in Heaven. I asked him to let them be my guardian angels, too, and to watch over Owen and Eugene as well. I asked God for them to watch over Pippa, and asked him that my parents and Jared be safe, also. I then thanked him for the baby food that I was forcing down, and I said a prayer for all the babies who should be eating it, but who weren't here, and never would be. And then I prayed for, well, everyone. I prayed to a God I was previously unsure about, and I prayed for everybody.

Chapter 5

It was a new day, and in our new home, Owen, Eugene, Pippa and I had quickly become a family unit. We established a routine of waking and mediating – a habit that I had gotten the guys into, or rather, a habit to which they begrudgingly caved. Pippa would just lay and watch. We still had green tea, and we'd re-use teabags over and over again until there was absolutely no flavor left. You'd be surprised how much use you can get out of a tea bag when it is necessary. After we were done using them for tea, we'd lay them on wounds or over our eyes when we had a headache. Sometimes, we'd cut them open and eat the loose tea leaves. After all, we had to conserve all that we had. Once or twice, we'd even eaten scoops of Crisco. Somehow, we were making it. We were alive, and we were functioning without fast food and electronics, without superstores and subway systems. We were getting by.

Sometimes, we'd decide to take a walk. We'd scour the area for any bits of food, or any signs of water. The landscape rarely changed. Owen would go through the pockets of the deceased, and we'd take the clothes off their bones. We'd use their clothing as blankets, or wear it ourselves, or we'd use it for rags. We got a green scarf for Pippa, taken off of a teenager who, in life, had worn it as a doo-rag. She wore it as proud as can be, strutting her stuff like a show dog.

Things weren't too bad, relatively speaking. Eugene was getting his strength back, and he still walked with a limp, but his leg was in a little better shape than it had been. We still had peanuts and baby food, and even a little jerky. There was also the fish food, of course, which I'd begrudgingly tried one day. It tasted like dirt mixed with sawdust, and had the consistency of confetti. We had to be even more frugal with all of our food now, with Eugene in the mix. We always made sure that Pippa ate, too. She was part of our tribe. We were family. I'm sure that survivalists elsewhere would scoff at the notion of providing for an animal. They would laugh at us trying to keep a dog alive, well, and nourished – and some extremists may even suggest eating her. I shuddered at the thought. It would be an option for some, but never for us. Pippa was one of us, and would be until the end.

We all liked the fresh air. The stench of death wasn't as pungent as it had once been, or maybe I'd just gotten used to it, and the dust had cleared almost completely. Somehow, this new world looked almost normal to me. Almost. The obliterated buildings became landmarks to us, and, since Eugene, we'd seen no other sign of human life. We'd find little treasures on our hikes: sometimes, a pack of gum; once, a bottle of half-drunk Coca Cola. We'd take any food we could: a half-eaten bag of Cheetos, an expired bag of sunflower seeds, a stale, almost unidentifiable piece of bread that even the remaining birds passed over, but, to us, everything was worth something – even old cigarette butts. We collected nails, pieces of paper, stray gloves or shoes, bits of wood, and we'd even found a piece of leather for Pippa to chew on. We had to steer her away from any bodies. We didn't want to risk her chewing the bones, or devouring any remaining flesh. (Though it may have been good for her.) Owen spotted her gnawing on a woman's leg, once. He let her go at it, as disturbed as he was by the sight. I was glad not to have witnessed it, myself, but it didn't make me think any less of her. Like us, Pippa had to fight for survival. We kept Pippa on a rope that we tied around her collar. We had two ropes: hers, and the one that we kept back at home base, just in case we needed it. Pippa's real leash was long gone, but her collar had survived. It made me smile: pink and sparkly, like something I would have enjoyed in my old life. I was glad that Pippa and I had the same glamorous and girly sense of style.

As I admired her collar, I realized that it was cold, but not unbearable. I wanted to run, but Owen and Eugene had become like father figures – or uncles, perhaps – and my bodyguards didn't want to let me out of their sight. On this day, however, I convinced them to let me go. Like a caged animal, I craved my freedom and just wanted to run wild. Pippa had given in to her animal instincts on occasion, and I needed to, as well. I promised only to sprint to the end of the remaining road, and to stop once I was out of their line of vision. Owen made me strap the knife to my belt, using part of the rope that he cut off. I couldn't blame him, but I guffawed uncomfortably at the notion, hoping that I didn't trip and fall. What would happen if I stabbed myself? Owen didn't care. It was a risk he was willing to take: he "wasn't going to have me out there, defenseless and alone."

Ah, yes, because I am a meek little woman who can't defend herself. I rolled my eyes. But, whatever: I'd take what I could get. Running felt magnificent. I felt powerful, free, and full of life. I felt the blood coursing through my veins, as my legs pumped underneath me. I envisioned myself as a race horse, with strong thighs, and a glistening mane waving in the wind behind me. The air felt awesome in my lungs, and my body felt grateful for the exercise. I felt alive, for the first time in a long time. Respectful of their wishes, I stopped at the agreed upon point, and took a rest before returning back home. One thing I noticed was what looked like a camp setup. It reminded me of what a homeless camp had looked like, before we were all homeless. There was a shoddy fire pit, a plaid blanket, and a thermos. There was a camouflage walkie-talkie, but the fire didn't glisten with the embers of recent use, nor did the camp look very lived-in at all. I glanced around. There were no signs of human life anywhere nearby. I looked at the ground. No footprints.

I wasn't sure what to do. In this new world, everything was free for the taking. But, I believed in Karma. If I took any of this, what would be taken from me? I weighed my options. When you're in survival-mode, – which, let's face it, was now our default setting – there aren't many options. Just like the run-compromise, I had to take what I could get. I took a closer look. We had a lot of blankets and clothing. Maybe I'd leave the blanket to be kind, in case there was, in fact, someone currently staying there. The thermos, I didn't really see a need for. We had a canteen, an assortment of mugs, and water bottles at home, a kettle over the fire, and I'm sure that we could come across another thermos in our now-daily walks. I thought the men might be mad that I didn't take everything, but, I still had a heart, despite our disheartening circumstances. Someone else may have really needed this stuff. It looked to be all they had, if they were still with us.

But the walkie-talkie could be a real find. We already had the handheld radio we'd obtained from the gruff stranger, but, despite having questionable outlets and Owen's expertise, we couldn't get it to work, yet. Maybe this radio would help us communicate with someone, or find out what was going on in other parts of the country, or even other parts of the world.

I grabbed it. It felt like a score. A rush of adrenaline coursed through my veins, and I wondered if this was a good idea. I don't know what I expected as I swiped the radio. An alarm, maybe, like the time I got caught shoplifting at age 14? Still, despite being fairly certain that no one was around, I ran. I took off faster than I ever had, and I felt victorious, like the lineman who picks up a fumbled ball and runs it 50 yards to the end zone. I didn't know what to expect from Owen and Eugene when I came back: would they be proud, excited, or pissed? I wasn't sure.

I could see Owen squinting as I came jogging towards them. Pippa's tail wagged excitedly, and I knew the men were trying to figure out what I was carrying. When I showed them, they both seemed pretty excited. However, Owen's mood soon changed when I explained the camp.

"Are you sure no one was there, Shelby?" he asked sternly, hands on my shoulders, looking me squarely in the eyes.

"I didn't see anyone. Besides, if someone was nearby, why wouldn't they have tried to stop me?" I asked.

He didn't answer, but I could see the wheels turning and the fatherly worry on his face. "Let's get home," he said. Yes, we all now referred to the place-of-nothing as home. For all intents and purposes, it was a cave, just a shell of an old bomb shelter, but, to us, it became home.

We made it a home. We had (some) food, our little faux family, and a pet. We had trinkets that we collected on our journeys. We slept there, and it sheltered us. It was home enough.

When we got back, the guys tinkered with the radios. I learned that my find was a handheld CB radio and walkie-talkie. Owen said it looked to be part of a set. I wondered how far it reached, or who had the other device. I honestly didn't know anything about radio waves, frequencies, and the like. I let them go about their business, and did some yoga, which had become my saving grace. The space wasn't large, by any means, but it was large enough for us to have some room. It was amazing what you could make do with when you were in a state of desperation. After my yoga session, I lie with Pippa, singing to her. I'd found, by accident, that it was something she enjoyed. This funny-looking little dog had quickly become my friend. I stroked her golden hair, and touched her short little legs, as I sang Beatles songs and Britney Spears tunes under my breath. She relaxed into a nap, snoring a soft little Corgi snore, and we were content.

I must have drifted off, too, because I awoke to an enthusiastic "woo-hoo!" from Eugene. This mild-mannered, quiet man was rarely exclamatory, and so I was certain that they'd gotten one of the radios working. I dare not touch them, for fear of ruining it, but what I saw was amazing. They'd put different batteries in the radio I'd found at the camp, and Owen had somehow gotten the other radio to work by doing God knows what with old copper wiring we'd found on a walk. They were both on, tuned to nothing, but on. "Oh my god...we may be able to hear the outside world," I muttered. "We have a way to communicate!"

I shook my head in astonishment. I didn't know what it meant for us, but I knew it was good.

Or bad.

CHAPTER 6

I didn't know what the radios would mean, or what news they would bring us, if any. I didn't even know if there was any "outside world" to speak of. I just knew that, good or bad, useful or not, they'd gotten them working, and that was an impressive feat. We chalked it up as a small victory, at least for now. I had to toss aside my uncertain thoughts of whether or not I really wanted to have any outside communication.

We built a fire, and to celebrate, we each took a swig of whiskey. We each grabbed a jar of baby food, and some peanuts. This occasion called for some of the remaining pieces of beef jerky; we each got about a quarter-inch square of it tonight. I decided that my previous fears were irrational. This was great. This was special. I had to be positive about it all. Really, there was such potential that the radios could bring. Would help soon be on the way? Was there any help out there to be had? I wasn't sure.

We filled the old mugs we had acquired with warmed water and days-old teabags, My cup was chipped and the handle was broken off, but it had a faded image of a palm tree on it, something that reminded me of happier times: spring break, family vacations, and when Ezra first told me he loved me, on the beach.

"Let's just talk tonight," said Eugene. We always chatted idly, but often one of us was asleep, trying to stay warm and keep up our energy. I knew Eugene meant talk, really talk, and I was fine with it.

"Let's." I agreed. Eugene reminded me of a beardless Santa Claus, or an older Mister Rogers. He made me feel cozy and loved, somehow. He was stoic optimism, in human form. Owen just sat and smiled his wide, pearly smile. He looked happier than I'd seen in quite some time. Pippa lay at his feet, snoozing again, and I swear it looked as though a smile was playing on her doggie lips.

"Tell us more about yourself, Eugene," I said, over the hum of dead air and occasional white noise coming from the radios. Eugene was so friendly, but he kept his personal life very private. We knew he was a retired science professor and researcher, who took Chinese and French classes "for fun," along with dancing lessons at the local community college before the disaster struck. We knew he used to read three different newspapers every day, and that he wore a suit any time he was out in public, and sometimes, even at home. He told us, "You have to dress for the life you want, not the life you have. And I want the life of a dandy," which made me laugh.

"Well," Eugene started. "I never had kids. Never married. Folks thought I was gay, but I'm not. I have no problem with it, mind you, but I am not. I loved a girl, loved her for a long time, but never told her, and she married somebody else. After that, I just stopped looking. I think we really only have one true soulmate, and I missed the boat, so why settle for second best? I was happy though. I had a lot of friends. I went on dates, but let the women know, I wasn't going to marry. It was fine. I took girls dancing, and to the museum. I'm always educating myself – need to keep that mind sharp to stave off the Alzheimer's!" he said. I felt a pang at his one-sided love story, thinking of my own with Jared.

"What was her name?" I asked.

"Adelaide. The most beautiful girl in the world. Curly red hair, and a real looker. She passed away a few years ago," he said, with sadness in his eyes since the first time we'd met him. Owen shifted uncomfortably; I know he was thinking of Marta.

"Anyway," he continued, "I was rich, you know. Am rich, I guess. Well-to-do, you could say. This situation we've found ourselves in, though, just goes to show that money means nothing, really. Monetary wealth is meaningless in the grand scheme of things. What good is it doing me now?"

There was silence. He was right.

"What's your favorite memory, Eugene?" Owen asked.

"Oh, there's too many to name. I hiked the Appalachian trail as a young man – that's something I'm proud of. Sat front row at New York Fashion Week. Visited the Holy Land. Went on a game show," he laughed. "I lost."

We shared a laugh. It seemed like Eugene had lived an interesting life, and his situation now was just as interesting, but sadly so. When I thought about it, everyone has an interesting life, really. We all have unique stories that make us who we are, and even if we think they are boring and mundane, they're intriguing to others. All of our little patchwork stories make up a beautiful quilt that is the human condition. I loved it. I made a mental note to include Eugene and Owen's stories in my memoirs, if I were ever able to write them, or perhaps, I'd share our stories in a screenplay, and the world could watch it play out on the big screen, if life would ever get easy again. I longed for normal. I smirked, thinking about how I'd bemoaned my life before. "Why isn't anything ever easy?" I'd ask. "Life is hard!" I'd proclaim. That was child's play. Cancer was hard. THIS was hard.

"Do you regret not marrying, and not having kids?" I asked Eugene. As soon as I asked it, I regretted it, because it seemed too intrusive and far too personal. "I mean, if you don't mind my asking," I added quickly.

"No problem at all, my dear." He patted my hand, "We're family now." That made me smile. Eugene continued, "I don't regret it. Not one bit. I had lots of nieces and nephews who I got to watch grow up, and I volunteered with the children at my church. Plus, I worked with young minds every day as a professor, and I volunteered at an animal shelter, too, so all of my paternal instincts were fulfilled, if you will. My heart was full, with my nurturing and mentoring. I didn't need my own biological kids to complete that picture. I'm a loving person and I was still able to love, even without children of my own. The only marriage and only children I ever wanted were with Adelaide. If it wasn't with her, it wasn't for me. And it was my own fault to lose her. My own damn fault. She didn't want me to hike the Appalachian trail, but I was too stubborn, and I did. And I was gone for months on end. It was too much for her. It was not like it is now – or was, at least – with cell phones and computers. We couldn't keep in touch. She moved on. I expected her to, but it hurt. There was always a small part of me that wished she'd just held on. That she'd waited for me. I've always beat myself up for not asking her to marry me before I left. She knew I loved her, but maybe she didn't know how much. So that, friends, is my only regret. I would have regretted marrying someone else, or starting a family with someone else. That's the honest-to-God truth. Adelaide was all I really wanted. But, now I have a new family, with you all, and I'm grateful. I never did properly thank you for rescuing me. Thank you, and cheers." He raised his half of a mug – adorned with ducks and gingham – and we clinked. Cheers, indeed.

I leaned over and gave Eugene a hug. He looked pleasantly surprised but appreciative. Owen smiled a sad smile and cleared his throat.

"I regret it, Shelby," he said.

Puzzled, I asked what, precisely, he regretted.

"Not having kids. I loved Marta. We always had dogs – before Pippa there was Bruce, a rescue pug, and Lovely, a King Charles Cavalier Spaniel. When we first started dating, I had a scraggly mutt named Cupcake. Our dogs were like our children, and we, too, had nieces and nephews who we loved dearly, but no children of our own. We couldn't. I don't know if it was me, or her, but I always felt to blame. Surprisingly, she seemed content without kids, but I always wanted them. I regret not trying harder. You know, adopting, or trying the new technologies that were available for infertility issues and such. But I'm glad I have a family now, too," he said, with a lump in his throat. His voice was cracked as he added, "I just wish she wasn't gone."

"Well, Owen. You would have made a great dad. I'll never be a mother now, either…" I said, trailing off.

We sat in silence. I could tell Owen and Eugene both wanted to say something, but neither could think of the words, if there were any to say.

"I'm afraid that I can't help you out there, my dear," Owen finally said, and we all shared a laugh.

"I guess it would be rotten to bring a child into this world right now, anyway," I said, my joking tone masking the truth.

"I miss my parents." I said, changing the subject. I had done a lot of thinking about my friends, and Jared, and even Ezra, but the thoughts of my parents being gone were far too painful to think of, so I just blocked them out, most of the time.

The last time I saw them was the night I'd driven from Brooklyn to their home in upstate New York, not too far from where I was now. It was such a long, tedious journey for me, and the weather was awful. My mother was absolutely overcome with emotion to see me on her doorstep. She ushered me in and we hid out in their basement until the storm passed. It was wonderful...she made me hot chocolate, with the mini marshmallows, and when we lost power, we told ghost stories like we used to when we would go camping. I took a photo of the three of us: me, mom, and dad, on my mobile phone, and wished more than anything that I could look at that photo again – but my cell battery had long died, and the screen was cracked. I still kept it in my pocket, and I tried to power it on, every day, to try to look at their smiling, loving faces one last time.

THEY were my home. And I was pretty sure I'd never see them, or my home, ever again. I was asleep down in the basement when they ventured upstairs to start cleaning up the mess that the storm had left behind. I awoke to my dad's old-fashioned battery-operated police scanner, with an excited man warning us of a terrorist attack. I thought it was a joke: some teenagers who were off school and bored, using some kind of radio to break in and mess with already-panicky suburbia. I remember thinking that no one would be so cruel as to kick us when we're down. Nonetheless, I stretched and slowly started towards the stairs. Next, I heard a boom, felt a rumble, and then the house and my life literally began to cave in upon me.

I shuddered. I wanted to stop thinking about it. But I felt like if I didn't talk about them, that they would disappear from my memory. "I miss my parents," I repeated. "The last words we said to one another were I Love You, though. We never said goodbye or went to bed without saying those words. I'm quite thankful for that," I said. "And I meant it every single time I said it," I continued. "My Mom made the most awesome lasagna. And pumpkin pie! And my dad, he was amazing. He never gave himself enough credit, but he could fix anything. They were superheroes to me," I said. I meant it. They truly were.

"It sounds like you had great parents. Any gentlemen in your life?" Eugene asked. Out of the corner of my eye, I could see Owen signaling for Eugene not to ask about it, but, Eugene missed the cue. It was okay. Sometimes, it was a relief to talk about these things instead of keeping it all bottled up.

"I used to be engaged. To a great guy named Ezra. We didn't work out, though. We were together for a long time, and we loved each other, but the fit was always off. Kind of like when you find the perfect pair of shoes...and you want to make your foot fit into them, but you just can't, and you buy them anyway, because they're just so cute and they're on sale, and you just have to have them, but you get home, and they just won't work." I explained, but I knew my analogy would have worked better with Tamra, Daphne, or even Davis.

"Anyway," I continued, "he was fantastic, and I wish him well, but we were just not right together. No romance, just routine. Towards the end, we didn't even have the passion to argue. It was just apathy. We were spending too much time trying to make it work, and as the time passed, we fell out of love, and were just too codependent to move on. I told Owen, there was another guy, though, who, whether it was right or wrong, I loved as long as I can remember, but the timing was always off, and I never knew how he felt about me, and he just never seemed…serious. I dream about him all the time; I have for years, it's almost unnerving. I don't know how I could feel so connected to someone – still – who I haven't seen in so long. His name was – is – Jared, and he's from my hometown. He actually was living close by, the last I heard. I do remember now that I was actually trying to find him after I left my parents' home. I needed to find someone familiar. But everything I knew was gone. I don't remember how I ended up in the bank building but I do know that I was searching for him. In some facet or another, I was always searching for him. Our souls were tethered. We grew up together and it's like he's a part of me. I can't explain it, and it isn't rational. We really didn't have anything official, but, at the same time, he was everything. I hope … I hope he's okay." I choked back tears. "Eugene, at least Adelaide knew you loved her. Maybe not how much, but she knew you did to some extent. I wish Jared knew. He didn't know, at least I don't think he did. I wish he did, I wish I could have told him, but now it's too late…" I couldn't help it. I started to cry. "It's too late for all of it. My fairy tale…it's a nightmare." Owen rubbed my back, gently, and in a fatherly manner.

"Honey, it's never too late. There's always hope. Just keep the faith," said Eugene.

I wanted to believe him, but I couldn't. Where was the hope in this situation? How could I have faith? I wanted Eugene to be right. I wanted the little girl in my dream to be right. I wanted my inner voice to be wrong. I didn't know what to say, so I just nodded.

"Speaking of faith, Owen, what's with the Bible?" Eugene asked Owen, bluntly. I was taken aback, as it seemed like an odd and surprisingly off-topic question to ask.

"What do you mean?" Owen replied.

"Well, I noticed a Bible, but it hasn't been touched. Is it yours, or Shelby's? Why hasn't it moved?" Eugene asked. "Can I read it? I've always been a man of science, but I never subscribed to the notion that science and religion need to be mutually exclusive."

"Well, sure you can. It was Marta's. I haven't opened it, just because it hurts. I'd watch her read a verse every night before bed, and every morning when she awoke. She was a way better Christian than me. Hell, she was a way better person than me all-around. But, yeah, it was hers. I'm somehow scared to touch it. It was the last thing I saw her hold," he said sadly.

"Well, let's open it together. Let's read it, and keep her memory alive. What do you say, Shelby?" Eugene asked.

I squirmed. I was just slowly revisiting my own faith, which was shaken and had been for some time. Though I wasn't a non-believer, I also didn't love the dogma and politics that surrounded organized religion. So the suggestion made me uncertain. Then, again, I wondered what it could hurt. "I suppose that's a nice idea. To honor Marta," I responded.

"To honor Marta," Owen repeated.

Eugene handed him the Bible, and Owen flipped open to a bookmarked page. "It's highlighted," he said.

"What does it say?" I asked.

"Psalm 71:14," he said, "But as for me, I will always have hope."

With that, he closed the book. He then grabbed both Eugene and myself by the hands, and repeated, "I will always have hope."

CHAPTER 7

The rest of our chat on that particular night was less serious. The fired blazed on, Pippa took turns cuddling up next to each of us. Most of the time we talked; during silent moments I'd absentmindedly pick at the frayed edges of the nubby old blanket of which I'd claimed ownership.

We were regaled with funny stories from Eugene's youth, and Owen shared with us another of his talents: telling jokes. My dating woes entertained the older men, with Eugene calling me a vixen, and Owen calling me a card. We avoided the elephantine topic of my cancer, for the most part. It carried with it too much heartache, and too much burden. Equally prohibited was further mention of Jared. Both subjects were off-limits for the rest of the evening.

It was fun, though: fun in the way that school could be fun. I remembered that I'd enjoyed school, but even on the most fun and interesting day, I'd still rather be elsewhere. That was the kind of fun that this was, but, nonetheless, it still felt right. I had more than an affinity for these guys: I was beginning to love them. And I did want to hope. So, that night, we all went to bed happy and relatively full; a little achy, but relatively warm. The ground was hard but I found comfort in its unwavering solidity. I never took for granted the luxury of rest, and I knew that, for better or for worse, tomorrow would be a new day.

A new day, it was. We took our usual walk, Owen with Pippa, me holding Eugene's hand. We were always wary, keeping a look out, for who knows what. Pippa was starting to further cave to her animal instincts, and she'd whine as we passed the long-rotted corpses, her carnivorous roots beginning to show themselves. The sky was dark that day, and there was an eerie essence surrounding us. The wind howled, and I felt my arm hairs prick up: whether from fear or the cold, I do not know.

Something felt off. I think that Owen and Eugene had to have felt it, too. They were quiet, too quiet, and it was slightly unnerving. Food was scarce back at our home, and we were running out of places nearby to look. We were unable to hunt, there was no life anywhere, and even the few animals that we used to spy were no more. It was inevitable: we were probably going to have to move, soon. Or die. Our sparse rations were not going to last forever. We were consuming, and we were not able to replace what we were taking in.

Lost deep in thought, I almost didn't notice the figure, at first. Pippa sure did. Her tail straightened, she began to quiver, and I heard her growling like never before. The man began to approach us. I saw a gun. Around his shoulder, I saw the red plaid blanket I'd left behind at the camp.

"Run!" was all I heard.

So I ran.

Panting, I was back at home. Pippa accompanied me. Owen and Eugene were not far behind. I heard a gunshot. It felt like all blood drained from my body.

"No. No. NO!" was all I could think. I didn't care if they wanted me tucked away, safe and sound. I had to go help, and, for the first time, I grew annoyed

and indignant at the fact that I didn't have more weapons on hand.

I would make do without. I sprinted towards the three men. What had happened? Who was shot? I couldn't stop worrying. Pippa stopped suddenly, yelping. She had stepped on a shard of glass. I picked her up – whew! She was quite an awkward load – and continued running. I saw Eugene clutching his chest. I saw Owen arguing with the man in the red blanket. The man's voice wasn't that of the gruff stranger that Owen had robbed days ago. This voice seemed to be familiar. I had no time to think. I watched Owen struggle with the man, and I rushed to help Eugene. A bullet had grazed his arm. As uncertain as I was about God sometimes, I had to thank him that it wasn't a fatal wound. The man, in a crazed state of panic, struggled to shoot Owen, too, – but luckily, the gun had run out of bullets. As the men struggled, and my sight became clearer, I shrieked. The blood drained from my face.

The man was Jared.

"Jared!" I gasped. It was a both a question and a greeting. Stepping closer to be sure, I squinted my eyes and further examined the scene before me. Owen had him in a headlock, and I saw, with certainty, that it was, in fact, Jared. My Jared.

"It's you," he said. But his voice didn't convey the familiar, friendly love that I'd expected from him. In fact, it sounded formal and unfamiliar. I didn't care. We'd all been through a lot; this world had changed each of us in immeasurable ways. A tone of voice meant nothing. It was him – HIM! – the love of my life. My addiction. My downfall. The yin to my yang. My Jared.

"Jared, yes, yes, it's me, Shelby! Oh my God! How are you? Wait, why the hell did you shoot Eugene?"

my anger flared, tempered with my love and lust for this man who I, disbelievingly, saw before me. I ran towards him, ready to lunge into his arms, when the look in his eyes stopped me cold.

He gazed at me warily, his eyes blank. "You know me?" he asked, slowly, like he was trying the words on for size.

"Very funny," I said, finally close enough to give him a playful punch on the arm. He stiffened up immediately, like a cat who is tolerating, but not welcoming, you. I sensed trepidation, but I was counterintuitively relieved that he gave off a standoffish vibe. Coming from Jared, standoffish was something that I was used to. My love and desire tangoed with his confusion and uncertainty; it was a dance that we'd done before – a dance of which we'd both taken the lead, at one time or another. But this time, it was different.

I was the only one whose mind danced with memories of our lifelong past. It was then that I realized Jared had no idea who I was. In fact, Jared had no idea who *he* was.

My insides deflated like the flower-shaped balloon he'd once won me at a state fair. It was really, truly too late for me and Jared. Too damn late. I felt my world crumbling from its core.

Owen watched me carefully. Eugene cradled his wounded arm. "Come on," I said to Eugene, "Let's get you back home."

I felt like I had been punched in the gut. It took every ounce of my being to fight back the tears: the tears for watching Eugene hurt, the tears for the realization that Jared was a shell of who he once was, tears for the fact that I didn't tell him how I felt before it was too late. Just, tears.

I heard Owen speaking to Jared in a menacing tone. They parted ways, and I feared that it would not be the last time we would see him. But, at the same time, I also feared that it would be. I didn't know which option would be worse.

Once we got back to our home – which once again didn't feel like home anymore – I poured some whiskey on Eugene's wound to disinfect it. He screamed in pain, and my soul ached. I didn't know what else to do. I cleaned the area carefully with a cold, somewhat clean cloth, and lay some green tea bags on it, then tied a shirt sleeve around the area to keep pressure on it. I moved on to Pippa, removing the shard of glass from her paw, cleaning it thoroughly, and using some Crisco as a salve. Eugene and Pippa were troopers, I knew they'd be okay. But, I couldn't lie: despite my attempts to act like a tough girl, the whole scene today scared me. Jared aside, the fact that someone could shoot an elderly man for, well, seemingly no reason, was quite frightening. What was this world (or what was left of it, rather) coming to? The fact that Jared was the shooter, and that he also seemed to have memory loss was equally heartbreaking.

"Are you okay, Eugene?" I asked.

With some ragged breaths and a shaky voice, he answered, "Of course, Shelby. I'm fine, I'm fine. Are YOU okay?"

I couldn't answer. I didn't know how to, or what I could say. There was no way to verbalize the emotions that were jumbled up in my mind. My spirit felt crushed, my head felt confused. Owen entered. "I think that we'll be free of him for a while. He had no other weapons that I could see, and his gun is out of bullets. Ain't many places for ammunition, we've looted as many shops and cars as we could. I'd imagine he's done the same. Scarce pickings out there. I think I scared him off for now, but if he has any sense, he has to be aware now that we have food and shelter, and it won't be long before he'll come looking for us. It could be a battle. We'd better get a plan in place," he said.

Suddenly, a thought struck me. "Owen, Eugene: it was fairly obvious that Jared didn't recognize me, right? So why would he have said, 'it's you?'" It made me nervous, somehow. It also made me wonder if he was faking, but why would he do such a thing?

"I don't know, darlin'. I just don't know." Owen answered. Eugene nodded, signaling his concurrence.

I was miserable. The whole situation seemed to be too much to wrap my head around at that moment, and I felt myself slowly transforming into the whiny, needy, obsessive girl – a version of myself that only Jared could conjure. I so wanted a shot of whiskey, but we were starting to run low on just about everything, and we needed it.

Like a mind reader, though, Owen handed me the bottle and ordered me to take a small swig. I did, and then I cried myself to sleep, and left Owen on his own to figure out a plan.

In what I presumed to be the middle of the night, I awoke to someone shaking me. "Wake up," a voice whispered.

Groggy, and woken out of a deep sleep, I peeped open one eye. I gasped, Before I could scream, there was a man's hand covering my gaping mouth. "Mmmmmm!!!" I tried yelling. It was loud enough to wake Pippa, who bit the man's leg. Owen and Eugene awoke, and before I knew what was happening, Owen was holding a knife to the man's throat.

The man was Jared. He put his hands up, but kept his eyes down.

"I mean no harm. I just ... I have information for you, and it seems like this girl has information for me. I'm all alone, and I have nothing. Absolutely nothing. I thought we could be allies. Please. I'm not armed. I'm alone. Please." He implored.

Owen dropped the knife, but kept a grip on it, and stayed close to Jared. I could see my own concerns echoed in his face. Eugene's brow was furrowed with worry. We didn't know whether or not to trust him – this was a collective feeling that went without saying, at this point. Pippa sensed it, too, sniffing him all over. She'd stopped growling, and let go of his leg, though, which maybe said something.

"Stay there," Owen ordered, as he patted Jared down. Finding nothing of interest, he allowed Jared to drop his hands. Owen and Eugene surely wouldn't have offered him food or water, but I had to. He was Jared. MY Jared. Or, at least, he used to be.

I knew that we had to look out for ourselves first, though. So instead of getting him fresh water, I squeezed what was left from some teabags we'd been saving. It was very little, but, it was better than nothing, I figured. Oh, how I wanted to hug him. Kiss him. Reminisce with him. My heart ached. My loins ached. My insides were crushed, but the waves of nostalgia that his presence washed over me were innumerable.

"Shelby, was it? How do you know me?" he asked.

"You first," Owen interjected. He could surely sense that I was getting all swoony – and he was definitely correct, to say the least. "What did you mean by, 'it's you,' if you clearly don't know the girl?" he demanded, toying with the knife as a not-so-subtle reminder for Jared to remain cool and play nice. He was on our turf now.

Jared cleared his throat, and began, "Well, there was a guy I met awhile back. Maybe a week or so ago. Maybe a week and a half. After the second blast. At any rate, we started off as allies, me and this guy. At first, people were still alive, and we were trying to make friends, to bond together, get food, share resources, set up camp, and so on. Raided cars together, tried to help stragglers we saw along the way. Just looked out for each other. We joined up with a few other men – all ages, I'd say from 16 all the way up to maybe 60-ish. We had a good little group going at first. One guy had a young girl with him. We did our best to keep her safe, you know, her being a kid and all. We saw all kinds of things: dead mothers with their dead babies, old couples laying side-by-side, holding hands, even in death. It was sad – but you guys know. It could make a person go crazy. The whole time, I had no clue who I was or where I was. Still don't. Talk about crazy!" He took a breath. I felt for him.

He continued, "I have no recollection of what happened or my life before it occurred. I only vaguely know what I look like because of a dusty, distorted reflection in a sheet of metal. It's now gone, I used to go look every day, to try to memorize my face, to try to use what I saw to piece together the puzzle of, well… me. I'm a stranger to myself, I really am, and, dude, it sucks. Anyway, this guy I met, his name was Thomas, he was a pretty cool dude. He was rough around the edges, but seemed to have a good heart. Ex-military. Seemed tough but decent. He filled me in on the events. And some of the other guys died off, some parted ways and went off on their own, but after a few days, there were a few of us left in our group. Me and Thomas – he called me Andy Amnesia as a joke – and then the dad Mitch with his daughter, Rory, this other guy Cam and then the teenager, Vince. We got along okay, and we even had a couple of long-range CB radios. The handheld kind. Like a walkie-talkie. We'd get snippets of news broadcasts and police calls here and there, but soon even those died down, and there was nothing to hear at all, really. Well one night, we all sat around the fire, drinking. Except Rory, of course, and Thomas started talking real crazy. Said he talked to someone on the CB, and that there were only men in their town, too. He started talking about Darwinism, and said it made sense that women would die off, with survival of the fittest and all." He paused. "No offense," he added, before continuing,

"But then he started going on and on about how humans would never survive without women. He became convinced that our species was just over and done with. I think he was blowing it all out of proportion but I guess he got caught up in this mindset. We had a few beers, and the more he drank, the worse it got. The problem became bigger, and more real. And his intentions became more disturbing. We all ignored him, basically, and went to bed. I mean, people blabber and bullshit when they're drunk, ya know. I woke up in the middle of the night, though, to see him standing over Rory, kind of leering and creepy-like, and when the recollection of what he'd been saying at the fire hit me, I feared the girl might be in danger. A fight ensued and pretty soon it was all of us versus Thomas. I had the gun and was ready to shoot, but then Mitch knocked him out cold with a piece of stone rubble. We had a talk and decided not to kill him, for whatever reason, for morals, for the sake of the young girl hanging around and having to witness it, whatever. Now, looking back, I don't really know why we didn't just off him. Guess the killing thing is new to me. Vince and Cam dragged him out in the middle of nowhere while he was unconscious, and left him with just his own canvas bag. Then, the two of them, Mitch, and Rory said they were heading West, and asked me to join, but I felt like I needed to be here. I couldn't remember anything, but this felt kind of like home to me, and I just felt like I needed to stay. I dunno why, really."

We listened, nodding, and all felt appropriately disgusted at Thomas' behavior.

"But what does this have to do with me?" I asked.

"A couple days later, Thomas came back to camp. I was repulsed by him, but he didn't seem to pose any harm to me personally, and the girl and her dad had gone away by then. Plus, I needed some help trying to find food and whatnot. I'm no pussy, but I'm not really the hunting, scrapping, fighting type from what I can tell. I kind of sense that I have never really had to work for food; Thomas had, so there's that. So, I figured it'd be better to put up with his creepy ass, than to make an enemy of him. I'd rather have him close and know what he was up to, anyway, y'know? So anyway, one day we were listening to the radio, and some other guys came on, one was saying there was a pretty, young girl with dark hair who they'd seen enter the old bank. There was a group of them looking for her, I guess they had the same mindset as Thomas. Maybe. It seems like their thought process was pretty provincial. Caveman-esque. Find a woman. Procreate. Some just wanted sex; some wanted to be heroes or whatever. Save the humans, save America, rebuild humanity. I don't know," he explained. I shuddered. I didn't like the thoughts of this, not by any stretch of the imagination. Jared went on,

"Apparently this dude and some pals went to look for her, and she was gone. Thomas also became fixated on finding her, spouting off the same bullshit as he had the night by the fire. Said he needed to find a woman to keep us alive. Us, I guess, being human beings, or at least the American people. Or maybe he just wanted booty. Thomas became convinced that the biochemical attack was somehow specifically targeted towards women and children since, well from our vantage point, it looks like barely any of them survived. Seemed farfetched but so does all of this. His other theory was that men survived because men are superior. But even so, we still need women. I guess I get what he was trying to say to an extent, but I didn't pay any attention to his ramblings, since I hadn't seen any girl, but when I saw you earlier, I knew it had to be you," he explained.

"Shelby, before my radio was stolen, I heard guys talking. There are no women to be found, anywhere. You're a sacred, rare commodity right now. As Thomas spreads this fanatical, barbaric mentality, they'll all be after you. You are essentially the holy grail right now," he said, solemnly. Then, his eyes turned friendly for a moment, as though his guard were let down, and I saw a glimpse of the Old Jared for one second. "You *are* pretty cute," he said. He wouldn't dare wink in front of the older men, but, I could sense a wink in his voice. If he only knew! I blushed, a deep, crimson red. This was so surreal.

I pushed my feelings for him aside. Owen rolled his eyes. He wasn't yet a fan of Jared, despite the information he was feeding us. "So this guy's still out there?" I asked.

"Well, he took his bag and the one radio with him one day to go look for food, and never returned. He always took that one radio, and left the other behind, I don't know if that was his way of being nice, or if he just never intended to leave camp for good and wanted to have one there as a backup in case he got robbed on the road. He was hooked on using them, almost obsessed with trying to contact others. Borderline crazy about it. I see, now, that you must have encountered Thomas," he said, nodding towards our radio setup, "and," he continued, "that you were my thief. Why didn't you guys take everything else?" he asked, with a genuinely puzzled tone in his voice.

I blushed. "I wanted to be nice. I believe in Karma," I answered.

He laughed, "A nice thief. Okay. Well thanks for leaving me the blanket," he said. "Can you tell me what you know about me, now?" he asked.

There was a war ensuing in my brain. Do I tell him everything? Do I explain "us" or the lack thereof? I decided against it. I figured that the watered-down version would be overwhelming enough.

"Well," I began, "your name is Jared Ketchum. We grew up together." I said.

He blinked with surprise. "I know you don't have any reason to believe me, but, trust me, I know you very well." I blushed as I said it, but continued, "we've known one another since we were about 2 years old. We lived at opposite ends of the same street, and we attended daycare together. Our parents knew each other, and our moms played cards together. We went to the same church, and had a lot of common friends. You are 31 years old. We graduated from Sunhaven High School, which isn't too far from where we are now. We grew up right here in upstate New York, but I moved to the city for college, and ended up staying there and living in Brooklyn. I was a production assistant on various movies, and in my spare time, a freelance screenwriter and aspiring novelist and filmmaker. You went to school for education, but against your parents' wishes ended up becoming a bartender and a freelance graphic artist. You did a lot of odd jobs here and there, and toyed around with the notion of going to graduate school for art. You even said you'd love to teach art or graphic design on the college level one day. You always wanted to own a comic book store, and have dabbled with acting, too. You have a lot of interests, kind of like myself — I think it's why we always got along. Quirky. Different. Maybe a little weird. But yeah - you like sports, you like computers, you're a little self-absorbed sometimes, but funny. Like I said — quirky. A little eccentric but not in a bad way. You knew my ex-fiancé, Ezra, but you hated him. You hated most guys except for your best friends Chuck, Todd, and Ray, and even them, you began to drift from. You liked the ladies. You used to date a girl named Katie, and another named Chelsea. They never lasted," I laughed.

He looked flabbergasted.

"Jared? Hmm. I was getting used to Andy."

I looked at him, blankly.

"Andy Amnesia," he explained. "That's what the crew was calling me."

"Ah," I said, nodding. "The crew. Ok. Well, it's Jared. Some of your friends called you J, or Ketch. I didn't."

"Were we … are we … good friends?" he asked, with trepidation.

Owen and Eugene stared at me, awaiting a response. I felt like my mouth was filled with cotton balls again.

I swallowed, nervously, and carefully chose my words.

"Yes. We were good friends," I said. In my mind, I added, "Until you just forgot about me, jeopardizing that lifelong friendship and potential relationship for childish reasons." But that was just in my head. I couldn't chastise the guy who was just re-learning who he was.

"You know, on a smaller scale, I empathize with you," I said. "When Owen first found me, I couldn't remember anything. It took me awhile to piece it all together. I can't imagine not knowing anything at all. It must be scary," I said, laying a hand gently on his.

It was electrifying. He must have felt it too. He quickly retracted his hand and got a scowl on his face. I don't know if he was disgusted by the feeling, or embarrassed that I said he must be scared. I should have remembered: Jared didn't like emotion, and he sure wouldn't want to essentially be called a wuss. *"Duly noted,"* I thought to myself, but there was no denying the sparks that flew from that one second of physical contact. That's how it always had been. Sometimes, even a second of our eyes locking could do it. I'd never had the feeling with anyone else.

We all sat there, awkwardly, for a moment.

As per usual, Eugene broke the silence in his quiet, funny way: "Well, that's some story. Now why'd ya shoot me?"

We all laughed, but I felt sickened at the memory.

"How are you feeling, Eugene?" I asked with genuine concern.

Again, he replied, "I'm fine, angel. How are YOU feeling?" with a barely perceptible nod towards Jared.

How was I feeling? I couldn't put it into words. It was a combination of "ecstatic" and "heartbroken." My face couldn't hide it, I'm sure. All three men were looking at me strangely, and Pippa even seemed to groan.

"Sir, I really am sorry I shot you. You had the hat on, and from a distance, from your build, I thought you were Thomas. I thought he'd stolen the other radio, and left me alone, and I was worried for Rory, out there somewhere, and for this young woman, who I now know was Shelby. I wasn't thinking rationally. I was going on barely any sleep, I thought he was a danger, and I thought you were him, and it scared me to see you with another man, I thought maybe you guys were ganging up on me. I really ... I must have been delirious. I wasn't in my right mind, man. You have to believe that. I couldn't make out what you were wearing from a distance, couldn't tell your age, and, like I said, I haven't been sleeping. This is all just really hard and... there's no excuse...I don't even know a thing about guns...I just..." his voice cracked, and he trailed off, uneasily. In his face, I saw traces of the little boy who I'd once known. We used to play house together, or sometimes superhero games. He was always rescuing me, his damsel in distress. That is, of course, when he wasn't teasing me or his sister mercilessly. I smiled at the happy memories. We really were some cute kids.

It was true that Jared didn't know much about guns. I had been shooting with my Dad many times before. I would never hunt animals, but I like to shoot at targets and clay pigeons, and I had no problem handling a gun for purposes of self defense. Jared came to the gun club with us once and, though he'd never admit it, was terrified. He was definitely more at ease playing video games or golfing than he was with firing a weapon. He hated that I was better than him at it, too. He always had that competitive streak. He was my biggest fan, and my biggest competition, all our lives. That's just how it was.

"It's okay, son. I just hope that you learned a lesson and that you end up where you need to be. It's never too late," he said, looking pointedly at me. It seemed that Eugene was warming up to Jared, and that he was hoping Jared would warm up to me. Owen, on the other hand, still wasn't as welcoming. I can't say that I blamed him.

"We're all exhausted. Jared, you can stay, I guess. We haven't much room, and we haven't much food, but we are a family. So we look out for each other first. But, it sounds like you're practically like family to Shelby, here, too, so, again, I suppose you're welcome to stay. We haven't got much, but we've got each other. But no more guns," Owen said, "and no slip-ups or you're gone. You're one strike away from being out. No warnings. Don't test me."

Jared swallowed hard and nodded. "I can see why you'd be leery. I won't disappoint. Thank you," he replied.

It was too much. Jared, staying with us? It was just unreal. But, Owen was right. He was like family. He was more than family. He was my heart. The fact that he didn't know who he was, or who I was, though … it was almost as bad as the fate I'd imagined he'd had: death.

I was exhausted. I was angry. I was sad. I was thrilled. I didn't know what I was. I laid down to sleep some more. Eugene went to rest, too. I could tell that

Owen wasn't yet sure about Jared, so he stayed awake and let the rest of us sleep. Jared lay near me on the ground, but not within touching distance. When I woke up, I was facing him, and was able to just look at his gorgeous face in the candlelight. How could he not know I loved him? How could he not know ME? It hurt so badly. His square jaw, slightly cleft chin, his full lips, long brown lashes, dark brown hair. Even his nose was perfect – and his body – well, if I needed proof that there was a God, there it was. He was perfect. A chiseled Prince Charming. My very own Byronic hero. Moody. Beautiful. He was kind of a jerk, and now an amnesic jerk, at that, but MY amnesic jerk, or rather, the guy who I'd so desperately wanted to be my amnesic jerk.

"Too late," I sighed to myself. My face was hot with tears. I was sick of being this weepy girl. I could be the damsel in distress in my story, or, I could be the heroine like the women that I wrote about in my screenplays: tough as nails, a bitch when she had to be, and sexy as hell while she's at it. I was a go-getter. I had overcome a lot. I would overcome this – with or without Jared. Who had time for heartbreak or love affairs when survival was on the line? No, I couldn't let myself be distracted. I wouldn't. I needed to focus on me. My health was still an issue with unknown proportions. I had to overcome that in addition to just surviving this new set of tribulations we were all facing.

I needed to focus on Owen, and Eugene, and Pippa. I needed to survive for my family and for my friends, especially if I was, as Jared had called me, "the holy grail." I could not allow Jared to cloud my vision or my judgement. Oh, we all know he'd clouded my judgment on more than one occasion. My love for him would have to wait. Shit was about to get real.

Feeling empowered, I got up with a start. Owen raised an eyebrow, "Energetic this morning, are we?" he asked, smirking.

"Owen, what are we doing? I mean, are we really prepared? Really, REALLY prepared? What if I'm being hunted? What if people want to…I don't know… take me? And- are we just going to wait to run out of stuff to eat, and just die? What are we doing? Are we going to stay, are we going to move? Can we defend ourselves? What if I really am all that's left? What if we run out of food? Come on. Man up, we have to think." I said, rudely pacing with my hands wringing.

He watched me bemusedly.

I paced back and forth, back and forth, biting my lip. My mind was racing, simultaneously ever-present and a million miles a way. The anxiety was creeping back up, and I was pushing it back down. "No, no, no." I told myself.

My thoughts were irrational, and fast-paced. I was feeling frazzled, and rather snarky, to boot. I idly wondered if it was my time of month. The notion grossed me out, to say the least. Tampons were things of the past. Relics of a different time, when hygiene was a priority.

"Owen, we can't just do nothing!" I exclaimed.

His look went from amused to angry. "Little girl, do you think we're doing nothing? Who's been taking care of you? I could have left you at the bank," he snapped.

I felt hurt; it was like a slap in the face. Then, I realized, I must have hurt him, too.

"I'm sorry," I said. "I don't know what's gotten into me today. I feel really on edge," I apologized.

"Wake up your little boyfriend," he said. "Let's do some meditation. You need it," he said, pointedly.

I nudged Jared in his ribs, with my foot. Any other physical contact would be too much to bear. "Wake up," I said.

He rolled over and peered at me through lazy eyes. "Good morning, Jared," I said with too much forced formality. "If you're staying with us, you're going to be one of us," I said. "We meditate in the mornings," I said.

He looked startled for a moment. (But oh, his large chocolatey eyes were to die for!) He blinked, "Um, okay."

Now, Jared was athletic, but, meditation? I laughed at the notion. It was close quarters, but Owen, Eugene, and I settled into our normal spots. Jared folded his tall, slender frame into position and sat there, awkwardly.

"I don't know what to do," he whispered after a moment.

"Just clear your mind," I snapped. (Why was I so testy that morning? The tension. It had to be the tension. One-sided sexual tension, that is.)

"Um...my mind is pretty clear. I don't even know who the hell I am," he said.

We all burst into laughter.

Jared was now one of us, and things were going to work out just fine.

CHAPTER 8

That afternoon, we decided to take a walk. Eugene stayed behind with Pippa, each nursing their respective injuries. Owen, Jared, and I ventured out and were surprised to find the sun shining for the first time since...before.

Though it had only been a couple of weeks, the storm felt like it was many lifetimes ago. The bombs were only a faded Polaroid photograph of a memory, and the time that had lapsed since seemed both molasses-slow and lightning-quick. The world around us looked inexplicably normal, yet startlingly different. Though the weather had calmed since the havoc it had wreaked not too long ago, this world felt colder. The emptiness was a shock to my system. Everything seemed more dismal. Things looked right, but they looked wrong, too. The convenience store near our hideaway still boasted a neon sign, the colors bright against the dreary terrain. Its once-overflowing shelves were now barren, the walls of the building were crumbling in. Stop signs decorated the street corners, still boasting their proud caution of red, a caution now dulled by a layer of dust. Non-working streetlights looked like ominous warnings, like tall strangers that were guiding our way into a place where we didn't belong. Bodies littered the street like something out of a horror film, but there were still cars intact and random personal belongings that we'd stumble upon: a handbag that had been emptied out, a man's wallet with family photos inside, cell phones that no longer worked. We'd find hair barrettes, random toys, pens, fast food wrappers, cigarette packs, and empty bottles of medicine. The things we'd come across were so mundane, and yet, they now seemed so foreign. Pens were a weapon. Chewing gum was food. Things had a new purpose, but not a new name. Things were normal, but not.

From time to time as we walked, I would notice Jared stealing sideways glances at me. He always was the master of sidelong glances. But I always knew he was looking – and I liked it. Now, however, it felt awkward, and he made it even more awkward when he refused to make eye contact. I tried to ignore him, to force his presence out of my mind. I was in hunting-and-gathering mode. Whereas before, I had enjoyed these walks, valuing them as exercise, taking in the dusty outdoor air and still trying to recover and refocus, now, I was in a different frame of mind. Meditation had calmed me down, a bit, but I was still more alert than ever: I finally realized the full scope of what was going on. The magnitude of the situation weighed heavily upon me.

The guys didn't even think I would venture out, but, for the time being, at least, they felt it was relatively safe. Just in case, though, I put my long, dark hair up under Eugene's hat, and layered myself in some baggy men's clothes we'd taken from some of the bodies. While I wasn't going to hide out 24/7, I wasn't going to flaunt my femininity, either.

The day wasn't fruitful. We roamed, and roamed, for what felt like hours. Owen was pensive, and Jared would make small talk, but there were no sustained conversations, for whatever reason. The gorgeous weather seemed like a betrayal. It was in stark contrast to the mood that enveloped us. The sun seemed to mock the desolation; it seemed to shine a spotlight on the lack of humanity. It was too pretty to be fair, when we looked at what was left of the life that we knew.

I began to wonder if Jared was perhaps better off not remembering. Was his amnesia a gift? Was he lucky to have no recollection of the life that he'd once had? Did it make it easier for him? I thought so. A part of me felt childishly envious.

"You know, Jared, you're kind of lucky that you don't remember life before. You just got thrust into this new normal without the burden of having to compare it to everything that came before," I said.

He stared at me, wide-eyed. "Are you kidding me, Shelby?" His argumentative tone sounded familiar, and I liked that. Familiar was something he knew nothing of. He didn't have to deal with the heartache of losing all that was familiar.

"No, Jared. I'm not kidding. I have memories, but they hurt. They hurt more than anything," I said, my voice cracking.

"But at least you have them!" he argued.

We were at a stalemate. I didn't know what to say. We both were a little envious of what the other had, even though neither of us had much at all. Jealousy was always something that plagued us growing up, and even as adults. But of course, he wouldn't have known that. How could he?

"Whatever," was my genius reply. Owen rolled his eyes; Jared glared.

My calves ached. My body was sore and weak, and my muscles cramped often, with the lack of nutrition, exercise, sleep, and hydration. I worried about my body. Was cancer spreading rampantly throughout it, or had the clinical trials helped me at all? I would probably never know, and that was something that was both rewarding and outright scary. None of us were in the best physical shape, and surely things were only going to get worse.

I wouldn't allow myself to whine, though this was a far cry from casual weeknights sipping coffee at the library, or swanky industry parties on the weekends. This wasn't what I was used to: mom's lasagna, workouts followed by manicures, shopping and gossiping with friends, teaching my dad how to send text messages. This time with Jared wasn't what I'd imagined, remembered, or hoped for, and it was a brand new world compared to the one we came from, which consisted of high school parties, the pool hall on the weekends, and playing in the sprinklers or sled-riding as kids. It wasn't the bar-hopping of our 20s, or the family get-togethers of our tween years. It was new, and it was certainly not what I'd wanted or expected my life – our lives – to be.

While I bemoaned my own existence, I worried about others even more. Were my parents alive? My friends? Was Owen okay, emotionally? Was Eugene healing alright? What became of all of the displaced pets who weren't as lucky as Pippa? The sick people with no hospitals? What was it like in other parts of the country, or in other parts of the world? We had no solid idea what was going on. I felt badly for the people – if there were any left out there – who had it worse than we did. I knew that in some warped way, we were lucky. I wondered how many people were like Jared, remembering nothing. Was it a blow to the head that caused the memory loss, or a coping mechanism that his mind constructed, to help erase the sheer horror of it all? At any rate, I had mixed emotions about whether or not he was luckier than me, or whether any of us were, in any way, lucky at all.

We hiked along in silence. There was no food to be found, anywhere. A Styrofoam cup blew across our way like a tumbleweed. Owen picked it up, out of habit. It was empty, of course, but he put it in his bag, anyway. There were not many plants for us to eat, and we had taken just about all there was to take in the area, at least as far as we knew. Even as we walked a little farther than usual, we came up empty-handed. We all knew it. Our shoulders sagged with the new realization that we'd soon have to leave our humble abode and traverse the terrain to hopefully find better sustenance and new shelter. We didn't know when, but I sensed it would be soon. We had no choice. It had to be.

The silence was deafening. All we could really hear was the light pant of our breaths, and the occasional wheezy cough from Owen. Jared said nothing, just spit occasionally, or kicked the dirt. I was lost in thought, and overcome with worry. Instead of letting it get to me, though, I was trying to think positively. My yoga instructor had always taught me that we grow our thoughts. I was trying to choose to let positive thoughts in, and to keep negative thoughts out. It was hard to do when everything around us was direly negative. I didn't know if optimism really worked in a life-or-death situation, but, on the same token, I knew that if it was ever needed, it was now. Cancer. Hurricane. Bio-terror attack. Perhaps the last woman left on earth. Love interest has no recollection of who I am. Everyone else that I loved? Dead. Yeah – life was a mess, but I had to hold on to what little was positive: Life itself.

New friends. Jared, in any form. Pippa. A slowly-renewed faith.

What else could I do but try to cling to the good, as scarce as it might be?

"Well," said Owen, "let's head on back, I guess." I could tell he was discouraged.

In silent agreement, we turned around, one foot in front of the other, our quiet little train heading back to its station, slumping, and empty, and bringing nothing along for the ride.

On our way back, we saw some cockroaches that Jared killed and threw in our bag. I, for one, wouldn't be eating any bugs, but the boys could have at it, if they so desired. On top of the aching, I did feel hungry, and the sun was blinding, even in the cold. I shivered, but refused to whine. I was getting a headache and just wanted to get back home to Eugene and Pippa, and relative warmth.

Jared threw an arm around me. I don't know why. Perhaps he sensed my discouragement, my chilliness, and maybe, even in his newly oblivious state, he could still see through my "tough girl" façade. He had always been able to, and after all, somewhere deep within, his soul knew me better than most, even if he forgot that. I didn't fight it. In fact, I appreciated the friendly gesture for what it was, and the extra warmth didn't hurt, either. Out of the corner of my eye, I thought I saw Owen give an ever-so-slight smile, but the whole thing just made me feel even more sad. This was Jared, and at the same time, it wasn't. Because of this, the gesture didn't mean as much to me as it could.

It was nice to have a piece of home with me, though. Jared might feel like a stranger, new to our gang, but he was a huge part of my life, and being with him was a little bit like having a slice of my mom's pumpkin pie. He was familiar to me, even as I was foreign to him, and so, there we were, an odd little pair, like puzzle pieces somehow fitting together. Our souls were reflections of one another. He was my mirror. He always had been.

When we arrived back at home base, we were pleased to find Eugene and Pippa, doing fine and snuggled up by the fire. He read the Bible; Pippa snoozed away.

"I take it you're feeling okay?" I asked.

"Yes, indeed!" Eugene answered, brightly. "Pippa, too," he added with a smile. "Any luck?" he inquired.

"Unfortunately, no," Owen replied.

"A whole lot of nothing," was Jared's response. I just shook my head, idly wondering if our luck had run out, and if luck had ever existed in the first place.

Owen removed the Styrofoam cup, and placed it with our assortment of misfit cups and mugs. He opened one of our last bottles of water, and split it between the 5 of us. (Pippa would never get neglected.) Before we drank, Jared raised his cup and said, "Cheers to new friends."

"To new friends," we chorused.

"And to overcoming tough circumstances," I added.

"Couldn't agree more," said Eugene.

I noticed beads of sweat on Owen's forehead, and grew alarmed. He appeared clammy, but then again, our walk was longer than usual today, and, though cool, the sun was beaming down on us the whole time.

"You okay, Owen?" I asked.

"Just peachy," he answered.

I wasn't sure whether to believe him or not, but really, what choice did I have?

We sat glumly for awhile. Isolation from the world entails a whole lot of boredom and self-reflection. Silence replaced noise. Stillness replaced motion. Stress replaced ease. I let my mind go blank after awhile. I didn't need to let the worries consume me every second of every day.

Our thoughts were interrupted by a scrambled noise coming across one of the radios. It was garbled; there was a lot of static and white noise in the background, but we could hear at least two men's voices going back and forth.

"Shhh!" Owen commanded.

We listened. I couldn't make out a thing. We heard a couple words here and there: "She" ... "camp" ... "alone" ... "tough"... and a lot of grumbling.

It wasn't enough to form a single idea, but, it was enough to let us know that there were more men out there. We did not know, however, who they were, how close they were, or even how many of them were out there. We did not know if they were potential friends, or potential enemies, and the whole thing left me more than a little afraid. I assumed, nowadays, that we had to treat everybody as a potential enemy. In my old life, I'd look at everyone as a potential friend. Doing so had hurt me sometimes. But, now, it could be a fatal mistake.

I was content with our little bubble and didn't want any outsiders intruding upon what we had built. On the other hand, people could equal food, if we were able to obtain it. But, people could also equal danger.

We contemplated the message that we'd listened in on. It likely wasn't Thomas – we had his radios. "Jared," I asked, "did the other men you were with have radios?"

He shook his head. "No," he answered. "Just the ones you found."

"Did you know of anyone else out there besides the men you'd mentioned to us?" Owen asked.

"Nope. I knew there was someone Thomas had communicated with, and I know he had referred to a group, but I don't know who or where he was, or how big this group was. It could have dwindled anyway given the conditions, I guess," Jared replied.

"I guess there's nothing we can do," Eugene said. "Unless we go searching for them."

It was something we'd have to consider. If these men were really searching for me, as Jared had alluded to, we were most likely going to have to encounter them at some point, anyway. Would we be the ones to hunt them, or would we wait, and be the hunted?

"We have a lot to think about," Owen said.

To lighten the mood, I joked, "Anyone up for a game of truth or dare?"

To my surprise, Eugene responded with a gleeful, "Sure!" We laughed.

Jared added, "Count me in."

Owen didn't look thrilled by the idea, but, not wanting to be a poor sport, agreed after a short protest. Though I'd said it in jest, it seemed that we all needed a distraction, as irresponsible and dumb as it may have been.

"You're going first," I said pointedly to Owen. "Truth, or dare?"

"Truth," he said, not surprisingly. I had to think for a moment on what to ask.

"Are you really okay?" I asked, thinking of his clammy appearance that I'd taken note of earlier.

He sighed. "Yes, Shelby. I'm just tired, that's all. I'm fine," he insisted.

Oh.

Despite his objection, I felt that my gut was right. I wasn't sure he was as "fine," as he proclaimed to be – health-wise or otherwise, and my heart ached for him. "Anything we can do?" I asked.

He ignored me. "Your turn," he said.

"No!" I interjected. "What can we do to help you?" I asked again.

"What do you think, Shelby? There's nothing you can do. Just pray. Worry about yourself. Worry about YOUR health," he said. "I'm not the one with cancer," he said lightly. He and Eugene knew, but Jared looked alarmed and surprised.

He cleared his throat. "I didn't know," he said.

"And why would you?" I asked, gently. He took it to mean that he couldn't have known given his amnesiac state; I meant it to mean that he didn't bother to check in on me, post-Ezra. "I'm fine," I said. "Let's change the subject. I'm just worried for Owen."

"Your friendship and support is enough," Owen said. "That goes for all of you. Now, truth, or dare?" he asked me.

"Was Ezra the love of your life?" he asked, knowing very well what the answer was.

I narrowed my eyes, and tried to control the uncontrollable flush that always crept across my cheeks and chest at the most inopportune of times. I swallowed.

"No, he wasn't. That's why I didn't go through with the wedding," I said.

"And?" Owen asked.

"And nothing!" I snapped, with a quick, uncomfortable glance at Jared who was taking it all in.

"Eugene, truth or dare?" I asked, more than happy to change the subject.

"Dare!" he said with a mischievous gleam in those old blue eyes.

I didn't expect that, and wasn't prepared. As I fumbled for a dare, Jared butted in: "Go streaking!" he laughed.

Ah, yes, that was like the Old Jared, who had dared me to strip down naked on a number of occasions. I joined in his laughter, followed by Owen, and we waited for Eugene to crack a smile. He didn't. His mouth lay in a flat, hard line, and the glimmer in his eyes were gone. Uh-oh. Had we offended him?

We sat silently for a moment, and just as I opened my mouth to speak, Eugene slowly began undressing. Carefully, he removed each piece of clothing, leaving only his boxer shorts on.

"Come on," he said, motioning towards our exit.

When we got outside in the night air, we expected him to run around in his boxers – he was an old man, we'd forgive him if we didn't want to go for a jog in his birthday suit.

Seconds later, in what seemed to be in the blink of an eye, there went Eugene, in all of his naked glory, running in circles outside of our makeshift home, laughing hysterically, tears running down his cheeks, his old-man parts flapping in the wind. Owen, Jared, and I couldn't contain ourselves. We collapsed in a heap of fitful laughter, Pippa joined in with an excited bark, and I shielded my eyes from the sight before me, though the image was burned into my memory both out of modest disgust and an affinity for this delightful old man who had no inhibitions and no clue how charmingly infectious his personality was to be around.

We needed this laughter, that was for sure. I hadn't laughed like that in ages. When I caught Jared's eye, my insides melted. I'd missed his quiet laugh and contagious, mischievous smile so much. He looked like my Jared in that moment – was he in there, somewhere? As our eyes met again, I hoped for a gleam of recognition. I didn't see that, but I did see – was it, appreciation maybe? Admiration? Whatever it was, I'd take it. As Eugene dressed, I helped Owen up, and gave him a hug. "I'm glad we're doing this. Making happy memories, you know?"

"Me, too," he replied. He put his fingers to his lips and blew a kiss up to Heaven. "Marta would have loved this. She was so funny, and such a prankster." He nodded his head, smiling.

We headed back inside. "Who hasn't gone yet?" Eugene said, with no shame about the show that had just occurred outside. "Jared!" I said, a little too enthusiastically.

"Truth, or dare?" Eugene asked him.

"Truth," Jared said.

"Okay, do you really have no memory of Miss Shelby here?" Eugene asked, in a gentle tone.

Jared's face grew hardened, and his eyes turned sad. "No," he said. A second later, he looked intensely at me, making extended eye contact with me for the very first time, "But I wish I did," he added.

I was thankful that the fire was dying down so he couldn't see the various shades of red that my face was surely displaying. He continued looking at me. "Truth or dare, Shelby?"

I panicked inside but kept my cool on the outside. "Dare," I proclaimed, boldly.

Eugene and Owen exchanged a glance, Owen whistling under his breath. Jared seemed thoughtful about his request. It was torture. A part of me immediately regretted my choice. Was he going to make me go streaking, too?

"Pick truth," he said. What? This was unlike him. The Jared I knew was full of dares, many of which had already humiliated me in the past. Then again, this wasn't the Jared I knew, and a part of me was quite relieved by that fact, in this context, at least.

"Okay, truth." I said. Why did this make me more nervous than picking dare? Why did I suggest this silly game in the first place?

"Were we more than friends?" he asked. His lack of eye contact bugged me before, now his intense stare was making me feel uncomfortable. I couldn't form thoughts, let alone sentences. Our little group awaited my reply, and Jared was the only one who didn't know the answer.

"I wanted to be." I replied. I left it at that. Suddenly, I was furious. I was furious at myself for not saying this sooner, when it mattered, and I was furious at him for constantly leading me on but never making a true commitment, when it mattered. "But, too late now!" I said, a bit too cheerfully.

"I think I'm done," I then proclaimed. "I want to get some rest," I said, and gave quick pecks on the cheek of each man, lingering a little too long, and yet not long enough, when it was Jared's turn. I couldn't really "go" anywhere, so I assembled a makeshift pillow, grabbed a shirt to cover up with, and lay down, turning away from the three of them. I was reticent in my efforts not to cry, and, internally, I was beating myself up for being such a *girl* this whole time, boo-hooing about love lost, having to get permission from the men to do what I wanted, being dependent on them for protection, and missing silly things like hair products, reality television, and Starbucks. I felt like the little girl stuck at a sleepover, who just wants to be at home with her mommy and daddy, but can't tell anyone lest she look "uncool." This time, though, I had no teddy bear or Cabbage Patch Kid to cuddle with. I did have Pippa, though, who was my girlfriend through all of this. I used to snuggle up on the couch with Tamra and a tub of Ben and Jerry's when I was nursing a broken heart or when I had a bad day at work. Now, I snuggled up with Pippa, on the dirty, hard ground.

"Light as a feather, stiff as a board," I mumbled in my half-asleep state, letting waves of rest crash over me as I drifted to sleep, dreaming of brownie ice cream and teenage slumber party games.

In the middle of the night, I awoke. I felt emboldened. The men were asleep, and Pippa was out cold. Before the disaster, I would head to the refrigerator for a snack when I awoke like this, padding in my socks or slippers across the linoleum, the warm glow of the fridge making whatever forbidden treat I was enjoying seem just a little more comforting. Tonight, I had no fridge, and I had no slippers. The only comfort I could get was solitude. I was grateful for these men, but I needed to be alone. Careful not to make a sound, I tiptoed around each one of them, and slid out into the fresh nighttime air. I inhaled. It was glorious. I glanced up at the sky. The night looked normal, as though nothing had happened, as though everything wasn't...over. The stars were painted across the bold black canvas sky, and for a second I did feel that refrigerator-glow comfort, imagining each star as a special someone: Mom, Dad, my grandparents, Tamra, Daphne, Davis, Ezra, Marta. It felt amazingly good, and I felt oddly at peace. The cold air felt brisk and nourishing in my lungs. I felt alive!

Always a victim of my own impulsivity, I decided to jog, just a little. I had the urge to run free like the deer I used to watch in the meadow near my grandma's house growing up.

I started at a slow pace, just enough to get my legs going. I picked it up a little more, lost in a sea of my own thoughts. I was gloriously alone. I used to be afraid of being alone. I would have panic attacks and fear would overtake me. But now, alone felt empowering. No Jared, complicating things. No Eugene or Owen, acting like my father. No Ezra, who was so anal-retentive and condescending. Not even Tamra, who sometimes was overbearing with her very bold opinions. No annoying boss, judgmental co-workers, helicopter mom, gossipy neighbors, or pushy salesmen. No politicians, no clients, no supermodels telling me I wasn't good enough from upon the pages of a magazine. It was just me, and the open air, and the new world in which I lived. I ran. I sang. I don't know where it came from, but there it came: Mariah Carey, just spewing from my mouth. I felt giddy. A little too giddy. I was undernourished and exhausted. I sat down on what was left of a curb to rest. Far off in the distance, I heard voices. I got my bearings about me – they weren't coming from my home base. At that moment, reality set in. I WAS alone.

Shit.

I took off again – this time in the direction of our nothing-home. When I got close, someone grabbed me.

I tried to scream, but his hand was over my mouth, tight. My eyes were clenched shut, but when I opened them, I was again looking into the face of Jared.

"We've got to stop meeting like this," I joked, knowing very well that a joke was vastly inappropriate at that moment.

"What the fuck is your problem?" he hissed. Yes, the Old Jared was in there somewhere, for sure. And he looked angry.

He then, quite literally, picked me up and threw me over his (sexy) broad shoulders, like a caveman. It struck me as funny, somehow, since we were basically living in a cave, after all. The irony of it, the runner's high, and the sheer, absolute terror must have gotten to me, because I burst into a fit of giggles. When he set me down in front of the concerned faces of Owen and Eugene, I tried to contain myself.

"She drunk?" Owen asked Jared.

"No, she's just an idiot!" Jared fumed.

"I just wanted to go for a jog, I wanted to have some time alone! I'm a woman! We need time to ourselves sometimes, you know!" I said, a little too defensively. I realized that my propensity towards acting like a spoiled child, at times, wasn't helping my cause or working in my favor.

"You ran out, by yourself, in the middle of the night, with no protection, no dog, and didn't let us know where you were. You call it alone-time, I call it insanity." Jared sniped.

The immature teenager that sometimes still lives inside me wanted to retort, "Ok, DAD," but I refrained. After all, this wasn't Old Jared, who just liked to mess with me, who was usually my partner in crime; this was New Jared, who seemed legitimately, and understandably, concerned. The worry and anger on Owen and Eugene's faces matched his, and I immediately felt bad, not to mention, stupid.

"I'm sorry. Really, I wasn't thinking…" I trailed off and Jared interrupted, "What were you running back from?" he asked.

They all waited expectantly. "I heard voices." As I said it, my own voice quivered. All at once, I recognized the immense danger that I could have put myself in, and I regretted the selfish ignorance of my seemingly-carefree act.

Chapter 9

I could feel their disappointment, and it stung.

"I'm not perfect," I mumbled. It was the truth. I was, indeed, far from perfect. Ever self-aware, I'd examine my flaws and accept them, even before all of this.

The men didn't respond to me. The silence was worse than a lecture, but they were too busy getting into warrior mode to waste time or words on a situation that was already over and done with. I decided to let them be. Owen sharpened our butcher knife, and his pocketknife. Jared toyed uselessly with the bulletless gun, and a stray bullet we'd acquired that was, unfortunately, the wrong size for said gun. Ammunition wasn't easy to come by. We weren't in an area where gun stores were common; and my Dad was only one of a few hunters in our community. In fact, we had to drive two hours to our gun club; we'd stay at a camp nearby the shooting range when we had gone. I figured if we could get up there, we may be able to help ourselves to some weaponry and ammunition. But we hadn't been there for years, and I couldn't remember where exactly it was, or how to get there. Reality slapped me in the face as I once again realized my Dad wasn't around to ask – and he never would be, again.

Eugene played around with the radios, trying to see if we could pick up anything. I went on somewhat of a cleaning spree. I didn't know what else to do with myself so I organized what little food and water we had left, with what little stamina I had left. It felt good tidying up the small space – I was never one for housework, nor was I anything even remotely close to a neat freak, but, it was giving me control over my environment. Control was something I hadn't had in a while. It felt nice to have order in the midst of chaos; it was refreshing to have control over anything at all.

With my heart still heavy, I remembered that my mom, too, would clean when she was overly stressed or anxious. I remembered my dad joking that he'd intentionally piss her off sometimes when the house needed to be spruced up. I missed them with every cell of my body, and it hurt. This type of pain was worse than cancer: it was the worst and most unimaginable kind of heartbreak, the deepest-set pain of all pains.

"Guys!" Jared said, and we heard some more rumblings on the radio.

"What is it?" I asked.

It seemed to be a news report in a foreign language. "America" was the only word I could make out. It sounded mildly Asian to my ignorant ears, but I couldn't even identify the language.

"It's Mandarin," Eugene said.

"A Mandarin newscast? Why would we be picking that up?" I asked, immediately anticipating the inevitable "Shhh!" that would follow. (It did.)

We listened. I didn't know why – none of us were fluent, but we listened nonetheless. When it faded out again, Mr. Interesting, the man of Appalachian Trails and New York Fashion Week, reminded us that Mandarin was one of a few beginner's language courses that he'd taken at the local library. Of course.

"Well?" I asked, impressed but impatient.

"Unfortunately, I don't know enough to help us out that much. I can tell you that they said America is no more, or something that would roughly translate to that. It sounds like they said Europe and Asia are okay but on high alert. They didn't mention any other regions – not that I could make out, at least. They also said that there were no survivors in Canada or the United States. That, I gathered for sure. They mentioned the storm but also spoke of a large-scale bombing. They used their equivalent of terror, and the word for chemicals, quite a bit, from what I gathered," he said. "But, I'm no expert," he added, "and there was a lot that kept cutting out."

"No survivors?!" I exclaimed with indignation.

"Well, Shelby, honestly, how would anyone know we're here?" Jared pointed out. "Look around."

It was true. We may as well have been goners. If no one knew that anyone was alive, no one could rescue us. "What else did they say?" I asked.

"I don't know. I think they said 9, purple, and Tuesday," Eugene replied.

I didn't know if it was his idea of a joke, but it didn't matter. The new information was neither encouraging nor helpful. As we were thinking about the new revelation, a harsh voice cut in on the radio, sounding much clearer and frighteningly closer. This was not part of a newscast.

"Thomas!" Jared and I exclaimed together.

"You know the plan. Is your clan ready?" he asked, someone, on the other end, who never answered. "Hello? Hello!" he demanded angrily.

"Here," came a reply. They all sounded echoey, and very far away. I hoped they were.

"Let's go find her," Thomas said, urgently. "We need to get her."

Suddenly I feared that they were closer than we'd like … perhaps too close for comfort.

My eyes grew wide. "Why are they after me?" I asked, more rhetorically than anything. "It's so cliché!" I exclaimed, half-joking, but mostly serious.

Owen did his usual eye-roll, and I allowed myself to pout for a moment. "Suck it up, sista," said Jared, handing me a 1/8 full bottle of water. "Drink this, you need strength." I took it, not knowing how water would help anything, but appreciating his effort. As I sipped, I made sure to savor it; we were almost out.

"Let's move. I'm not taking no for an answer. These guys probably have at least an idea of where we are. We can't stay here. Plus, we're nearly out of food and water. We can't just wait to be found. That's not my style. I play hard to get. I lay down for no one," I said, with a pointed glance at Jared, although, he didn't quite get it, since he was New Jared. (And truth be told, I probably would have laid down for him, old or New Jared. But he didn't have to know that!)

"Who's with me?" I said. Owen shifted uncomfortably. Eugene solemnly nodded. Jared grabbed my hand. For some reason, I jerked away. I was the heroine in this story. I didn't need a man holding my hand the whole time – even if I did kind of like it. Why was he always making me contradict myself? He made me feel so conflicted. With my mind already in a fragile state these days, I didn't need further confusion. Any lapse in judgement could be problematic for not just me, but for all of us.

Pippa must have sensed that I needed some reassurance. She jumped up, pawing my legs. "You with me, girl?" I asked, affectionately patting her head.

I knew she was.

They all were.

I was glad I'd organized, as it made it easier to pack. We only had a couple of bags, so we would have to leave some things behind. We piled on as many layers of clothing as possible, fashioned a bag out of a shirt, stuffed our existing bags full of as much as we could: the last couple bottles of water, the rest of the baby food and the fish food, the Crisco and the batteries and the cloth. We waited to pack the radios: we wanted to have them on and leave them out for now, just in case. We had the knives, the rope, and the empty gun. We strapped the bible to Pippa. Owen had his photo of Marta, and I had nothing to speak of besides myself and my anxiety and my possible tumors. For the first time in my life, I was okay without material things. I was okay with just me.

I couldn't say that I wasn't scared – of both the cancer and of Thomas and his men, but my will to live outweighed those fears. My instinct was that we should move, and I knew the others agreed. We didn't have much more of a game plan beyond that, but sticking together was good enough for me. Whatever and whomever we encountered, I was pretty sure we could take them.

Or was I? I couldn't imagine Eugene fighting, and had never witnessed Jared in a real altercation, either, so I was hoping that Owen could throw down, if necessary. As for me, I could play the tough girl when I wanted to. (I wasn't sure how convincing it would be, but in my mind, at least, I was a total badass.)

It was still dark outside. We collectively decided that it would be best to start out on our journey while it was still dark, to make it harder for anyone to spot us. We didn't know how many hours we had left of darkness, but it couldn't have been many. Before we left our home – possibly for good – we got in a circle and held hands. Pippa with the Bible stood in the middle of us, and, without words, we said a silent prayer. I had been questioning my faith a lot before this all had happened, especially given my illness, but now that we had nothing, I could see how important it was to turn to God – whatever god you believed in, no matter what kind of god that may be. When you had nothing, it was somehow easier to believe in something. If this journey had taught me anything, it was that we had to believe.

I wasn't sure of anything in that moment, though, except that this could very well be our last moment of peace. I wanted to linger there, to live in that moment for as long as time would allow. I was choked up, but wouldn't let them see me cry.

"Please, God," I said to myself, "Whatever God you are, just, please keep us safe." I quickly added, "And thank you. Thank you for these people. I don't know if you're a Christian God, or Allah, or Buddha, or a Goddess, or the Universe, or what, but I do know you're there, in some way, and always have been, and I need your help. We all do. Please. Thank you. Amen." It was a plea of desperation, and not the most eloquent prayer, but I knew that it was necessary. I hoped there was someone or something out there who was going to hear us. There simply had to be.

I took a deep breath, and slowly locked eyes with each one of the guys. This was real. With a slight nod, I said, "Let's go."

For some reason, they listened. Perhaps I exuded more self-assurance than I felt; perhaps I came off as more powerful than I was. The truth, though, was that I didn't feel in control, no matter how much I wanted to be. I hadn't felt in control other than when I was tidying up our home, and even that was fleeting and futile. Even before all of this, I would often struggle to feel in control of my own life, and would struggle even with controlling my own thoughts, at times. But now, confidence and self-control were necessary. Being able to stay calm, cool, and collected could be a matter of life and death for me – literally.

I took one last glance at the nothing-home that had since become a real home, against all odds. I thought that when we left that place, I would think, "good riddance," but it felt bittersweet, instead. We were moving on – but to what, I did not know.

We started on our journey. We hadn't intercepted another message on the radio, and so we had no way to know what the others were up to. We just started walking. We walked in the opposite direction of our usual path – we certainly didn't want to head towards Jared's old camp, for fear that Thomas could be set up there once more.

For a while, we were silent, and worried about being found. We were on high alert, and the silence only heightened our senses. We still hoped to score some food along the way, but in the darkness, it was hard to unearth much of anything. We were simply focused on finding our way, and hopefully finding a new place to hide – a new place to call home.

The darkness began to fade into light. Our journey was, so far, uneventful. I was as tense as could be, just waiting for something dramatic to occur, but, at the same time, I was beyond grateful for the lack of excitement thus far. The soles of my feet ached, but what was worse was the weight of the world on my shoulders.

I glanced at the guys. I seemed to be holding up better than the three of them. Owen was sweating, and to me, taking on a gray pallor to match the gray landscape we'd become accustomed to. Eugene's limp was back, and he would occasionally give a subtle rub to the area where the bullet from Jared's gun had grazed him. Jared, who was in phenomenal shape physically, just looked beat. He looked exhausted, aged, and more haggard than I'd ever seen him look. We all were tired, and weak. By this point, we'd been walking for hours. Pippa was still trotting along, but I knew she needed a break, too, judging by the occasional whimper she'd let out between ear-perks and tail-wags and panting. Why were we still going when everyone was in bad shape? It then dawned on me that, for whatever reason, they may have been waiting for me to give them directions. I was the leader. My heart swelled with pride, but my mind was baffled by the notion. Still, if the roles were changing, and if I was to lead, then a leader I would be.

"Let's rest," I suggested.

"We can't. We have to get as far away from town as possible," Owen said, but the look of relief that swept across his face betrayed his words.

"Are you sure?" Eugene asked, his voice peppered by barely-perceptible hope.

"Yeah. We need a break!" I said.

We spotted a large tree stump up ahead, next to an upside-down bench, in an otherwise-barren area. I tried to get my bearings about me and estimate where we were. Everything seemed foreign, but I surmised that it must have been a park, once.

Before. I'd idly wondered if I'd been there as a child. Though we had been walking for a long time, it wouldn't have been too far outside the realm of possibility that my parents had stopped there at some point. Perhaps Jared had been with me. Most recognizable landmarks were gone at this point. My sense of direction had failed me, and all was foreign in this disorienting new world. My rusty memories did me no good now. It'd been years since I lived in the area, and Jared didn't remember.

"Guys, where are we going to stay?" Jared asked.

For some reason, his question annoyed me. It seemed that everything he did or said lately either made me all swoony, or annoyed the hell out of me. Today, he was irritating. Scathing, almost.

"Jesus, Jared. That's what we're trying to find!" I snapped. In addition to being tired, hungry, and stressed, I was PMSing. If life ever got back to normal, I would never complain about my period again. Battling cramps on the couch in my Victoria's Secret sweats and a heating pad with the luxury – yes LUXURY! – of a tampon was nothing compared to this hell on earth. I tried to remind myself to be nice. Jared hadn't done anything wrong. (Other than lose his memory, and, prior to that, make no real romantic gesture of any kind, ever.)

He looked taken aback, like a wounded puppy, and I had to laugh.

"I'm sorry. This just..." I shrugged.

"Sucks?" he finished.

"Yeah," Eugene chimed in, "this sucks."

We sat in silence for a bit, taking turns dozing off to nap. I leaned on Jared's shoulder for my shift. He and

Eugene would keep watch while Owen and I got some shut-eye. I don't know how much time passed but I jerked awake, suddenly. I smacked Jared. Everyone was asleep – even Pippa! "Jared! Eugene! Owen!" I yelled. Jared awoke groggily.

"You fell asleep. You let us all fall asleep! What happened to shifts?" I barked.

"Sorry," he grumbled. It didn't seem sincere. I was annoyed.

My frustration turned to concern. "Owen! Eugene!" I shook each one of them ... but only one of them responded.

Everything went white. I was in shock. I just kept repeating, "No, no!" in between heart wrenching sobs, as I realized what I was seeing. Jared held me close, stroking my hair.

The three of us cried over the loss of our friend. We were really a family, and now one of our own was gone. Pippa lay her head on his leg, her eyes sad and uncertain. We were at a loss. What did we do now? How did we go on from here?

"It was almost inevitable," Jared said, "that not all of us would make it."

It may have been true, but it wasn't reassuring. I didn't need matter-of-factness right now. I didn't need logic. It did nothing but piss me off and make me cry harder. "I wish it was me!" I yelled. "I'm the one who was sick! My clock was already ticking! It should have been me."

Both men looked at me like I was insane. Jared shook me, "Why would you say that Shelby?" he demanded.

"Because! Because it isn't fair! He was a better person than me. He was so good to me, to all of us! I have nothing! It's too late for the life I wanted. I'm just causing problems for all of you! You all would be safe back at our place if those guys weren't looking for me. ME! Not you guys. ME! I'm putting you all in danger and why? WHY?" I sobbed uncontrollably. I didn't know what truly uncontrollable sobs were until recently. Now they came so easily. There was so much to mourn, all the time. "If it was me," I continued. "I'd be with my parents. With my friends. In heaven or wherever people go, and I wouldn't be here without people who loved me."

Now they both looked angry – disgusted, actually. Was I being selfish? I was so upset and emotional that I didn't know what I was saying or feeling. I was taking on the role of the hysterical woman that I so hated to write about in my screenplays. But here I was: her. The madwoman in the attic. I was a literary device sprung to life in an age of death.

"It isn't fair, it isn't fair!" I repeated, falling to my knees and clutching my chest. The hurt was real.

"We're all sad," Jared said gently. "But this wasn't your fault. And we want to protect you. Why else would we be doing this?" he asked.

I couldn't think straight. I was overcome with grief.

I looked at my two accomplices who remained – three, if you counted the dog – and I took a long, deep breath, reminding myself not to dwell.

"Ok. He would have wanted us to keep moving. But please - let's have a memorial," I said.

With that, we lay him across the bench, in a peaceful position. Pippa moaned, and licked his face, as we removed the Bible from her back and placed it across his chest. The other men sadly said quick yet respectful goodbyes, but I wanted some time alone. Pippa stayed by our side, whining. She knew this was a time to mourn. I kissed his forehead, my tears hitting him on his chapped lips, and, for a moment, I lay my cheek against his, whispering "thank you," in his ear.

Before leaving, I removed one of my shoelaces, tying it around his finger, as a reminder for him to never forget me, as I would never forget him, and I checked his pocket, making sure the photo of his beloved wife was still there. I silently hoped that, where ever he was, he was reunited with Marta. "Always have hope." I said aloud, through my tears, and for a second, I basked in the sun's rays, hoping and praying that my dear friend Owen was at peace.

We sat without talking, shocked and depressed. No words seemed to suffice. After enough time had passed, Eugene, Jared, Pippa and I decided to let Owen be, and to continue on our journey, as he surely would have insisted upon. We walked for a long time in silence, mourning the loss of our Owen, considering whether it was our dire circumstances, or outright heartbreak, or a combination of both that did him in. We were all saddened by the loss, and no words or actions could make it better. My heart ached for Pippa, but she seemed to know that she was needed here, with us. Every once in awhile, she would stop, turn around, and cast a long glance back towards the direction of her owner. But then, she'd look up at me, with her sweet doggy eyes, and I think she knew that I needed her now. So on she continued with her new human pack, but surely feeling the same pain as all of us, if not more.

With heavy hearts, and hungry bellies, we continued on. Owen's death was a surprising but stark reminder of our own mortality. At times, I forgot about the state of the world and the crushing enormity of our precarious situation. I was stunned by how seemingly easily it was for us to just gloss over this gigantic loss and this depressing reality – but we had to. We had no choice. But, the reminder was all too real. I did worry. I worried about Eugene. Youth was not on his side, and he'd sustained more injuries than Jared and I had over the course of this whole disaster. All of us now had more to carry, too, in the way of material goods, and in the way of emotional burdens. What I would have once deemed formulaic nonsense in my writers' circles was now the reality of my life: traveling on foot, in the midst of a post-apocalyptic event, with bad guys after me, unrequited love unfulfilled, and my good friend and caretaker dying off like he surely would in some sappy movie. In fact, it all seemed so unreal and farfetched and contrived that I almost hoped I was in some kind of coma or nightmare. Or perhaps I was on some kind of trip from a roofie in my drink at a chic Manhattan nightclub. But then the ache in my legs and the growl of my stomach reminded me that this was real life, and that there was almost certainly no happy ending in sight. This was no movie.

I had to, for lack of a better term, man up. We all did. We were in a dire situation, and my inner dialogue was getting us nowhere. We needed a morale boost of some kind, but, there was no hope in sight, even as we passed a desolate convenience store, and even after we scoured it for one sliver of food, one ounce of water, or anything, really, that could help us on our way. Morale, it seemed, was a hot commodity, of which there was scarce availability. (Kind of like myself, apparently.)

Walking along, we found some cardboard that we figured we'd pick up to later start a fire. Nearby, we spotted a brightly-colored box, and I picked it up. It was a disposable camera! I didn't even know that they made those things anymore. It reminded me of high school, taking fun photos in the cafeteria at lunch, and waiting with my girlfriends as we got them developed in one hour at the supermarket, showing them off the next day during study hall in our pretty plastic photo albums and carefully-crafted scrapbooks. I smiled, and unwrapped it. We'd never see these photos, of course, but, I felt the need to capture what was left of us while we still could. Was this the morale boost we so needed?

"Say cheese!" I said, clicking the button and aiming the camera towards Eugene. He smiled his charming, contagious smile, and posed for another one, holding Pippa, and sticking out his tongue.

"If only we had this during truth or dare!" Jared joked. We laughed. I knew that Owen would like our laughter, but thinking of him laced mine with pangs of sadness.

Eugene grabbed the camera from my hands and shakily took a shot of me mid-laugh.

"Gorgeous, darling!" he exclaimed.

"Get one of us!" Jared said.

I posed with him, and wished I'd been able to show him one of the gazillion other photos we'd gotten together in our lives. Maybe that would jog his memory.

The quasi photo session was what we needed to boost our spirits. Who knew that morale could come in such surprising packages, on the side of a road, in an abandoned town, from underneath a sheath of cardboard? It was pointless and weird, but it felt almost normal, if only for a moment.

"You know, guys, things are going to get better," I said, and I hoped it was true.

With that, I blew a kiss up to the heavens, the way I'd seen Owen do once before, and I hoped that he was there somewhere, with Marta, smiling down upon us, as we continued on our way.

"Things have to get better." Jared agreed.

"They will," Eugene assured.

CHAPTER 10

They didn't.

The weather was iffy – moody, almost. Very "Wuthering Heights." Sometimes, the sun shone upon us like the skies were celebrating a new day, basking us with warmth. On these days, Mother Nature it seemed, was giving us a hug, and embracing us with her nurturing essence. Then, these maternal skies would darken, and, in the back of my mind, I feared her wrath upon us once more. Only this time, I wouldn't have Tamra's jokes and hysterical forecasters and Mommy and Daddy's basement to help me through it.

Another big storm never did come, but in typical fall fashion, the days grew shorter, and colder. Rain was sporadic. Thankful for the layers of clothes and Crisco, we trudged on. We were just about completely out of food, and so, the time had arrived. I could not avoid the inevitable anymore. I'd have to lower myself to eating insects and rodents – this was what it had come to. We had to do what we could to survive.

We made a fire – it was not as good as Owen's were, but it did its job – and Jared put the freshly-killed mice on a stick and roasted away. I, for one, barely ate meat in my life before, and yet, here I was, about to eat a sweet, innocent mouse – a BABY mouse, nonetheless. It made me think of the human babies who had perished, and left me to wonder whose fate was worse.

The irony wasn't lost on me, either. Had we seen a mouse in our Brooklyn abode, we'd have the mouse traps laced with cheese, waiting to trap the little, terrifying critters, no problem, and yet, here I was, defending them, begging Eugene and Jared to find another way for us to survive.

"It is what it is," was Jared's genius response. Sometimes, I had to remind myself what exactly it was that attracted me to this man. Sometimes, I just didn't know.

I sighed. My stomach felt nauseous, and the tears welled up in my eyes. I didn't know if I could do this, and yet, we were the living, breathing picture of desperate. Our situation was, in fact, dire. I was emaciated. We were cold. We hadn't seen people, we were basically out of food, we got no other correspondence on our radios, and, we were in pretty poor spirits since Owen passed away just days before. I was at my wit's end. We all were. These were grave times.

"I want to give up," I whispered.

"What now?" Eugene asked. Jared ignored me.

"Never mind," I answered, but my words were becoming more true by the day: I wanted to give up. I sometimes begged God to take me, and feared that my mental anguish would eventually consume me.

As we watched the little family of mice char away over the flames, I once again considered their fate. The mouse population was probably struggling, just like their human counterparts were, and so, maybe they were the lucky ones. Maybe everyone who wasn't stuck in this new world were the lucky ones. Those who weren't with us anymore surely had been dealt the better hand, or so it seemed. So maybe the mice were lucky in that way, too. I now prayed regularly, and so I found myself saying a silent little prayer for the rodents. After all, humans weren't the only of God's creatures who were suffering. We all had a cross to bear.

Pippa hungrily licked her chops. This was a true treat for her, and a real challenge for the rest of us.

"I don't know about you," Eugene said, "but, this is nothing. I've eaten escargot, frog legs, octopus, and, even tripe."

"I tried dog food once," Jared said.

I laughed. I remembered that.

"Wait! Jared! How did you know that?" I asked.

He shrugged. "Some things, I just seem to know ... but I don't remember them, and I don't know how I know them," he said, as though this were a quite natural, simple phenomenon.

If Jared was remembering some things, maybe he would remember me! Maybe he would uncover feelings for me, that have stayed hidden for far too long! I tried to contain my girlish excitement. I hated that he always made me feel that way to begin with; I hated it more given our circumstances and the world around us.

"What's the weirdest thing you've eaten?" he asked me, as we all stared hesitantly at the mice.

"Umm...caviar, I guess. Or sushi." I said. "I also had duck once," I added, cringing.

"Snob!" was his reply. He said it in jest, but it irked me: Jared always used to make fun of me, calling me a girly-girl and a yuppie. Calling me hoity toity made no sense, since were of the same socioeconomic status, had the same background, and ran with mostly the same crowds. I suppose my sometimes-pretentious language and my affinity for designer duds had perhaps pushed me a bit farther across the snob-line, but still, it wasn't fair. That label was simply inaccurate. If anyone was a snob, it was him. He was an egomaniac, endlessly self-absorbed and, at times, quite antisocial. (Again, I lamented: why did I like this guy?)

"Well, let's do it!" I said, suddenly feeling brave, or, maybe just to prove to Jared that I wasn't some wimpy yuppie.

Jared handed out the mice, taking them off of the makeshift-skewer, and distributing them to us and Pippa.

"On the count of three?" Eugene asked. "1, 2, 3…"

Pippa didn't wait for three, devouring what was surely a gourmet treat in her mind, in one gulp. I doubt she even tasted it.

I hesitantly put the baby mouse into my mouth, all at once, to try to get it over with. I had to fight my gag reflex multiple times before being able to chew. I tried to chew quickly through the bones and the gristle, but it was difficult. The texture was sinewy but luckily all I tasted was…"burnt." I'd insisted they char them, hoping that the carcinogenic blackness would kill off any germs or disease that the rodents carried. I also correctly speculated that burning it would mask the taste a bit. I got it down quickly, and prayed that it stayed down. We needed protein.

Jared also seemed to be struggling. He was taking smaller bites, and looked as though he may spit it out, throw up, or both. Eugene was a pro about it, acting as though it was no big deal. I wasn't surprised, Mr. Interesting was game for anything, it seemed – including streaking, as we'd learned. I laughed at the memory.

"What?" he asked, looking at me with a twinkle in those old blue eyes.

"I was just remembering truth or dare!" I said. "This would have been quite a dare! Eat a mouse!" I said.

"You have to do what you can to survive," Eugene said, sadly. I could tell he was probably thinking of Owen. I put an arm around him.

"True. At first I was afraid. I was petrified…" I started to sing.

"Kept thinking I could never live without you by my side..." Eugene continued.

I grabbed the stick/skewer/mice-roaster and used it as a microphone.

"But then I spent so many nights thinking how you did me wrong, and I grew strong, and I learned how to get along…" I continued, adding in a few hip wiggles and hair flips along the way.

"But now you're back, from outer space, I just walked in to find you here with that sad look upon your face, I should have changed that stupid lock, I should have made you leave your key, if I 'd known just for one second, you'd be back to bother me!" I sang to Jared.

"Go on now! Walk out the door! Just turn around now, 'cause you're not welcome anymore, weren't you the one who tried to hurt me with goodbye? Did you think I'd crumble? Did you think I'd lay down and die?" Eugene sang.

Simultaneously, we belted out, "Oh, no not I! I will survive! Oh, as long as I know how to live I know I'll stay alive! I've got all my life to live, I've got all my love to give," we sang in unison, and finally Jared joined us, "And I'll survive, I will survive, hey, hey!"

Pippa barked gleefully. We were swallowed by laughter. I smiled, thinking Owen would have enjoyed our little show, and then, my smile faded as I realized that he didn't. He didn't survive.

It was late and dark, and we needed to rest up. We were very careful to sleep in shifts – one person slept, two stayed awake. We decided to let Eugene rest first. Jared and I spoke in hushed whispers.

"How are you holding up?" he asked me.

I casually leaned against him, ignoring the pitter-patter of my heart.

"Fine, I guess." I answered. "It's scary to think that people could be looking for me, and it is frustrating not to know who exactly attacked our country, or why, or if they could be plotting to do more. It's hard not to know if anyone we loved is still alive. So, mentally it's rough. But I guess you know that," I said.

We sat in silence for a minute.

"Physically, I feel okay as can be expected, though." I said with false cheerfulness. "Which, is pretty crappy, but, I'm still here. For better or for worse, I'm still here," I added.

Pretty crappy was putting it mildly, to say the least. I hadn't really shown the extent of my suffering, which was vast. I was nauseated every single day. My skin itched, all the time. My mouth was dry, and the sores inside felt more raw by the day. Above all of that, my bones ached right down to the marrow, a deep-set ache that can't be adequately described to someone who hasn't felt it on their own.

"Can you tell me about it?" he asked.

He didn't say as much, but given the hesitancy in his voice, I intuitively knew that he was referring to the cancer.

"I had the breast cancer gene. I thought nothing of it. But, I began to feel lumps. Some were cysts, but, my doctor insisted I have further testing done. My mammogram showed some areas that were complex and likely malignant. So, they wanted me to have a surgery – lumpectomy or mastectomy, it was up to me – followed by radiation and chemotherapy. But, I always try to practice holistic health, and so the thought of undergoing chemo and radiation? I wasn't a fan. So, I did some research, and I found this one clinical trial. It was through a practice that does more integrative and translational medicine, which made me feel a lot better about it. Only a handful of women were selected to partake. Maybe 75 or so, and then a portion of them got the placebo. I don't know. This new therapy was supposed to stop the cancer from growing and diminish symptoms. It would somehow "turn off" the breast cancer gene. I know that it worked similarly to some other meds that are out there, but it didn't seem like it was as harsh as the other options, especially since it was through the integrative department of the hospital. We weren't allowed to learn a lot about the treatment, and, in fact, I don't even know if I got the real infusion or not. We didn't really know what the outcome of it would be, what the side effects would be, and so on, but, it just FELT right to me. It felt way better than the alternatives! And now, ha, who cares about long-term side effects. None of it really ended up mattering, did it? I'm closer to dying now than I was before. But yeah, I'm okay. Physically, I mean. I'm okay," I said.

It was a half-truth. A part of me was always trying to keep up with him, and even Eugene, who was in surprisingly good shape for his age. I didn't want to admit when I needed a rest, and it was taking its toll on me. My knee ached from an old ballet injury. Headaches were a constant. My stomach hurt all the time, from hunger, probably, in addition to the medicine that was still coursing through my veins. I was exhausted, physically and mentally. Emotionally, I was just beaten down. I was losing my will to go on, but I couldn't let anyone see my weakness, even my friends. As usual, I didn't even like to admit my weaknesses to myself. Being self-aware was a gift of mine, but that didn't mean that I enjoyed dwelling on my shortcomings.

"You're amazing," Jared said. "So strong," he said, brushing a strand out of my eyes. I didn't respond. I didn't know what to say. His eyes melted me, but my mind was elsewhere.

I did not feel amazing or strong. We shared the leader role for the most part, but, inexplicably, it seemed like the guys most often depended upon me for guidance, and to make decisions. I felt even more burdened with this duty since Owen left us. The truth was, I didn't have a plan, I didn't have answers, and I didn't really want to be the leader. The responsibility of that was just overwhelming, but I didn't want to let them, or myself, down. So, I had to stay strong, and just told myself to "fake it 'til I make it."

I asked Jared how he was doing.

"Fine, I guess. I wish I felt more comfortable in my own skin," he said. "All the other stuff, the shitty stuff that we're all dealing with – I mean, it's just awful. That goes without saying. But, that's what is hardest for me. I can't reconcile my flashes of memory. I can't FEEL who I am," he said.

It was poignant, even if he didn't mean it to be. We all think we know who we are, because, we just ARE. We just exist, and we accept it. But if that security were taken from you, how would you know who you truly were at your core? How would it feel? You'd feel like a body without a soul, or a soul without a home. My heart broke a little for Jared, in that moment. I had once considered him lucky for his lack of memory, and, I can see why I felt that way, at the time. But now, I finally understood how very lost he must be. He has no points of reference, and no foundation on which to build. It was sad, really.

I gave him a hug. I didn't let go. He lay his head on my shoulder, and I stroked his hair. The energy between us was palpable. No one knows what a real spark is until they feel it firsthand. We had a spark that was inarguable. When he touched me, I felt sure that God had a hand in it. It was undeniable that the universe had meant us to be one, like we were two pieces of one heart. Star-crossed no more, he was my true north. He was my anchor. He was my vibration – a sensation and a part of me that no one else could feel. With the slightest brush of his hand against mine, I felt him flow through my veins. Jared was the medicine I needed, the drug that I craved. And right now, he felt like my favorite cozy blanket on a fall day. Jared was my home. And it felt sad that my home was shaken to its core.

"I'm sorry," I whispered. Those words seemed so inadequate lately, and so insufficient, but sometimes they really are the only words there are to say.

"I wish I knew you," he whispered back with a crack in his voice.

My heart that was breaking for him suddenly went whole again. It melted into itself and spilled over with joy. Joy, in such a desolate, hopeless time, was a rare, welcomed commodity. I reveled in it, being mindful of the feeling, in case it never came again. The warmness I felt was from my love for him; our fire was dying down but that spark between us was alive and well.

"Jared," I said, and before I could get any words out of my mouth, he kissed it. Our lips felt like they were meant to be one, and, in that moment, it was as though some beautiful, passionate prose was being written in the stars. It felt timeless and perfect. It was comfortable, but new, all at the same time, and, in the flawless physicality of our connection, I momentarily forgot where we were, who we were, and what life had become. I just wanted to take the moment and lock it up safe in my memory forever. I didn't want it to end. Jared's mouth felt fiery on mine. I felt the longing that we both shared. There was a burning passion, and a lifetime of love and connection in that one interaction.

I didn't know what the kiss meant; I didn't overthink it. I just enjoyed it. It seemed to last an eternity, but it wasn't actually a long, drawn-out, soap opera kiss. It was just right.

We looked at each other, breathless and glassy-eyed. I felt flushed and flustered, but somehow whole again. I smiled, shyly, and we didn't bother with words. I'd once read that kissing originated as a way for mothers to transfer food to their babies' mouths, and thus was a lifeline. This kiss, too, felt like survival. It had felt like LIFE. We leaned against one another, and tried our hardest not to drift off to sleep.

But I did - I dreamt of Owen in the Technicolor field again; of high-school Jared and I dancing at a Prom that we never attended together; and of ballet dancers wearing red plaid. It felt nice.

It was short-lived. I awoke with a hand over my mouth – this was becoming routine. I opened my eyes. Everything was black. I panicked. "Jared!" This wasn't funny.

I tried to call for him through the gloved hand. I'm sure he was trying to be playful – naughty perhaps

– but, I was growing annoyed. I then became aware that the grasp seemed aggressive. I began screaming, as much as I could whilst being wrangled and muffled. My mind raced; I kicked my feet; and realized my hands were bound, too. Oh my God. I immediately grew scared; were we moving? Who was taking me? Why was I blindfolded? Why was I bound? Where was I going? Couldn't Jared and Eugene hear me? Where was Jared? I needed my lifeline.

I felt a blow to my temple. I was nearly blinded by the pain and was slipping in and out of consciousness. My breaths came out raggedly; I was beyond the point of panic. I prayed that it was a nightmare. But, no – this hurt too badly to not be real. My very own screams sounded like distant wails. I felt like no sound was coming out of my lungs, as hard as I forced it, but at the same time, I felt my throat aching from the shrill shrieks that I was indeed emitting. It hurt. It hurt so very badly. I couldn't touch my face, but I felt the hot tears that were steamrolling down my cheeks. He was pulling on my long, dark, now-matted hair; tugging so hard that I thought it would be ripped from my scalp in a big, knotted mess. His manly fingers were rough and unwelcome against my ample breasts. His gripping, groping hands hurt my butt as he squeezed, hard. Too hard. His kisses were demanding, violent, almost darting. These kisses choked me and weren't like Jared's by the fire. His caresses weren't soft, and his fists were a striking danger. I felt them come down on me, relentlessly. Unwelcome. I knew what was coming. I licked my lips and tasted a mixture of blood, sweat, and tears. His voice tickled my ear in an unpleasant manner. I vomited and allowed myself to slip into the abyss of the unknown, where I heard bits and pieces of a muffled, violent whisper.

"Shut your mouth! … Don't fight it. We need this."

Fade to black, again. Awake, again. My insides felt like they were on fire. A searing, thrusting pain tore through me. A part of me begged for total unconsciousness, or, perhaps even death. A part of me knew I needed to stay awake.

"You like that? You better. You're mine, you're mine. We're going to do this…it's okay…" the man said, his urgently whispering voice conveying power, hate, and a strange vulnerability all at once, a combination that I had a hard time understanding. "You're it, you're it, and now you're mine.." he said, gruffly, menacingly, in the same eerie, harsh whisper.

I tried to bite him. "You bitch!" he hissed.

It was hard to make sense of any of this; I was in a state of shock. I was disgusted, and I prayed that death would come grant me some respite. The contradiction of unwanted pleasure and undeniable pain ripping through me became too much to bear. I felt my pride leaking out of me, and right before I was about to pass out in the pool of my fluids and my shame and my blood, I silently wished that God — if there was one — would just take me away right then and there.

CHAPTER 11

I was mildly aware of some kind of commotion going on around me. God had failed me, and, once again, I questioned my faith. I was still alive – and my body let me know it. The physical and emotional torment that I was experiencing was otherworldly. I didn't know that it could exist. I wasn't sure if I was fully conscious. I couldn't see, and my hearing was muffled. All I heard was a piercing, shrill ringing in my ears, and I felt pain radiating off of me – every square inch of me – in waves. I had the urge to get up and run, much like the urge I had felt in that first day in the demolished bank, but I had absolutely no strength left to do so, nor any literal or figurative light to run toward. My will to survive was weak, at best.

I didn't know what was happening. I couldn't organize my thoughts; I couldn't process my feelings. I was the living dead.

I felt dust kick up in my mouth. Should I play dead? I was careful not to sputter. I didn't want to make a noise, let alone make a move. I tried to listen above the ringing. I heard scuffling – a fight, perhaps? Then, I heard men's voices. I couldn't quite make out what they were saying, but it was clear that the discussion was heated, crucial. I struggled to maneuver my bound hands up to remove the blindfold, but it was to no avail. I was afraid to move, or to even make a peep, in case the man wanted to come back for round two.

There was a bark. Was that Pippa? Yes, Pippa! If I had been able to feel anything, I would have felt touched to know she was here. I pictured the beautiful, loyal dog protecting me and defending my honor. I hoped she wasn't in danger. Surely, she was alongside my Prince Charming, Jared. I wanted to rush to him, to hug him, and kiss him, and thank him for being my savior, but I could barely move, and I didn't want to risk being seen awake and conscious. I tried to listen to my surroundings. The voices, I now recognized, were Jared and Eugene. Relief washed over me.

I heard footsteps rushing towards me. Hurriedly, Jared removed my blindfold and the ties. I couldn't stop shaking, but attempted to give him a trembling hug.

"Thomas." Eugene said, sadly, shaking his head back and forth, with a sheen of tears caressing his eyes. "Jared noticed you were gone and came to find you. He tried to fight him off, but Thomas got the best of him, and ran away," Eugene explained. I glanced at Jared, who looked dazed and deflated. His eyes were glazed, his face was reddened, his jaw was tightened with barely-contained anger. Something in his face looked stunned, and something about him looked dangerous. He was livid, and we were all in shock.

My hopes crumpled. This whole situation was worse than I'd thought. My stomach was in knots, and I was breathless, shaken to the core. What would have happened had Jared not come to my rescue? I shuddered, a shell of the Shelby I once was.

CHAPTER 12

Water was scarce. All I wanted to do was wash away the blood, to wash away the sticky. I felt like I was retreating into myself, like life was just swallowing me whole. I was numb. I never envisioned myself a rape victim, let alone a rape victim in a post-apocalyptic world, fighting for my cancer-ridden life, and perhaps being the only hope for a repopulated America, either.

I wanted to make someone feel as violated as I felt. I longed for revenge. I wanted explanations, but, at the same time, I didn't. There was no explanation or justification for what had been done to me. I'd been taken, abused, and left for dead. My rapist was still at large, with God knows how many other men yearning to do the very same thing to me – and I had wonder: had he succeeded in his mission to impregnate me? And was this only the first attempt of many?

As we walked back to where we had, just hours before, happily sang Gloria Gaynor, bravely ate charred mice, and, where Jared and I had finally given in to our romantic desires, I was silent. Eugene and Jared repeatedly asked me if I was okay. I wasn't, but there was nothing anyone could do or say to fix that. I wished that they would stop asking. I wished that I wasn't once again a damsel in distress. They helped me walk; it took us awhile. The incident had taken place not too far from where we were that night, but, my legs and torso hurt so badly, and every movement was shockingly tender and insurmountably painful.

The emotional torment was worse than the physical pain, though. I kept getting flashes of memories, and I wondered for a moment if that is what it was like for Jared. Everything had happened so quickly, and in my mind, seemed so fragmented. The kiss with Jared. Awaking, thinking he was just messing around with me, only to realize that it wasn't him, and that it most certainly wasn't a game. The feelings of abuse, embarrassment, helplessness, and disgust. How could a night transform itself from happy to tragic during the brevity of a quick sleep?

I wanted to cry but I couldn't. Not anymore. I felt too much – there was no way for me to express it. I now fully understood what people meant when they said they were numb. When we got back, the men insisted that I try to rest, and that we'd start moving at sunrise. They urged me to try to sleep, and I refused. I sat, mutely, in a daze. Images, sounds, smells, and feelings played over and over again in my head, flooding my brain and my body. I tried to focus on the positives, like the kiss with Jared, and the fact that he and I, Eugene and Pippa were still here. But, as much as I tried not to dwell on the negatives, they kept flooding in. Now it was not just the storm, the terrorist attack, the cancer, and the unknown fates of my loved ones. Now it was all of that, and then some: the death of Owen, a rape, a group of men still out there somewhere who wanted to capture me and knock me up, and so on. How much could one person take? This was not life – this was hell. And now, I was a game; I was prey to be hunted; I was a means to an end. A resource. I was no longer human, at least it didn't feel like it. My emotions were scattered. I was in love with a man who didn't really know who I was, and I was in excruciating physical pain, to boot. These same thoughts just kept recycling themselves in my brain. There was nothing else to think of, because this was my existence now. And I was losing the will to exist.

I tried the word out in my head: "rape." Had that really happened? Had that happened to ME? The girl who refused to carry pepper spray or a whistle in Manhattan because it made her feel ridiculous? ME? The girl who pretended she was some kind of badass? How could I have let that happen to myself? How did Thomas manage to kidnap me without Jared and Eugene knowing? I became enraged. I was mad at them, and I was mad at myself. Ironically, and inexplicably, more anger was directed at myself than Thomas. I couldn't believe that I'd just … taken it. How could I let that happen? And how did Jared let him escape? I knew I'd never seen him fight, but if ever there were a time, that was it. I was struggling with all of it. It all seemed too surreal.

Jared gently laid a hand on my shoulder and I jumped, recoiling at his touch. I suddenly didn't trust anyone, and was turned off by any physical contact at all. The current from earlier had dulled; I no longer felt the spark. I felt disgusted and disgusting. I was ashamed and embarrassed that they knew what had happened to me. I couldn't even make eye contact with the dog. I knew that I couldn't play the victim role forever, but, the fact remained that I was a victim; a victim of something horrific, and I just needed to dwell for a moment and feel what I was feeling. I needed that and I deserved to dwell and mourn and cry and scream and sulk as long as I wanted to. There wasn't a "Rape for Dummies" book that I could check out of the library or download on my Kindle. I didn't know how to act, and I didn't know how I needed, wanted, or expected them to act, either. My own thoughts felt like they would be the demise of me, but after all the things that could have and should have killed me by now, I wondered if I were somehow invincible – and that notion scared me more than anything else. I didn't want to be invincible. I always would have preferred to die young than to be immortal. Growing old used to scare me, and now it seemed to be both an impossible and a sickening notion.

I felt like I was slowly unraveling, but I couldn't let them see that. The conflict of feelings I felt within was unbearable. Jared seemed to understand that I didn't want to be bothered. I couldn't help that any touch felt repulsive; I didn't want to feel that way towards him, of all people, but at the time, I also harbored resentment that he didn't stop it sooner, that he just let Thomas take me. I also wondered if Jared still desired me after knowing what had just went on – forced or not – with another man, mere hours after we shared a lovely, meaningful kiss.

Through pursed lips, I let out a sigh. Jared may have often felt like home, but if there were ever a time for a hot bath, this was it. Ice cream, flannel pajamas, and a stiff drink wouldn't hurt, either. Instead I had tattered, blood-covered layers of men's clothing; stubbly legs; grimy teeth; dirty hair; a swollen eye and a swollen vagina – not to mention the bruised ego and mental scars that would never fade. Jared and Eugene began fashioning spears out of sticks we'd gathered. I watched them shaving and carving, focusing on the knives.

Right then, those knives seemed like a great tool that I could use to just end it all for myself.

I was desperate, and I was mad at the entire situation, from cancer to storm to bomb to rape. I was mad that Owen died, that Jared had amnesia, and most of all, that I was vulnerable even in the presence of these two men. I was mad at them, at Thomas, at myself, at God. I was just mad.

"How didn't you guys hear Thomas coming to get me?" I levelly asked the both of them. My steely eyes demanded an answer.

They sat silently, and stared at me with no reply. The answer was obvious: they were both out cold. We were all so exhausted, and right then, I realized that they probably felt exceptionally guilty about what had occurred. Though I knew that it was absurd for me to apologize, I felt that I had to. I was always like that: apologizing profusely even when there was no need.

"Sorry. I know it wasn't your fault, guys. I can't blame you. If anyone is to blame here, it's Thomas. Not us. We're a team, and I appreciate you guys coming to my rescue! My knights in shining armor!" I said, woefully but gratefully, and I meant it.

Despite my feelings of anger and resentment, on some level, I forgave them. I knew that they would never purposefully keep me in harm's way. But, I couldn't forgive Thomas, and, I didn't know if I could ever forgive myself, even though I knew at my core that I didn't do anything wrong. My self-loathing at this time was a weird, unwelcome feeling. I patted Pippa on the head, and rubbed my nose against hers, "You're a good, good, girl, you know that?" I said, and gave her a hug.

I made the decision not to let these events define me. It would be hard, but I would, someday, have to move on from this night. It wouldn't be tonight, though. I sighed. The fatigue was getting to me. I lay my head on Pippa's squat little Corgi body, and drifted off to a dreamless sleep until it was time for us to move once more.

After an indefinite length of slumber, I awoke and stretched. I felt sore all over, and the breeze had picked up, making it much cooler than when I was last awake.

Jared laid a gentle hand on the small of my back as I stood. "How's it going?" he asked.

I still felt numb. I still had no words. I, once again, withdrew from his touch. I felt that I owed him something, though.

"Fine," I said, with a curt nod towards him and Eugene. I couldn't muster a smile or a cheerful tone, and hoped they didn't expect either from me. I patted Pippa on the head. The dog had been my pillow all through my rest, and I wanted to let her know that I'd appreciated it. She lifted her eyes, peering lazily at me from under heavy lids. The poor pup, as hardy as she was, was utterly exhausted – we all were. It hit me hard to think of this sweet little dog's journey – what a trooper Pippa was! It was just unfair that she – or any of us – had to be.

"I hate to do this to you," Eugene said, "but we have to move."

"Yes, we do." I replied. "Let's get ready to go," I said in a monotone voice, and began apathetically packing up and prepping. Mindless motions seemed to help me through all of this, especially now. It was when I started thinking that things went south. When I began to think, the feelings of panic, and the storm cloud of dark thoughts would consume me. I had to constantly remind myself not to dwell. I had to constantly remind myself not to stop breathing – even when I wanted to, so, so badly. I was consistently on the brink of going crazy. I was consistently on the brink of death.

We gathered up the last of our very sparse earthly belongings, and set out on our way. My steps were taken quite tenderly; my pace was slower than usual. My inner thighs and swollen eye screamed with pain, but I kept silent. We walked and walked – the men discussed what sports teams they'd followed before this all happened. It was idle chatter, but a welcomed distraction, which I assumed was the purpose. I could sense that they were very actively trying to let me be and were careful not to bring up any serious topics just yet. Pippa sniffed every piece of debris we'd pass, as though she felt it were her job. I didn't mind the small talk, but I didn't participate, either. I just idly watched Pippa, and tried to keep breathing. Tried to stop the crazy. Tried to fend off the death.

We were out of the system of small towns and were approaching forests and countryside. Hopefully, this would allow for more food sources, and perhaps a stream or river for us to get some water, or, better yet, follow to civilization, if there was any left. We didn't know the true magnitude of this situation, but it couldn't hurt to try to find out at this point. We just had to be careful and choose our company wisely. After all, we didn't know if we'd encounter the group of men that was looking for me, and we didn't know if the fragments we'd pieced together were even true. Was I the last woman? Maybe here, but what about in the state? The country? The world? We were so isolated that we had no points of reference regarding anything.

It was mind-boggling, at times, how out of touch we were, when our former lives were so connected. Twenty-four hours a day, seven days a week, and 365 days a year we'd be online, receiving emails and text messages, phone calls and notifications. We went from being able to communicate with friends around the world from the comfort of our couch, to not being able to pick up a phone and call a friend across town. We couldn't even call 911 – the number we'd learned to call in case of emergency. We were taught that as children: if you are in danger, simply dial 911. It comes engrained in our minds early on in our lives, and it makes us feel secure: call that magic number, and help is on the way! This time, though, we couldn't call, and even if we could, it was very likely that no one would be there. If they were, who knew if they could help. We had no idea what the world was like now, and the isolation was stifling.

I was lost in my thoughts, but at least they weren't of the rape, or Owen, or my parents. I no longer obsessed over Jared – somehow his being here made my mind stop the fixation. Don't get me wrong: I was still in love with him, but his constant presence helped to ease any excitement or anxiety that I would have felt about him previously. He just felt normal.

"Check this out!" Jared said excitedly, stooping to pick something up. My curiosity was piqued; I wondered what he'd found.

What he held up was a mirror. The smile on his face was exuberant, and I'd remembered then that Jared didn't have a very solid idea of what he looked like. He peered into the mirror, studying his face for what felt like an eternity. He'd run his fingers over his lips and his eyebrows, smile, frown, touch his now-bearded cheeks, squint his eyes, run his hands through his hair. He looked amazed, enthralled, and, for some reason, scared. I couldn't wrap my head around what that would feel like, and how simultaneously traumatic and exciting this must be for him. I felt really guilty for insinuating earlier that he was lucky for not remembering anything. At least he was good-looking.

I couldn't recall the last time I'd seen Jared cry in our former lives – it was probably as kids, or, during a Rocky movie, but there they were: tears.

"Are you okay, Jared?" I asked.

"I'm just so...relieved," he said. "Happy. This somehow makes me feel complete – like a real person. Even though I don't remember my life before, I look at this person in the mirror and he – I – look familiar to myself," he said, smiling somewhat sadly.

"Not too shabby looking," Eugene chimed in.

"Not at all!" I agreed.

I gave Jared a hug. This time, I didn't mind the physical contact. I initiated it, and, I was just happy that he was happy.

After a couple of minutes, I couldn't stand it anymore: I had to take a look. I was always that girl who looked in every mirror or window that she passed – it was just my nature. I wasn't shallow, and valued character over looks, but, I was a little bit vain, and put effort into my appearance. I needed to see if I was still the girl I remembered.

I held up the mirror, but it took me a moment to have the courage to take a peek inside this strange, foreign looking glass. I gasped. I felt like the Evil Queen in Snow White, once she sees how she truly appears to the outside world. I was no longer the fairest of them all, and I was aghast at the face I saw staring back at me.

I stared. I studied. My face was dirty, tear-stained, and the hair at my temple was caked with blood. I looked closer. I saw the fine lines forming around my eyes, across my forehead, near my mouth, like spider webs. I saw the thinning of my glorious raven hair, no longer thick with its trademark shiny glaze. I saw a unibrow, dry lips, and dry, red eyes, with dark circles around them, one swollen shut, bruised, and drooping. I looked like an owl. My teeth looked yellowed and grimy with almost-fuzzy filth, like they were wearing little sweaters. I was pale; I was gaunt. My tall, curvy-yet-athletic frame was always slender, and trim, but this was a new look. I appeared to be emaciated, like the anorexic ballerinas I'd once shot a documentary about in school. I didn't look fit or toned; I looked sickly and frail. Gone was the sexy, athletic girl I once was. Where was the muscle I'd worked so long and hard to build? I looked pathetic. At least, my outsides matched how I felt inside: downtrodden. Fragile. All used up. Grim.

"Bella," said Eugene.

"Molto bella," Jared chimed in.

Internally, I scoffed at them, but, I knew that they were just trying to be kind. So, I lifted my head high and decided to embrace the new me, as hard as it was.

"Those bags under my eyes had BETTER be designer," I joked.

We shared a laugh, but it was demoralizing. Looking into the mirror and seeing a practical stranger is not anything you could ever get used to, really. I wondered, then, how Jared felt. If seeing a ghost of myself was so hard on me, I imagined seeing oneself for the first time would be even more difficult. Or would it?

We offered the mirror to Eugene, who shook his head and held up a hand, "I'll pass. I want to remember myself as young, and handsome," he said with a wink.

We took it with us, for some reason – maybe to remind us of who we now were, in this strange new world. Plus, on a practical level, we could break it, and use the shards as weapons.

As we continued walking on, I let my mind drift back to the last time I felt truly beautiful. It was my engagement photo shoot with Ezra. He was a gorgeous man: a blond Adonis, a bit on the hipster side, but well-dressed, and well-versed. I really did love him, and he made me feel like the most beautiful woman on earth. I remembered our edgy engagement shoot around New York City, the bright lights faded out in the background, and us at the forefront kissing, holding hands, him holding me, me on his shoulders being silly, us holding a red heart-shaped balloon. It was a fun time, and a great memory. I sometimes wondered why I let him go. I could have stayed with him, and had the life I'd envisioned, and maybe had the experience of having a child – but at what cost? Would sacrificing my happiness at the time have been worth it, especially if it were all to end up like this, anyway? In a way, I was glad I didn't bring children into this horrid world. I felt grateful that they weren't experiencing this awfulness that was now life as we know it, or, dead. Ezra was great, though – a bit pompous, but very loving. He was flattering, he adored me, and he always let me know it. It was fabulous and stifling all at once.

I remembered Jared's odd reaction to my engagement to Ezra. There were no congratulations, and no mention of it at all – not to me, at least. I heard from mutual friends that he was bad-mouthing Ezra and me all over the place. In comparison to Ezra, Jared never told me I was beautiful, or really expressed any feelings towards me, aside from jealousy of any new relationship I was in that didn't involve him. He didn't want anyone else to have me, but he didn't want me, either. In some ways, he was so egotistical and immature, and I'd often wonder why I cared for him, at all. Many of our friends had stopped bothering with him and his eccentricities and childish habits long ago. I, however, couldn't do that. I felt magnetically drawn to him for reasons I couldn't explain, and even at points in my life when I wasn't romantically drawn to him, we were still somehow connected. I always felt the need to reach out to him, and to let him know I was there, even if I didn't necessarily want to be. The instinct was almost primal. Our souls were intertwined so powerfully, and yet, so pointlessly.

Sometimes, as I lay in bed at night, even if I had Ezra or another man by my side, my thoughts would waft over to Jared. I'd have this almost-otherworldly sense of electricity come over me, almost like I could *feel* him. In my mind, I was feeling him thinking of me, too, like we were plugged into one another, magically. I'd try to send him simple thoughts: "I think of you all the time." "I hope you're okay." "I love you." "I miss you." Sometimes, I'd just send him a feeling: love, well-wishes, good vibes, regret for what could have been. I often wondered if he'd ever received my psychic bedtime messages, but, of course, I would never have asked. The nearly-supernatural scope of my deep-rooted love for him seemed downright insane. And maybe it was ... unless he felt it, too.

But of course New Jared would sweet talk me, compliment me, and be tender towards me — I *was* the only woman within God knows how many miles, after all! I may be the last female he ever laid eyes on. I rolled my eyes and sighed out loud.

"What's wrong?" Jared questioned.

"Nothing!" I snapped, exasperated. "It's just...old you. Old you is pissing me off," I said.

He looked wounded, "Oh."

"I'm sorry," I said. "I can't really help it. I know it isn't fair to blame you now for things you did before, but it's also hard not to."

"It seems like I might deserve it. That's okay," he said, and he sounded like he meant it.

I hadn't seen this kindhearted side of Jared in a very, very long time, if ever.

An old memory popped into my head just then, making me smile. Flashes of happier times were so welcomed nowadays.

"You know what, though, Jared?" I said, "You were the first guy to ever tell me I was beautiful. In 2nd grade, Mrs. Bonnatunni's class. I wore a floral dress and a big bow to school, and you had one of our classmates tell me that you thought I looked pretty!" I laughed, recalling how shocking that was during a time when boys were gross and girls had cooties.

"Was I your first kiss, too?" he asked, and I couldn't tell if he were serious or not, but, he asked it almost eagerly, with a twinge of hope.

"No," I said, ferociously blushing. "I would have wanted you to be, though." I mumbled.

"What was that?" he asked, playfully poking me in the side and then, eyes widening, saying, "I'm sorry!"

"It's okay. I'm not that sore. You're fine," I lied.

The brief zing of pain brought back highly unwelcome flashes of memory:

Half-consciousness. Begging. Crying. The tearing sensation. Blinding pain. Crippling humiliation. The feeling of indignation and helplessness. Blood.

I literally felt a chill go through my body. I shivered, and took note of my arm hairs dancing on end.

I shook my head as though to erase the Etch-a-Sketch memories. As I peered out over the horizon, I gasped at what I saw.

"Jared, Ezra, look!" I pointed... and then we just stopped and stared.

Chapter 13

The smoke billowed in thick tufts up out of the forest trees. It seemed dangerous and threatening, but also hopeful and life-giving. Smoke meant fire. Fire meant food … warmth … destruction … death.

Pippa started barking. "Shhh…" we hushed her. I picked up a twig and absentmindedly threw it for her to chase while we pondered what this smoke could signify. What would it mean for us?

"It looks like there could have been a small plane crash," Eugene observed.

"Nah," Jared argued, "I think it's someone signaling for help."

I studied the scene, hands on hips, and blew my bangs out of my eyes.

"Lets go," I said, marching towards the smoky horizon.

"Shelby Weiss, stop it. Just wait a minute," Jared said, grabbing my arm.

Had I told him my last name? I couldn't remember. There was a small part of me hoping that he'd suddenly remember things on his own, and then, another small part of me hoping he'd never return to his less-than-flattering ways. But, then again, THAT was the Jared I had loved for a lifetime. I loved this Jared, too, but I wasn't so sure that it was quite in the same way, just yet.

"Why?" I asked. "Listen – if someone needs help, we should help them. Or - maybe they are nice people who just made a fire in order to eat, and so maybe we can form an alliance with them. Maybe they can offer us food, or protection. Worst-case scenario is that they're the proverbial bad guys. Then, I think it's better we find them, rather than them finding us, unsuspecting and unprepared," I said matter-of-factly. "Plus," I continued, "What's the worst that could happen? I've already been pillaged," I said, haughtily, with more than the hint of a snarky tone.

They both looked at me blankly. Eugene stroked his stubble, Jared shrugged, and Pippa stood there, staring at me, twig-in-mouth.

"I suppose you make a good point there, m'dear." Eugene said.

"Let's just chill for a second, Shel." Jared said.

I agreed, and perched myself atop a rather large rock nearby.

"Food?" I asked, digging through the measly rations that we had left. I found some loose sunflower seeds at the bottom of my bag, and handed one lone seed to Pippa, dividing the rest of the modest find amongst us humans.

"How far do you think we've walked?" I questioned. We'd been walking for days now, but it was hard to consider what actual distance we had covered, and, with the barren state of everything we'd passed, it was equally hard to pinpoint where exactly we had been throughout our journey.

"Well, it has to be well over 100 miles," Eugene stated.

"I'd guess 140," Jared chimed in.

"What?! I am worse with distance than I'd thought. I would have guessed, like, 50 miles," I said.

The boys, as I was affectionately referring to them, stared at me incredulously for a second, and then laughed out loud.

"All the bumps and bruises you've collected, and nothing has knocked any sense into you?" Jared joked.

He then winced, as my temper flared for a moment at his insensitive remark.

But, then, I burst into laughter. He was right.

"Well," I said primly. "I guess we're always learning, now aren't we?" I unsuccessfully tried to hide my smirk.

"You know, we ran a half-marathon together once, Jared!" I told him. It was such a great memory, and such a fun accomplishment – and one of the prouder moments in my former life.

"Well, good for me!" he said with a smile. "That's pretty awesome," he said.

"You know, Shelby, it sounds like I've been lucky to know you – then and now," he added, almost shyly.

Whoa. The things that came out of New Jared's mouth were insanely unlike anything "Old Jared" would have ever said. At times, I missed Old Jared, but this upgraded version was definitely not too shabby.

"Well, I guess I got lucky, too, then." I said. Eugene smiled as he watched the two of us. I quickly changed the subject.

"I ran my first 5K with my Dad. It was a great memory. I had a lot of great memories with him, and my Mom. I really miss them," I said, my eyes welling up with tears. I can't imagine what my father would have done to Thomas had he found out what he'd done to me. I remembered at time he intimidated one of my exes with a shotgun, and laughed a little at the memory.

"They would be quite proud of you, and the way you have been handling yourself in adversity," Eugene said. "I certainly am!" he said, giving me a hug.

We were sharing our very last bottle of water. Jared raised it, and said, "To Shelby!"

"To Shelby," Eugene chimed in, raising an imaginary glass alongside him.

"To us," I said, joining in, and adding, "and to Pippa!" as I threw her now-beloved stick.

"And to Owen!" Eugene and I said, simultaneously.

"Jinx! Buy me a Coke," I joked.

My heart still ached a bit, swollen with memories of my parents and Owen and Old Jared, but it was also bursting with something else: a renewed sense of hope. After all I'd been through, I was uncertain how hope could ever again thrive within me, but there it was.

"Ok, then," I said, stretching, and brushing off my dusty clothes.

I tucked my hair up into my ball cap, lest I give myself away to any woman-hunters by way of lustrous locks. "Let's go!"

"Let's go," my boys echoed; Pippa chiming in with a bark.

I thought about my friends back home. I tucked my hair up into a ball cap another time, too, back in my old life. Aside from my usual clique, I hung out with the local filmmakers' crowd. Being an aspiring screenwriter, and dabbling in documentary filmmaking myself, I just clicked with them, though I didn't really fit the stereotypical mold. They'd initially received me with hesitation, casting me almost undoubtedly as the pretty girl who had little substance. Sweet, but not legit. Not authentic. Not hip. Their acceptance of me was muted, almost wary, but don't we all tend to reject that which we're not used to, at least at first? Isn't it human nature to be leery of those who are unlike ourselves?

I smiled, woefully, remembering how I'd stepped in, last minute, to help a woman named Darlene to complete her short film submission to a regional festival. I did so graciously, but with trepidation, as the character I was to play was, surprisingly, an adolescent boy. I remember the debate: could I pull it off by just tucking my hair and taping my boobs? Was I too girly? Should I cut my hair? Should we just try to find a boy to replace the original actor, and could we do so when a deadline was looming? It was so last-minute and such a conundrum. At the time, it had seemed like quite a debacle. I recalled, sheepishly, how important it seemed to us. I felt like I was really sacrificing something for this lady, hiding my beauty, dulling my femininity, and playing a boy, and yet, I'd never really sacrificed much in my life, at all. Now, I found myself making sacrifices every day and, however ironically, portraying a similar role as I routinely muted my womanhood from the outside world.

After a day of filming, I recalled letting myself daydream about what it would be like to do it for a living – acting, that is. I'd never been a serious actor, and had never been one to work onscreen, so it was a different, albeit welcomed, change of pace. Jared had always aspired to it, but, I wasn't sure I got the hype until that experience when the acting bug bit me hard. Prior to that, I had always been a behind-the-scenes kind of gal. I remember lounging in bed after my performance, which, in my mind, was artfully delightful and deserving of critical acclaim. I lay there, flipping through the channels, seeing all of the teasers for "awards season," as we called it. I'd never told anyone, aside from maybe my diary, but, even before that short film, I'd always had this inkling, this underlying feeling – just a sense, really – that I'd be famous one day. I wanted to just will it into action, somehow. I spent my teenage years trying to figure out what for: I couldn't sing, I was too short to be a model, and, I liked eating far too much to be one, anyway. I couldn't paint or play guitar, and my ballet skills were average, at best. I dabbled in theater arts at my school, but I was never the lead and didn't feel that my place in our choir would afford me the opportunity to see my name in bright lights. So I kept my aspirations private. No one had to know that I was planning (as if you could really plan those things,) to someday become a celebrity of some sort. I walked the walk, and talked the talk, though. I had that so-called x-factor. People were awed by me. People cared about what I said, wore, thought, wrote. People truly liked me, but I was never really certain as to exactly why they felt that way. I was cool and all, and I liked to think that I was good enough, if there really is such a thing, but I wasn't special like the people on the late-night talk shows and inside the glossy magazines. At least, I didn't think so.

I remember begging my parents to let me go into the city, though, to camp outside the television shows for just the chance to be in the audience and maybe eek my way on to TV. I made them drive me to concert after concert, always having some devious plan to get myself backstage. As I got older I'd schmooze my way into radio events and fashion shows and industry parties. To glance through my photo albums, you would have thought that I was actually someone important. After all, I was my own best paparazzo. The memories made me smile to myself. They warmed me. But they also made me sad at the same time.

Was it just a front, though, that magnetism that I thought I'd radiated? Was I important? Surely, I was to my family and friends, and, at one time, Ezra. I may have been important to Jared, but I could never truly tell. I certainly wasn't a real star, though. Not the kind that I wanted to be. My grandpa used to tell me that I was a superstar in his eyes, going so far as to name a star for me on my 16th birthday. But, I surely wasn't. Though I'd rehearsed many an Oscar acceptance speech and practiced many a Vogue magazine cover pose in front of my dusty, smudgy full-length mirror, I was basically a nobody. I was a single, wannabe, yoga-doing, aspiring screenwriter – just like everyone in New York City – and now, honestly, none of that mattered at all, now did it? No Pilates class could have prepared me for the physical feat that I now faced: the physical feat of simple existence in this new world.

The irony, though? Now, I *was* a star, in a sense. I was the most sought-after celebrity of the day. I was the one that everyone was after. Instead of clamoring to capture an unflattering photo to write a made-up tabloid story around, they were after me ... and not just a photo, but the real me. Celebrities always complained about not having privacy, about no one leaving them alone, about being followed when they got their coffee or their morning paper or their pedicures. I wondered how the starlet of the day would self-destruct if they were *really* after her: her ovaries, her being, her womb. So many actresses and athletes would grace the cover of books and magazines, being touted as heroes. Were they heroes, though? Where were they now? What did they do? They were providing entertainment. I could provide life.

As I mulled it over in my head, suddenly, my role in all of this seemed more clear. I had shifted from daydreamer to lead role, and I recognized my newfound position to be of utmost importance. Yes, in the past I'd aspired to walk red carpets with camera bulbs flashing as I smiled my pearly smile and tossed my silken hair over my toned and tanned shoulder, showing off my perfect collarbone and my perfect cleavage, with perfect diamond earrings to match. But now, *now* I realized how superficial that all seemed. People were after me – but not for my photo. They were after me because I actually meant something. My role of a lifetime could actually be life-giving. I had something that they needed, that we all needed, and I realized that I was, perhaps, a true hero, a true star, and that was somehow both insanely nerve-wracking and truly fulfilling, as I'd always imagined a life in the limelight would be.

CHAPTER 14

I let my mind settle back into the here and now. We'd been walking, and I was so absorbed in my thoughts that I barely even noticed. I chastised myself: I needed to be more present, more mindful of my surroundings. We were moving towards the source of the smoke. Our journey had gotten progressively more rural, and as we walked, we'd seen less signs of life, past or present. Bodies that we'd passed were skinless, fleshless, devoured – whether by animals or other human beings, we'd never know. I shuddered at the thought. I cringed at the idea of having no identity attached to me, and being a pile of bones along a desolate pathway.

That wouldn't happen to me, though – not now, I was too important. Somehow, though, that thought was just as scary.

The solitude that our sparse surroundings afforded us was simultaneously comforting and panic-inducing. After my breakup with Ezra, and my disconnection from Jared, my anxiety had worsened. I was never all that good at being alone, and I remember once turning down a glamping (yes, "glam camping,") trip with my girlfriends because I was terrified of being in the middle of nowhere, with no connection to the outside world, far away from cities and hospitals and cell phone towers. My anxiety would overcome me in situations such as that, and here I was, in this new world, with no forms of communication, with no hospitals in sight, and I was relatively fine, all things considered. I suppose that my abnormally strong "fight-or-flight" response and over-analytical nature was helpful in this situation; whereas, when it was unnecessary in my former life, it was detrimental. I felt self-satisfaction at that thought, and gave myself a mental pat on the back for being a survivor, even when I, at times, didn't want to be.

The question of our existence, literally to be or not to be, plagued me. An endless game of ping pong, I would bounce back and forth between desperately wanting to be, and then aching not to be.

"Do you guys ever wonder why we're suffering like this?" Jared asked, interrupting my thoughts with one of his own that was eerily on the same wavelength. "Why we're here and other people aren't? Do you think they're better off?" He was asking a question that we'd all mulled over, time and time again.

"We're not suffering," I said. "We're surviving!" I said. This time, my sense of cheerfulness wasn't exaggerated; it was authentic. The renewed sense of hope I had in my heart was real; and I hoped that my intuition and newfound positive attitude were not going to let us down or do us any disservices.

Jared and Eugene glanced at each other and smiled. There was no further conversation on the matter, and I think that they both enjoyed and accepted my succinct, uncharacteristically optimistic response.

"It's weird that we don't really know what happened, though. Not totally, at least." Jared said.

Weird didn't begin to describe it. We'd discussed these same topics many times before, but we never came up with any conclusions.

"It is what it is," was usually the standard response.

"We know about the storm. We know there was an act of bio-terror. Chemical warfare maybe. But who? How? Why? Could they be plotting more? How much of the country is demolished? Honestly, guys. I can NOT literally be the only woman left on earth. I'm probably not even the only woman left in America, or even on the East Coast, even though it seems that way. What would the chances of that be?" I mused out loud. But then again, what were the chances of any of this?

"We can't lose focus." Eugene interjected. "You may or may not be, but the fact is that people in this general vicinity believe that you are. That alone puts you in danger. It would be helpful to know the facts, though. In this case, ignorance is far from bliss," he said.

Jared and I agreed. But, then I glanced at Pippa, trotting along happily, tail wagging, despite sores on her paws and an inarguably empty tummy. Maybe, for dogs at least, ignorance was bliss.

We weren't dogs, though. Human nature involved the need to know. We wanted to know everything, and we wanted to know it FAST. We were used to instant gratification, and an endless stream of information at our fingertips infinitesimally. Constantly. Without fail. The problem, however, was that it did fail. Where was it now? This information that we lived by and lived for was simply gone. Vanished. There was no live streaming feed of events for us to read about or watch on television. There was no alert system to which we could respond. There was no social network of survivors. There was no cutesy, cringeworthy media nickname for this apocalyptic event that wiped out our livelihoods and our lives. That information that we so needed, and so craved, had vanished, and it was as useless to us as a screen door on a submarine. Yet, somehow, this nothingness and the not-knowing of it all was, in some sense, freeing. It was a kind of pure awareness, undiluted by constant connection, and any knowledge that we gained was blissfully unbiased, not skewed by this media outlet, or that one. Knowledge in this new world was organic – and that was, in some odd way, bliss, I supposed.

As we approached whatever unknown danger or sanctuary awaited us, a thought hit me like a truck: "Guys, what if it IS them?" I asked.

The "them" in question was, of course, the men with whom Thomas had been communicating. Or, worse yet, Thomas himself.

Both Jared and Eugene gave me looks that simply read, "duh." I could have even sworn that Pippa raised a little doggie eyebrow at me. In my attempts to not dwell on negativity, I was trying to focus on the good. When I saw the smoke, I immediately thought of possible rescue, of people needing our help, or people being able to help us. I thought of allies; I thought of, possibly, other women. I obviously knew there was a chance it could mean danger, but, I'd talked myself into believing that it would serve our best interest to find them, and not the other way around. The closer we got to the smoke, though, the less certain I felt. My bravery was wavering, and that survivor spirit was wilting along with it. I just didn't know what to think or feel at that point.

"We just have to stick together," Eugene said, "like we always do."

Jared added, "Are you okay to go on?"

"Sure." I said. I was okay, of course, because this new life gave me no other options but to be okay: to accept what was handed to me, and to just do what I could do get by. Now, "getting by" wasn't about struggling to make a car payment, or living on Ramen noodles for a couple weeks in college so that I'd be able to save up for a New Year's Eve outfit. This getting by wasn't about student loans or water bills; this was about living. Every breath we took, and every second of our days was life or death. My perspective had undergone a mammoth shift, and I was guessing that every single person who was left likely felt the same. These days, I wouldn't take a peanut shell or breadcrumb for granted, much unlike the leftovers I used to haughtily refuse to eat, as I wastefully dumped them down a garbage disposal to nowhere.

Now, we were living in nowhere. We were the children in the commercials, who were starving as they showcased their prominent ribs, hollow cheekbones, and distended bellies. We were the homeless men with shaggy beards, rancid stenches, and yellowed teeth, surrounded by flies. My hair was greasy, and bore that fried-chicken scent, when it used to smell like lavender-mango. Yes, THIS was "getting by." Yes, I was okay. because I had to be, not just for me, but for our little troupe, and, quite possibly, for the future of the United States of America. Or, who knows: perhaps, for all of humanity.

"Onward," I said, forcing a stiff smile. It hurt to smile. It hurt to breathe. It hurt to talk. It just hurt to be alive. But, alas, on we went, step by step, each foot's length taking us towards new possibilities. It was a risk: we were gambling with our existence. We were soon going to be known by even more people — this could be good, or this could be truly, truly bad. I realized, though, that we had to just make decision and face the consequences, whatever they may be. It was almost as though we were living on borrowed time, thus every passing second was crucial, and we had no time for option-weighing or second-guessing. So, onward it was.

As we walked together towards our fate, I grabbed Jared's hand in mine. He looked startled at first, but then a huge smile danced on his face. I could tell that Eugene also approved. My emotional pain was easing, though the physical pain wouldn't let up, and I knew I'd have scars from both aspects for a long time to come. I tried to push any doubts out of my mind as we made our way, and I was comforted by the fact that, whatever this new chapter was that we were walking in to, we were facing it together.

Chapter 15

My senses became fine-tuned and focused, as we proceeded towards our target destination. I heard the dried leaves crunch under my feet, felt the thorny bushes brushing up against my legs, and the spider webs tickling my face. I heard nothing but wind, but with each breeze, all I could smell was smoke. I could feel my arm hairs standing up on end, in anticipation of what was to come: was it danger we were going to face, or a welcoming new place to call home? Would we meet friends, or foes?

Pippa sniffed around in the woods. There were bugs here and there, but no sign of animal life. Animals were just as scarce as we humans were at this point. Jared was still holding my hand, leading the way, with Eugene right behind me.

"Jared, do you have a knife ready?" I asked, a bit louder than I'd anticipated it to come out of my mouth.

"Shh!" He gave me an annoyed glare, putting his a finger from his free hand to his lips. "We have to be quiet," he whispered. Eugene patted my back: a silent, "It's okay, Shelby."

I felt lightheaded. I didn't know if it was due to nerves, lack of food, or exhaustion. I presumed that the answer was all of the above. "Jared, I don't feel good, I'm dizzy," I said.

Did I see him roll his eyes? I think I did. *"What was with this guy?"* I thought to myself. *"Prince Charming one second, and Lord Grumpy the next."*

"Let her sit down for a moment," Eugene suggested. "We aren't in a rush. We have all the time in the world," he said.

"I want to get there before it starts to get dark," Jared said, but his voice indicated that he felt badly and was going to relent a bit. "But, okay. You're important. Sit, sit." he said to me.

I found a stump to rest on, and put my head between my legs. The blood rushing to my head felt good. My hands were numb, and I shook them out to get the blood flowing there, too. I was still in pain – there was no doubt about that – but more than that, I was worried about my overall health. My body had been through so much, and yet here I was, not taking care of myself at all. I couldn't, I didn't have the resources to do so. I remembered how I used to make excuses not to exercise, or eat well. I didn't have time, it was too expensive, and so on. Now, I wished more than anything that I could nourish my body, and to once again become strong, fit, and healthy. I was amazed, however, at the fact that I was, as they say, still alive and kicking. It was truly mind-boggling what the body could withstand, and how the human body will fight to the very end, with every ounce of its being, to live. The end goal is simply survival, and, as uncomfortable and ill as I was becoming, I was doing just that: surviving. And I had this body to thank. I cursed myself for ever bemoaning my body's appearance and physical imperfections. This was what it was all about; this made me realize that the body is just vessel for life. It IS a temple; we do need to care for it. But, was it too late for that, too?

I recalled the trials. The smell of the nurse's latex gloves, the pinch as they inserted the IV. I remember the cool sensation as they let saline solution course through my veins before administering the infusion, or perhaps, the placebo. I remember watching the drip-drip-drip and reading the magazines as I waited for the magical potion to start to heal me. It was fear and hope, that IV. It seemed to me that my existence was hinged on whatever was in those little plastic pouches, hanging there proudly in the fluorescent lighting of the infusion center that felt so stale and sterile, yet, at the same time, so safe. It was like another life. How was I so dependent on that medicine, needing it to survive, and yet, here I was, without a balanced diet, without soap, and, certainly, without medications?

I sighed. I thought about Eugene's remark, as I sat there, moving in awkward ways to try to dissipate the pain and stop the lightheaded sensation. We *did* have all the time in the world – but, we didn't know how to measure that time, anymore. We didn't know how much time we'd have left, at any given second. There were no clocks with minute hands ticking away. There wasn't an hourglass, or a calendar, a stopwatch or even a sundial. We didn't know what day of the week it was anymore; we didn't know the date. We could only guess the time based on our environment, and even then we weren't sure. Yet, time moved on. It trudged forward like a devoted soldier in an unwinnable war. Even though we didn't know how much it was, we did, in fact, have all the time in the world. We had nothing but time. The only certainty we could really hold on to, was that.

"Time sure is loyal," I mused out loud.

Jared looked caught off guard if not slightly confused, Eugene just nodded in agreement. "It just ticks away, not even mindful of all that has happened," I said.

"Even when we die, time will still just keep going," I said. "But what will become of us? Is there another side? Is there time there?" I wondered.

"Shelby, are you feeling okay?" Jared asked quietly. He seemed genuinely concerned, with worry furrowing his brow.

He didn't know about my fleeting suicidal thoughts that constantly ebbed and flowed, or else he would have a reason to worry, (as though the cancer and my prey status weren't reason enough.) But, on the other hand, he also didn't know about my lifelong propensity towards philosophizing on vague and unanswerable topics such as this one. So, to him, this was all out nowhere, and probably seemed a bit odd. But it wasn't. I was always one for sharing what I was thinking with others. Old Jared would have been neither surprised nor concerned by it.

"I'm fine, I'm just wondering," I said.

"Well, stop talking. I told you, we have to be quiet," he said in a harsh whisper that made me uneasy.

He paused. "Are you feeling better? Physically, I mean?" he asked me, in a tone that was a little more gentle, but still laced with impatience.

"Yeah let's go," I said, rather annoyed, and exaggerating my whisper simply to be a brat.

"You know, Jared, I could use a few more minutes of rest," Eugene said, winking at me behind Jared's back. I knew he was doing it for me, and I appreciated it greatly. Jared wouldn't deny rest to Eugene, after all.

I don't know exactly why I was stalling. It could have been the sudden fear of the unknown, but then, that wouldn't make sense. Everything was unknown and always had been; the fear of such wasn't exactly a novel concept. I think that the physical and emotional burdens I'd been carrying were threatening to soon become too much to bear. Truth be told, I wasn't sure that I could make it, in any sense of the phrase. My optimism was off and on, and my hope wavered, too. I wondered how my emotional state could fluctuate so much and without warning. It made me uneasy, and I wondered yet again about the state of my mental health on top of everything else we were dealing with.

We all sat in silence, and soon Pippa began to whimper. We took that as our cue to begin to move once more. I noted that Jared didn't take my hand this time around, and I was okay with that. I steadied myself, taking deep breaths, and began to walk.

I fell behind the men and Pippa, trying to meditate and re-center myself as we moved. As I was so mindfully concentrating on my breathing, I felt someone grab my arm. Startled, I glanced to my side, expecting it to be Pippa or Jared. I screamed. It was a stranger.

Jared and Eugene looked back and came charging at the man who immediately dropped my arm. He didn't come off as aggressive.

"I'm sorry, m'am," he said. "I just wanted to stop you guys. We have a camp set up. Perhaps the lady and old man could use a rest?" he asked. "And the dog," he chuckled blatantly, paying no mind to Jared.

"I'm sorry, you just scared me," I explained. "What's your name?" I asked.

"Paulie. There's a few other fellas back at the camp – Dustin, Ted, Neil, and Garbo. I can tell you more once we're there, but we're trying not to be out in the open, roaming the woods too much. I was on a hunt for some berries and heard whispering. I thought it may be some new folks," he said.

Jared glared at him, obviously sizing him up. I also didn't know whether we should trust him or not. I'd seen enough movies and knew enough about "stranger danger" that some skepticism seemed appropriate at a time like this. Paulie looked friendly enough, though: a shorter guy, stout, and a bit pudgy, with shining green eyes and a slight gap between his two front teeth. He was balding a bit, but what hair was left was strawberry blonde. His face was smudged, and his calloused hands were dirty. I noticed he was missing half an index finger, and had a pink handkerchief with a duck on it hanging out of his back pocket. He wasn't exactly intimidating, but, I did smell a bit of alcohol on his breath. He smiled broadly at us, and I nonetheless took a liking to him in spite of myself. I gave a slight nod to Jared, giving my stamp of approval. I'm not certain that he cared.

"What are you guys up to?" Jared asked Paulie, who replied,

"Well, we're not having a video game tournament, I'll tell ya that much. Wi-Fi isn't great in these parts," he joked.

I smiled, Jared scowled. I wasn't sure what his problem is, but it was apparent that he wasn't taking to Paulie in the same way that I had.

"Nah, man, just kidding. We are a small group of survivalists who have been together since the apocalypse. You know, Doomsday preppers?" he said, with one of his signature winks.

Eugene's eyes lit up. "Ah! I watched a documentary on you folks before," he said, with a smile. "Must be beneficial during times like these," he added.

"Hey, whatever you gotta do. You guys are still here, too; must be doin' somethin' right," he said. "But we'd love to help y'all out. Especially with a pretty lady and a pretty puppy in tow!" Paulie said, bending to pat Pippa on the head.

Her tail was wagging, and I took that as a good sign. She wasn't standoffish at all, and I firmly believed that animals had a good sense about these things.

"Guess we could stop by and at least rest there, meet the others, eat something," Jared offered up.

"Sure thing! Got some berries here, and we have some Spam back at the camp. So cliché, I know," Paulie joked. "But true," he added. "That shit really holds up!"

We followed him towards the direction of the smoke. He seemed friendly enough, and, it seemed like, if nothing else, we could learn something from these guys.

"How much do you know?" Jared asked him.

"'Bout what?" Paulie replied.

"Anything, I guess," Jared shrugged. "What happened, who's out there, all that stuff," he said.

"Well," Paulie began, "I do know that a multi-national bio-terrorist group bombed multiple locations in the United States, two or three times a piece. The bombs were chemical bombs whose effects went on for hundreds of miles in every direction, and, for whatever reason, the compound seemed to mainly effect our women and children. Or, so we thought," he said, with a perplexed glance at me. "I don't know anything about them, really – who financed them, who gave the orders, what the name is, or what the point of the attack was. Is there ever a point with these things?

We suspect it's that MARF group, 'cuz I do know it's a group of different people from different countries who apparently hate America and saw fit to kick us when we were down – after the big storms, you know. They did the job, though. Between the effects from the storm and then the bombings, the good ol' US of A has pretty near been wiped away. Can't find nor contact no other humans nearby. We got radios and CBs, and ain't nothin'…no one," he said.

"You Thomas?" he asked Jared.

Jared looked startled. "What? No!" he growled angrily. I gave a small gasp and Paulie's eyes widened. He blinked, silently.

After an awkward pause, he said, "Okay, then…" and drifted off into silence. "Sorry?" He said it like a question.

"Paulie, Thomas attacked Shelby," Eugene chimed in, as if to explain Jared's rudeness and our obvious discomfort.

"I'm sorry," Paulie said with a baffled little head nod towards me. He seemed concerned, and confused. "You're that girl he was rambling about finding, then?" he asked me.

I nodded, and swallowed. My throat suddenly felt dry and sandpapery. The anxiety was threatening to rear its ugly head once again.

"Yeah," I squeaked out. The mention of the attack made my stomach go into knots, and I felt not butterflies but vampire bats, fluttering around wildly inside of me.

"Well, we haven't found no other ladies, neither," Paulie said. "My wife Courtney and my little daughter Alyssa were traveling with us," he said, tearing up. "Alyssa passed away peacefully in her sleep the first night. Won't ever know why, but we guessed it was the after-effects of the bio-attack or some such," he said, sadly.

"And Courtney?" I asked, gently, immediately regretting it.

He answered anyway. "She survived the attack, initially ... seemed immune to the chemical compound like I was ... but she couldn't bear the loss of our little girl. Did herself in," he said shakily, almost gasping through his words. I didn't know the man, but I tenderly lay a hand on his shoulder, as he stroked the pink duck handkerchief.

"I'm sorry," I said, and I meant it.

"Were there any other women with you, or that you saw?" Jared asked, brusquely. I choked back tears. There was just too much sadness.

If Paulie was caught off guard by the quick change of pace, he didn't show it.

"Only the first day. A bald Indian girl named Sahel. She kept going on about her sister Awa. Separated from us to go find her, and a couple days later we saw her dead body on the side of the road, her head bludgeoned in. Not sure what would provoke that," he said. "She was a beautiful, young girl," he added, shaking his head.

"There was also an elderly woman we heard of," he continued, "Marlene. She survived for a while with her son Benson, but he got shot and she had what we presume was a heart attack."

"Oh," I said solemnly. It was all I could muster. My head spun: could I seriously be the only woman left? And why had some managed to survive at all after the attacks, if they were targeting women and kids? It made zero sense.

"So it is feasible, then, that Shelby is the only woman left around here, or at least the only one of child-bearing years?" Jared asked Paulie. I couldn't read the tone in his voice, but it was odd. Flat. I took it as, perhaps, concern.

"I guess so," Paulie said. "So I'd like us to help protect her," he said. "Lots of crazies out there. I heard that Thomas and some of his men talking back n' forth about us needing to repopulate, needing to find her for that reason. Hell, I'd rather help protect you and make you our queen!" he said, giving me a sad smile.

I liked that idea. For a moment, I let my imagination run wild: me in a warrior princess outfit, big bejeweled crown on my head, sitting atop a gilded throne, with sexy men in sexy gladiator costumes fanning me as they fed me grapes. And wine. Lots of wine.

I saw a movie in my head, "Shelby: The Last Queen." I idly wondered who would play me. It's too bad that Elizabeth Taylor and Audrey Hepburn were long gone, even way before all of this. "*Maybe someday, I will write the screenplay,*" I silently mused.

"Here we are," said Paulie. I pushed some foliage out of my way and glanced around. I didn't see the others, or any sign of life, aside from the fire. All I saw was a large, spacious patch of rolling green grass with tall trees surrounding it, and a fire pit in the middle. I was a bit baffled. Paulie could sense my amusement, and his eyes glistened with humor.

"Underground bunkers," he explained. "Grass rooftops," he added. "For the illusion."

Wow. I now took note of the bumps in the landscape, the mounds that had to have been the roofs of their cubbies. I was impressed. These guys *were* professionals!

"Hang here for a minute, guys," he said, "I'd offer you a seat but the property didn't come fully furnished," he joked.

I was beat, and took a seat on the mossy ground. "How about that? A subterranean survivalists' warren," Eugene mused out loud, "I really have seen it all!"

Pippa lay down beside me, and Eugene stood solemnly while Jared paced with his hands on his hips. Jared seemed on edge, and slightly agitated.

"What's wrong with you?" I asked. I was used to Old Jared's moods, but New Jared was usually a bit more mellow, and a bit more likable.

"I just … I don't know if we should trust these guys," he said. I thought I'd sensed panic in his voice.

"I know. And I get that," I said, "but, what do we have to lose anymore?"

"I have to agree with Shelby," Eugene added. "We don't have to trust them 100%, but we can give them a chance and take advantage of what they have to offer us – while keeping our eyes open and guards up, of course."

Jared nodded, "Yeah, I guess you guys are right." But his eyes looked wild.

A moment later, as Pippa lay snoring and Jared continued to pace, Paulie crawled up out of a hatch with a few other men. I was still amazed and slightly taken aback by what I was seeing. I stifled a giggle as, for some reason, I was reminded of Snow White and the Seven Dwarfs. It seemed like something straight out of a cartoon, this assortment of characters seeming to just pop right up out of the ground.

"Dustin, Ted, Neil, and Garbo, I presume?" Eugene asked, extending a friendly handshake to each of them. I was impressed with his memory; I was awful with names.

"Yuppers," said a blonde-haired, dreadlocked man who looked like a surfer or a stoner, or perhaps both. "I'm Garbo," he said in an exaggerated Southern drawl. I kind of loved it.

"Uh, Neil," Neil nodded at us. He was slight in build, pasty white, with matted mousy brown hair. I would have avoided casting him as a nerd in a movie, solely for the fact that he looked exactly like a stereotypical nerd. It was almost too much, and judging by his shy demeanor, I guessed that he very well could be the living embodiment of that exact nerd stereotype. I also kind of loved this.

"I'm Dustin," said a younger guy, probably in his mid-to-late teens. He had dark skin, and jet black hair and eyes. I couldn't quite pinpoint his ethnicity, but he was handsome and exotic and looked to be pretty athletic.

"Ted," said a tall man with a wild, bushy gray beard that I could tell had been growing long before all of this. His was legit. The others' were beards of necessity. His was a beard that was once carefully cultivated out of love. He resembled Santa, minus the paunch, and he seemed curt but kind; brisk, but good-hearted.

The writer in me loved what an interesting and diverse crew they were. I was reminded of the Island of the Misfit Toys. We had the stoner-surfer, the computer nerd, the teenage jock, the bearded, woodsy dad-type, and then, of course, Paulie, who reminded me of a jolly Irish elf.

I giggled in spite of myself, "I'm Shelby," I said, "and this little Corgi here is Pippa, our mascot!" I said, gleefully gesturing towards the dog.

"Jared," Jared said, nodding, and quickly shaking each man's hand.

"I'm Dr. Eugene MacDougal," said Eugene, and I smiled at the formality of his introduction. "The educating kind, not the stethoscope kind," he added, charming as ever.

"So, I was telling the guys about you all," said Paulie, "and we want to invite you to hang here for awhile. We'll be eating dinner shortly, and we thought you may want to rest up a bit," he said. "Plus, we can get to know each other better; I'd like to hear your stories."

"I'm up for it. We really appreciate it!" I answered for us. Jared and Eugene nodded in agreement – I couldn't imagine they'd want to pass up the free food, regardless of what their feelings were about the guys.

"Safety in numbers," I added, with an efficient nod that I hoped seemed official. I didn't want these men to think I was some dumb, flighty woman. I needed to get in boss-mode. Queen Shelby had arrived.

CHAPTER 16

We sat around the fire pit.

"Is this safe, to have a fire? We saw the smoke miles away," I said.

"Well, yeah, we have weapons and shelter just in case, but in general, we want people to know we're here. They could be rescue, or, they could need rescued," said Paulie, and I sensed that we was the leader of this little group.

"Gotcha," I said.

"What's for dinner?" asked Eugene with a smile, rubbing his hands together and licking his lips in an exaggerated fashion.

The men chuckled.

"Berries, fish, and spam!" said Dustin.

"Fish!" I exclaimed, my eyes widening.

"There's a river nearby. Fish are hard to catch, they're pretty scarce after everything, but you can do it, plus… water!" explained Garbo.

I had not felt as excited since I saw Jared. That seemed like ages ago. This excitement was different, though. It was less emotional and more carnal. My mouth was, quite literally, watering, and I felt so over-stimulated in anticipation of this delectable delight that was coming my way.

"We don't have a lot to contribute," Eugene said sadly.

"Nah, we're good here. We are all family now, and we'll stick together and help one another survive," said Paulie.

I felt overwhelmed with gratitude and was counting my blessings to be in this environment that felt homey and safe. I couldn't help it; I felt the tears coming. I tried to command them to stop, but, they just wouldn't listen.

So much for Queen Shelby.

I began to cry. What a girl.

"What's wrong?" said Jared, somehow managing to sound both alarmed and annoyed.

"No," I said, "Nothing is wrong. I'm just so grateful to have found some new friends and to feel safe and to get to EAT!" (I practically yelled that last part.)

What could I say? I couldn't help it, I was excited for food.

Paulie gave me a hug. "We welcome you, honey," he said. While I knew it was naive and unwise to be so trusting right away, I felt like everything was going to be okay, and I felt in my bones that Paulie was genuine.

I thought I caught Jared scowling but I ignored him. He was reverting to his old, jealous ways.

The food was passed around, and it was worth the wait. The white fish flaked apart with perfection and seemed to melt in my mouth. Additionally, Spam had never been something I'd been accustomed to eating before, but it was now a much-welcomed treat.

We took the time to share our stories, and we exchanged a bit of small talk about our backgrounds. It was idle chit-chat, but, it was a nice change of pace from the heavy topics I'd been sifting through in my brain lately. Rape. Suicide. The repopulation of the earth. You know, the usual.

Everyone seemed to be getting along fairly well. Almost all of these new men were likable, and, Jared was finally being mostly-agreeable to all of them, as well. Eugene, of course, was liked by everyone, and liked everybody in return, so there was no surprise there. I thought it was a nice group, but I wondered how they'd come together in this seemingly strange lifestyle. I had to ask.

"How did you get into this prepping stuff?" I asked. "What makes one become a Doomsdayer?" I was intrigued.

Garbo chuckled, "Never heard it called a Doomsdayer, but I'll take it." He gave me a warm smile. A warm, handsome smile. I blushed a little. This guy was kind of charming. Jared scowled.

"We started a group in this area after 9/11. The Northwest New York Region Preppers Society. There were about 10 of us who regularly attended meetings and who kept up with the forums online and whatnot," said Paulie. "Unfortunately, some people dropped out after a couple of years, and then when shit got real, some of them decided to do their own thing, or got too scared to come with us, or whatever," said Paulie. "But we've had this planned out for awhile now. This exact spot and everything. Built these hidden underground bunkers a couple of years ago. Been storing up Spam and canned goods for quite a while too. Picked a location in the middle of the woods, not too far from a river, but not too far from the roads, either. Familiarized ourselves with edible plants and berries, taught ourselves to hunt, how to make spears, how to do CPR, and so on. A lot of us had experience with camping and scouting, which helped too. We never wanted to have to really use this spot. Hell, we never even wanted to have to use our knowledge, but, as batshit crazy as most people thought we were, we wanted to be prepared in case of a disaster," he said. "And this was a disaster," he added, flatly.

Garbo added, "Yeah, Neil was even on a talk show! They did a segment about extreme survivalists! He froze up on air, dude!" he exclaimed, poking Neil, who was apparently not amused by the reminder.

"It was Extreme Survival Experts," said Neil, "and I told you, it was the editing," he said.

We laughed as he reddened. I truly liked this group.

"We've stockpiled First Aid stuff, blankets, and water; took self-defense classes, read all about what to do in disasters and planetary crises. In other words, you'll be safe with us," said Ted.

"Sounds like it," said Eugene. Jared and I nodded in agreement.

"Was there anything you wish you had now that you didn't think of?" I asked.

"Yeah, electricity," Paulie joked. "Actually, I'm serious; we had a generator that was working for awhile after the storm but then once the bombing came, it went out. It'll spark now and then but there's not enough power for it to really be useful. We got a shitload of batteries, though!" he said. "So power up. Flashlights, radios, whatever you need 'em for. We got all sizes."

"Any way to charge a cell phone?" I asked hopefully. You never know.

"Got a boyfriend to text?" Garbo said, jokingly.

""No!" I said haughtily. "I have a photo I want to see," I said, sadly. I still did miss my parents, so, so dearly. Jared saw my sadness and gave me a squeeze.

"No working phone chargers," answered Dustin, glumly.

"Wish I'd prepared more for the economic effects. I was prepared for an economic collapse in general, but now...I mean...what good is cash that you can't spend? We all have cash buried in different places, though, in case order is ever restored, and if life ever returns to normal," said Ted.

I could tell Eugene could relate, and he nodded to show his agreement.

"Don't get any ideas, guys," Paulie said, wagging his finger at Eugene and Jared with a friendly glint in his eye, "none of that moolah is buried around here, I'll have you know!" he said, clucking his tongue.

"Oh, money's not an issue for me," Eugene said with a wink. "Besides, I doubt I'll live long enough to be able to spend it, anyway. I'd bet that I've spent my last dollar," he said.

It made me sad. I didn't like thinking about a world sans Eugene. He was truly a precious gem of a man, a diamond in all this rough. I thought of Owen, and said a silent prayer, asking God to make sure Owen's soul was safe and reunited with Marta. I also sent a prayer up to Owen, asking him to continue to be our guardian angel, as I knew he was.

My faith had been tested time and time again throughout my life, but specifically in recent times. I wondered why God had let Thomas rape me, why he didn't just let me die, why he took my parents and friends, and why he stole Jared's memories, and Paulie's family, and Owen's life. But, I thought of my grandma who would always clutch her rosary and tell me that everything happened for a reason. I had to believe that old adage these days – I simply had to. Maybe I was meant to be Queen Shelby now, after all.

"Where's your money, Eugene?" Jared asked, giving his elder a sidelong glance.

"Oh, I've got some offshore accounts, and, in typical old-person fashion, I'd hid some under my mattress. Now my bed is probably in Nebraska, so that doesn't much matter, now does it?" Eugene replied, laughing.

"Offshore where?" Jared pried.

"Jared!" I interrupted. "Stop being so rude. You know, you've always been a little too invasive," I said, exasperated by his lack of manners.

"Geez, sorry! Just asking," he said, looking wounded. "I was just curious," he explained.

Eugene looked a bit relieved to be off the hook regarding his personal finances, but, I was admittedly curious that a retired professor was seemingly so wealthy. He didn't like to discuss it. I wondered if it was old family money, or if Eugene was more important or successful than he'd let on.

Paulie, thank goodness, changed the subject.

"So, how do you guys know Thomas?" he said, "What's the affiliation there?" he asked.

"Ugh!" I said out loud, cringing.

"Do you want to excuse yourself?" Eugene asked, soothingly.

"No, no…go on," I said. I'd have to get used to hearing the story, eventually.

Eugene looked indescribably sad. Jared seemed uneasy. It couldn't be easy to be a man and have to listen to the horrors of what a fellow man has done to a woman that he cared about. The act was pure, unadulterated evil. Thomas was a black mark on all that was humankind. It made me sad, not just for me, but for other women who had gone through the same horror that I had so recently experienced myself.

"At one point, Thomas and I were camped out together with some other men," Jared started, "we had CB radios, and caught word that there was a woman out there. Some of the guys wanted to find her and protect her but Thomas was crazy about it. He was taken over with this ... lustful ... I don't know ... rage, I guess. Seemed like he wanted to possess her," he said with a disgusted, hateful tone in his voice, almost spitting out the words. "I told him he couldn't do that to Shelby. Well, at the time I didn't know it was Shelby, but still. I felt an urge to honor her, whoever this girl was, and to stop him, but he didn't take kindly to my noble idea. Thomas went out on his own, and encountered Shelby's group. He got in a fight with Owen and Owen shot him. Owen was our friend who is dead now. Thomas didn't die though, and still kept looking for Shelby. I ended up finding Shelby, Owen, and Eugene, and teaming up with them, but we heard some stuff on the radio that indicated Thomas may be trying to assemble a team of guys to come after her and capture her. To fulfill his mission to repopulate and help humankind, yada yada yada," said Jared. He seemed exhausted just explaining it all.

"Huh," said Garbo. "We heard some interceptions and thought the Thomas guy wanted to find Shelby, but only to protect her," said Garbo.

"No," interjected Eugene. "The rest of the story goes like this: Thomas did catch up to us. He kidnapped Shelby while we slept, and..." He trailed off.

"He attacked and brutally raped me," I finished. "Then escaped," I added.

There was stunned silence all around. The tension hung in the air like stagnant clouds. The "r-word" will do that to a room. Talk about a buzzkill.

"And that's all, folks" I said with facetious charm.

"So sorry you had to go through that," said Ted, who I thought was aptly named, due to his rough exterior but warm teddy bear soul. "My daughter…my daughter was a rape survivor. She died in a car accident a few months before the storm," he added. "That girl, she went through so much. I am a survivalist, but Tessa… Tessa was a survivor," he said. "At any rate, so sorry, Shelby," he said, kindly.

Sadness was just splayed across every inch of every life we'd come in contact with. Was there any human who remained untouched by tragedy, by loss? I thought back to life before, and wondered if any of us had known how charmed our lives were. If only we hadn't taken it for granted back then. If only.

"Well, I'd like to kill that son-of-a-bitch," I said. I gasped, slightly, surprising myself with the words I hadn't yet thought, let alone planned on saying out loud.

"Understandable," said Dustin agreeably.

"Me too," said Jared.

Despite their agreement, I felt inexplicably ashamed at what I just said, no matter how true it was. I wrestled with right and wrong all the time these days.

"Well, we'll do what we can to keep you safe," said Paulie. "But we'll need to come up with a long-term plan. For now, though…let's sing," he said. Ted, Dustin, and Neil rolled their eyes. Garbo seemed game. We all looked at him blankly.

"Be right back," he said. He went into the underground bunker, re-emerging with a miniature banjo.

"Was that on the prepper's list?" I joked.

"Only his," snapped Neil, quietly, before retreating back into his shy little shell. The jury was still out on that guy.

"Any requests?" asked Paulie cheerfully.

"How about I Get By With a Little Help From My Friends?" I suggested.

"Great choice!" Eugene exclaimed.

With that, as corny as it was, we sang together into the wee hours of the night.

As I curled up to sleep in the safety of the bunker that evening, I let all fears slip away, and a feeling of serenity washed over me. I eased into sleep, feeling hopeful that I was protected. Queen Shelby was being watched over, for sure.

Chapter 17

I awoke peacefully hours later. I wasn't sure what time it was, but I felt far more rested than I had in a very long time. The swelling in my eye was going down, the pain in my crotch and my legs was subsiding. I felt less lightheaded, less nauseous, and less empty. I glanced around. Paulie and Eugene were missing; they must have been awake already. I stretched, yawned, and tried to run my fingers through my tangled hair. It was of no use. I climbed the makeshift ladder up out of the bunker, and poked my head out like a little groundhog.

Paulie spotted me and waved excitedly, "Good morning, princess!" he said. "Sleep well?" he asked.

"I thought I was a queen?" I said in jest, winking. "But, good morning to you guys too!"

"Shelby," Eugene nodded towards me with a warm, grandfatherly smile.

"I slept great!" I exclaimed. "Who's up for some yoga?" I asked.

"Psssh… no thanks," said Paulie.

"Not today, dear," said Eugene.

"Okay, I'm going to get in some flows. I need to stretch," I said.

"Alright, be careful darling," said Eugene.

I found a spot nearby. It was far enough for me to have some peace and quiet, but close enough so that I was still in their line of vision, under their watchful, protective eyes. The old me would have resisted being in the care of men, but the new me realized that they were my friends, and my allies, and that I needed to accept any help, and any protection, that was offered to me.

I concentrated on breathing in the cool, crisp air. It felt good in my lungs. I noticed how beautiful the early morning sunlight was as it bounced off brown tree limbs and golden-amber leaves. It amazed me that, after so much destruction, nature could still prevail. I took a breath. It felt nice to stretch, to feel my muscles fill with warmth as they relaxed. I needed to let go of the tension, to expel the pain and negativity, and to breathe in goodness, wholeness, and life. With each motion I felt calmer, more serene, and more present. I was ridding myself of all that had happened to me, inviting in possibility, good energy, and healing. My body needed this, as did my mind and my soul. The nourishment was unparalleled. I was feeling at one with the universe and at peace with this new life. I felt alive. I felt God.

Towards the end of my yoga session, I decided to meditate a bit. I usually shied away from conventional prayer, but I needed the meditation to refocus, to gather my thoughts, clear my mind, and to try to practice gratitude – especially in this time when it was hard to find much to be grateful for, at all. However, as I was meditating, I found it turning into prayer, nonetheless: "Dear God, please bless my new friends and guide us all. Please forgive me for the thoughts I have towards Thomas. Please help Jared regain his memory. Please take care of my friends and family up in heaven. Please don't let the terrorists attack again. Please don't let anyone take me or rape me again. Please watch over us," I said. I guess my faith was really returning, bit by bit, and I was okay with that. I needed it. I needed something and someone to believe in, in these dark and dismal times. It made me feel like a hypocrite or a fraud, but, I supposed it was better than nothing.

"Amen," I said out loud, quickly adding, "Namaste." I wasn't sure just how to end these little sessions anymore, but that was okay. We were anew in an age of uncertainty.

I walked back over to the site, realizing that everyone was up by now, except for Jared. High-school me wanted to wake him in some obnoxious manner. College-me wanted to go snuggle with him. Grown-up me knew I needed to let the man sleep.

"Eugene," I said, "Do you want to walk Pippa with me?" I asked.

"Sure," he replied. "Anyone else?" he asked.

"No, we're going to go fish," said Garbo, pointing at himself and Dustin.

"I'm good," said Ted.

"Go on," said Paulie with a smile and a wave.

Neil just shook his head.

Okay, then.

"Let's go, girl!" I said, enthusiastically. Pippa really was a great dog. It absolutely amazed me that she'd held on this long. Then again, animals never ceased to amaze me.

We barely had to hold the rope; she walked right by our side.

"How are you holding up, Eugene?" I asked. Our pace was slow, and comfortable.

"I'm good darling, but I could certainly ask the same question of you," he said.

"I'm fine," I said. I mostly meant it. "It's just been hard, ya know?" I said. I knew that I did not need to elaborate. He got it.

"I know," he said.

"You know, Shelby," he said, "I was talking with Paulie and we think we need to come up with a plan for you, for your future and your safety," he said.

"Yeah?" I asked.

"Yes. Now, I'm not sure what's going to happen, or how any of it is going to work, but if you truly are the last woman standing, things could become very bad for you. Not everyone will have Paulie's mindset of protecting you like a holy grail, and treating you like a queen. I'd venture to say most men will become animals as reality is faced, egos will get in the way, they will give in to their most basic human instincts, and the hunt will be on, with you, my dear, as the prey. This is very real," he said. I let it sink in, as he continued, "Shelby, I don't know how we're going to get you there, or if we even can, but if you EVER have the possibility to make it there, well, there's money waiting for you in Switzerland."

I gaped at him. He reached his hand down his pants.

"Eugene!" I exclaimed, "what are you doing?" I asked, flabbergasted.

He pulled out a gold I.D. tag on a key chain. On one side were engraved numbers, on the other side, some kind of computer chip.

"Clip this inside your pants, or to your bra. Somewhere where no one can see it and where hopefully no one can grab it!" he said, pointedly.

I didn't know what to say. "This is your offshore account?" I asked.

"Yes. They are very discreet. No questions will be asked. If you have this, you gain access. If not, make sure you have the numbers on the tag memorized, and, when they ask you the security question, just answer orchid longchamp."

I didn't ask any questions about the strange code. "Orchid longchamp," I repeated.

I wondered how we didn't notice the gold tchotchke when he'd stripped down in truth-or-dare, but, to be fair, we were caught a bit off guard in that wildly inappropriate and equally hilarious moment.

"Eugene, are you sure?" I asked.

He looked at me, earnestly, and I sensed a sentimental speech of some sort coming on.

"What the fuck am I going to do with it?" he asked with a laugh.

I was shocked at his language, and it struck me as hilariously funny.

"Well," I said through giggles, "I don't know. Why can't you come with me if I am ever able to go?" I asked, knowing the answer all too well.

"Honey," he said, somberly. "I'm an old man," he said, grabbing onto my hand as we continued to walk.

There was nothing else to say. I understood that Eugene's days would have been numbered, even in normal circumstances. Now, all of our life expectancies were most likely greatly diminished. It was a sad truth that we needed to accept.

"Well," I said. "In that case, I accept," I said.

"Now, don't get too excited," he said. "I don't know precisely how much is in there," he said, "it's an inheritance, plus some money from a research grant I'd won, but, you aren't going to be an overnight billionaire or anything. It will be enough, though, to get you back on your feet, one would hope," he said.

He shook his head, "Maybe it will give you a fresh start. I sure hope so. I just don't know what the world will be like, or what the future will hold for anyone. I don't know what to tell you, I just hope you can use it, and I want you to have it," he said.

We continued walking in silence.

"I really appreciate it," I said, my voice cracking a bit.

"I knew you would, sweetie. You deserve it," he said. "But, can I ask you a favor?" he asked, stopping and facing me.

"Of course!" I replied. Whatever he needed, I was game. I was overcome with gratitude.

He placed his hands on my shoulders and stared directly into my eyes.

"It's a condition of sorts. A kind of … mandatory … request. Please don't tell Jared about this," he said.

I stood open-mouthed, not knowing what to say. My mind was racing, bursting with questions.

"But…but why?" I finally mustered, asking the most obvious one. "What happened to we are family, we are a team? I love him, Eugene, and beyond that, we are best friends!" I said.

I didn't know if I could keep this promise, and I told him that.

"It isn't anything against Jared. He's a great guy. I like him, I respect him. But this is for you, and you alone, and I don't want to risk ANYONE else knowing. Not Jared, not Mickey Mouse, and not the Queen of England. It has nothing to do with Jared or these other men specifically. I don't even know that I would have shared this with Owen. This is for *you*. You're already a target, and if anyone else were to find out about this, it could put you in even greater danger. So please, please, please, Shelby. Keep this to yourself. If Jared finds out in the future, if you are, God willing, together, and find yourselves in Switzerland, wanting to start a family, or whatever, that is one thing. But right now, just … until that time … don't say a word. To ANYBODY. Got it?" he said. His voice was stern and I knew that he meant it.

I was unnerved by how emphatically he was driving home this point. His request was almost begging, pleading.

"I promise, Eugene. I promise," I said, and I meant it. For whatever reason, whether for my own safety or otherwise, Eugene wanted this to be a secret between us, and I respected that. I didn't need to understand why. I would just have to fight the urge to share this news with Jared. I was a big girl. I could handle that.

I gave Eugene a long hug. When we broke our embrace, I noticed a tear rolling down his cheek. I wiped it away with my hand, and planted a kiss where it landed. "I love you, Eugene," I said.

"I love you, too, Shelby," he said, with a bigger smile than I'd ever seen him smile, as we turned around and headed back towards camp, Pippa happily trotting by our side. We were startled by a figure running towards us.

I gasped, and then realized it was Jared, out for a jog. "Hi, Jared!" I said cheerfully.

He gave Eugene and me a wide smile. "Good morning, guys!" he said, sounding unusually chipper. Maybe a good night's sleep had done us all well.

"Out for a run?" I asked, immediately feeling stupid. The answer was obvious.

"Training for a marathon," he said with a wink. "Want to come?" he asked.

I refused. The news of the bank account was too new, and I was afraid that, despite my promise to Eugene, that I'd spill the secret in my excitement. I needed time for it to settle in, if I was really going to keep it between us. "Thanks anyway!" I said.

He peered at Eugene. "I'll pass," Eugene said with mock seriousness.

When we got back to camp, I asked Paulie if I could help with anything.

"Nah, sorry. Not much for you to do right now," he said. "What did you have in mind?" he asked.

"I don't know," I said. "I can shoot, but I'd like to learn to hunt or fish, or to go out with you collecting berries and plants that are safe to eat. I know nothing about that stuff," I said. I figured it could come in handy.

"Well, I can take you to where the boys are fishing," he said. "I'm sure they might like the company, plus, it'll be fun to watch you try!" he said with a laugh. "No offense!"

"None taken," I responded.

"Okay, then, give me a minute. I'll bring a bag, that way, we can see if there are plants, berries, or animal carcasses we can grab along the way," he said.

I cringed at the thought of eating an animal carcass, but, in reality, isn't that all that meat ever really is, anyway? In essence, the filet mignon I'd once desired was, actually an animal carcass, when all was said and done.

"Sounds good!" I said, choosing to envision said carcass as an expensive steak versus highway roadkill.

Paulie appeared with a spear, a canvas bag, and a small net. "Let's go!" he said, enthusiastically.

We walked towards the river, stopping along the way to forage berries and greens. "How did you learn which plants and grasses were safe to eat, and which berries aren't poisonous?" I asked.

"Eh, it all comes with the territory," he said. "It's all a part of being a prepper," he explained. "You educate yourself on what you think you need to know. And I'm glad I did. Some of these other guys didn't bother too much with learning about edible plants. Now they're thanking me," he said. "But, I'm not too much of a fisherman or a hunter. So, it all evens out. I'm not a tough guy either, but some of those boys, woah, they'll have your back in a fight, that's for sure. Just make sure they're on your side!" he said.

"I'd like to learn everything I can," I said. "I like learning about these plants, and I want to learn to hunt, and I need to learn to fight. Or at least basic self-defense," I said. I winced, "I could have used it with Thomas."

"Don't what-if yourself. It'll kill ya. I'm sure you did all you could in that moment," he said. "Did the guys, though?" he asked.

I was taken by surprise at his question and how intensely he asked it.

"What do you mean?" I asked.

"You know. The guys. Eugene and Jared. Did they do all they could that night?" he asked.

"Well...yes!" I said defensively. "I mean, Eugene can't do much...and Jared, well, he was the hero! He fought Thomas, and scared him away. It wasn't his fault that Thomas escaped!" I said, haughtily.

"I'm not implying anything, sweetie. I am just asking. I didn't know the details of the situation. I'm glad they were there to defend you. We will be, too. Always. You don't have to worry with us guys around. We're survivalists and we'll help you survive. And protect your honor," he said, with a genuine caring concern that I appreciated.

"Thanks, Paulie. I can see that. And, they did try. We were all so exhausted from our travels, though. I don't blame them at all. We were all in the midst of deep sleep. The kind where you're practically comatose," I joked.

"Understood, missy. Understood," he said. We continued to walk and pick, and he taught me a lot in that brief little jaunt.

Almost at the river, we stopped to take a little rest, and I noticed, as Paulie wiped his brow with the pink handkerchief, that, in addition to the yellow duck sewn onto it, the underlying pattern was that of pink breast cancer awareness ribbons.

"Huh," I said out loud.

Paulie stopped mid-wipe, and looked at me, puzzled. "Yeah?"

"Oh, nothing." I said. "It's just...well, before this all happened, everywhere I looked there was a reminder of breast cancer, or, at least, cancer in general. I guess you can't escape that anywhere. Cute hankie, though. Was it your daughter's?" I asked with trepidation.

"Yeah, it was hers, given to her by Courtney. You had breast cancer?" he asked.

"Yeah. Have it. Well, I think. I don't know. I was in a clinical trial before all of this, and I'm not sure that it helped," I explained. I didn't feel like discussing it, and regretted bringing up the topic.

Paulie's eyes widened. "No," he said, "wow..." he trailed off. I could see the wheels turning in his head.

He looked at me and said, "My wife had it. She was in a trial for women who were genetically predisposed. Something with B-cell and T-cell inhibitors. I guess the treatment was similar to one previously used for autoimmune conditions. It involved some estrogen targeting, too. Anyway, just thought that's a crazy coincidence."

I was speechless.

I put it all together. His wife had survived the attack. She survived an attack meant to target women and children. She died from suicide, not from chemical warfare.

"Do you think whatever the medication was, or, something in our genetic sequence was what allowed us to survive when most others didn't?" I asked.

"Yeah, I mean, there's a chance. And if not – it's a small world, and a weird-ass coincidence," he mused.

We didn't know what to make of the information, except that it was a very small trial and not everyone had the actual drug. I wondered about the other women he mentioned, and remembered he said Sahel was bald. I gasped audibly.

"Sahel!" I said. "I remember her!"

He looked at me, incredulously.

"No shit," he said. "This is wild," he said. "Stranger than fiction, that's for sure."

"Yeah, I remember thinking that, if I did end up having to shave my head at some point that I hoped that I'd look as fabulous as she did. She looked like a supermodel," I said.

"So it must be true, then – something about you guys – either the trial or the illness itself, made you survive," he said, with disbelief. "But, if it's the trial that made you survive the attack, well, then there definitely aren't many of you out there," he said. "I'm sorry," he quickly added, perhaps sensing that this information may just be too much.

"That's okay," I said. "I'm okay with this, it's kind of better than not knowing," I said, but, I didn't know how much I really believed that.

"It's a lot to take in and a lot to consider," he said, tenderly stroking the handkerchief that once belonged to both his beloved daughter and wife. "We can drop the subject for now," he said. I was kind of relieved. We just walked, and pondered. I knew that Paulie was mulling this over in his head as much as I was. Could the cancer actually be, in some direct or even a roundabout way, what ended up saving my life? The irony wasn't lost on me. I nonetheless still felt a twinge of jealousy, though, that Courtney had the courage to end her own life. Or, at least I would have, had I not seen the sadness that it had caused Paulie.

We soon arrived at the river bank. "Have you guys seen any boats today?" I asked, changing the subject. I didn't know what else to say about our discovery just then.

The guys all shook their heads. I guessed that there was no hope of any civilization nearby.

"Shelby here wants to learn how to fish. Teach her well," Paulie said. "You good?" he asked me, before heading back into the woods.

"Yes, sir!" I answered. I didn't know why, but I wasn't ready to share our secret revelation with anyone, yet, and I was glad that he didn't mention it. It seemed like added pressure, that my cancer was meant to happen, so that I went to the clinical trial, and thus would survive the biggest catastrophe the world had ever seen. Oh, God, maybe I really was the holy grail! I didn't know what to make of it. I couldn't be the last woman here, I couldn't be the lone vessel. On top of that, I now had two huge secrets to keep: this new information, and Eugene's Swiss bank. It was too much.

I needed to focus on something else.

Garbo and Dustin welcomed me, and showed me how to try to hunt fish with the sharp spears, fashioned by hand with care. They instructed me to then place the fish in the net, and explained that they'd cook them when we got back. That was it? It wasn't as complicated as I'd thought, and I was surprised that there were more fish still alive than they'd let on. This was fishing in its most rudimentary form. I had to ask the obvious question.

"Why didn't you guys just bring fishing rods, bait, and tackle?" I asked.

"Preppers pack as minimally as possible. If it is something we can make on our own, we do that. Even a fishing pole could slow us down. It might be light, but it's awkward, and then, we'd still have the supplies to worry about," he said. "So, we decided to make spears and fishing rods out of sticks," he explained.

"Where are those, can I try one?" I asked.

He handed me an old-fashioned fishing pole: literally a stick with a string tied to it, and a hook at the end.

"Why aren't you using this?" I asked.

"We haven't had luck with it. We have had more luck with the spears, as far-fetched as that may seem," Dustin said.

"Ok, what do I put on it?" I asked. They both laughed.

"Grab a beetle or a worm if you can find one. You won't catch a minnow to use, it's pretty hard," Garbo said.

They did not offer up assistance in baiting the hook or locating said bait. I had this. Queen Shelby could do this.

I hunted around for any sign of a bug or worm to use as bait. It was harder than I thought, and soon my back and knees ached from crouching over.

"Any luck?" Garbo hollered.

I raised my hand to shield my eyes from the sun and looked back in his direction.

"Nope," I answered. "You guys catching anything?" I called.

"Nada," said Dustin. It seemed as though none of us were having much luck.

It was cool by the river, the breeze radiating off the water. I longed for the Crisco we used to have, to shield my face from the elements. I was sure I'd be wind-burned with chapped lips in no time. I was determined not to complain – and I sure as hell wouldn't give up.

Finally, after probably an hour of searching, I found it. One lone beetle, its shell gleaming in the sunlight. "Yay!" I said out loud.

The men watched as I stooped carefully, with catlike mannerisms, stalking my prey. I waited patiently for just the right moment, and set aside any girlish fears of holding a creepy, crawly creature in my hands.

The time was now. I clasped the beetle between my two hands, and, slowly, walked back towards my makeshift fishing rod while cupping my prize, with care.

The guys clapped.

"Way to go!" said Dustin.

"Right on!" said Garbo.

I had to admit, it felt good. I felt proud of myself. It was nice to do something, no matter how small, that showed I could survive on my own. This girl didn't need a man, especially one who was as moody as Jared (both the Old and New models.)

It was then time to put the beetle on the hook. Another challenge – and one I was up for. The bug was tickling my hands.

"Any suggestions for how to put mister bugger on the hook?" I asked.

"Make like Nike," Dustin said.

It took me a second – but, I got it. "Just do it," I said, perhaps to myself, perhaps to no one in particular.

I pinched the beetle between two fingers and, without overthinking it, stabbed the hook through him. I felt badly for the poor little thing for a moment, but then imagined the feeling of triumph I'd feel if I caught a fish…and then how yummy said fish would taste over an open fire, so I got over it pretty quickly.

"Another step complete. Now catch a fish, woman!" Garbo joked.

Some people would have been offended by his teasing, but, even though I hadn't known him long at all, I found it quite endearing, and sensed that he was as harmless as they come.

I threw my line into the water.

"Now what?" I asked.

"Just wait," they said in unison.

"Well, what else do I have to do? We do have all the time in the world," I said with a smile, thinking of Eugene. I sat on the ground and let the sun bask on my face. It was cold out, and the cool air off the river wasn't helping, but the sunshine was mildly warming, and very welcomed.

"I don't know about all the time. We'll have to head back as dusk approaches, and hopefully before if we get something," Dustin said.

Of the two, he was the more serious one, despite being younger. That being said, they were fun guys, with a great sense of humor. We mostly sat in silence, but occasionally one of them would tell a funny story, share a joke, or make a funny noise just to break up the monotony.

I didn't mind the silence, though. I found being by the water extremely relaxing. I loved watching the light reflect over the glass-like surface; I loved the poetry behind a ripple through the water. I liked the serene atmosphere and the soothing lull of the sloshing water up against the riverbank. This body of water was somehow calming. It felt like peace. It felt like life. I shuddered. Again, I felt the presence of what some would call God. And I wondered how long I'd ignored it in the past.

Chapter 18

I must have dozed off. I jerked awake to consciousness with some confusion.

It took me a moment to shake off the dust and acclimate myself to my surroundings.

"Shelby! Pull it in! Pull it in!" Garbo yelled.

"Yeah, girl!" Dustin chimed in.

I was confused for a moment, and then realized I had a fish.

"What!?!" it was more of an exclamation than a question, and I excitedly pulled in my prize.

A teeny, tiny, disappointing little fish hung, half-alive at the end of my shoddy fishing pole as he flapped madly to survive in this cruel world. I could relate.

"Congratulations," said Garbo. "Your first fish!"

"He's kind of pathetic," I said.

They laughed.

"I've seen bigger but it'll work!" said Dustin.

I resisted a classic, "that's what she said" joke and watched as the men removed the fish from the hook and placed him in the net. I noticed that there was another admittedly bigger fish already in there. They must have caught it as I napped.

I was more excited about the fish than I'd let on, and I think they knew it. They started hooting and hollering, and there we were, three of us dancing around and whooping with joy over a sad little fish.

But, it was MY fish, and so it felt special. It felt important. I'd never caught a fish before, I'd never baited a hook before, and I'd never picked wild berries before. It was a day of firsts. I loved it.

While we were celebrating, we heard a familiar bark coming through the woods.

"Pippa!" I yelled, genuinely excited to see her. "Hey, girl!" I said.

She came over and sniffed the fish.

"Noooo!" I said, warning her away from our catches.

Jared appeared moments later, sauntering over with a casual, sexy stroll, and those smoldering eyes. Oh, and that body … sigh. Greek gods themselves would have been green with envy.

"Hey, you!" I said.

"What up," he answered, giving me a quick hug, and fist-bumping the guys.

I was pleased to see my new friends and my love getting along. Jared had a long, complex history of being "iffy" around other guys.

"I caught a fish," I proudly proclaimed.

"Better than catching crabs," he said.

"Eew, Jared. You're gross," I said, "Tsk, tsk."

However, inside I was overjoyed. Crude jokes were reminiscent of Old Jared. Maybe my baby was coming back!

He laughed. "Nah, that's pretty awesome," he said. "Good job."

"Thanks," I said, smugly. I did feel rather accomplished and pretty darn pleased with myself.

"Guys, what's up with Neil?" he asked.

Dustin and Garbo exchanged sideways glances.

"Uh…what do you mean?" asked Garbo.

"Dude seems off," said Jared. "I just don't know. I don't feel like I get a great vibe from him. I can't get a read on him. He reminds me of someone who would have had, like, a hit list in high school, or who collects cat skins or something," he explained.

Dustin stifled a laugh. Garbo let out a chuckle.

"Don't say anything, but he's definitely the weird one of the bunch," said Dustin.

"The guy is harmless, though," said Garbo. "Just a strange character," he said.

"Ah, gotcha," said Jared.

"Whatever," I said. "Everyone has quirks," I added.

"Yeah, but Shelby you always see the best in people," Jared said. It was true, I did.

"Not a bad quality to have!" Garbo said.

"Not usually," Jared said.

"I'm bored with fishing, and it's slow today," said Dustin. "Let's just head back," he said.

"Don't stop because of me," Jared said.

"No, I'm tired," said Dustin. "We've been out here awhile."

"You two can stay, if you know your way back," Garbo said.

I was pretty sure I remembered the way home. (Yes, now THIS was starting to feel like home.)

"We'll make sure the fire is a-blazin' so you see the smoke, just in case," Garbo said.

"That would be helpful," I said.

"Yeah, we're good," Jared added quickly.

I felt a silent little thrill at the prospect of, finally, being left completely alone with Jared. A small, albeit electrifying, shiver of excitement rippled through my body. The anticipation was exhilarating.

"Okay, then," said Dustin, as they packed up their stuff.

"See y'all later," said Garbo, and off they went.

Pippa stayed with us, but I didn't mind. I loved her company, and, between her and Jared, I felt really safe. Plus, the dog didn't make me feel embarrassed. If Jared wanted to make sweet love to me right then and there by the river, then so be it. Let's get it on.

"Can we talk?" he asked.

"Talk? That wasn't what I was thinking," I said flirtatiously.

My boldness seemed to catch him off guard. He fidgeted and cleared his throat.

"Um..." he started, and suddenly I felt like an idiot. Why, oh why, did he always make me feel so silly?

"I mean…well…I just had a couple questions first," he said, almost shyly.

He peered at me through those lush, dark lashes. It almost wasn't fair how beautiful he was.

"Go ahead," I sighed, but I knew that I wasn't quite ready for that kind of intimacy just yet, neither physically nor mentally. I wondered what he'd had to say. Jared was historically not a talker.

He smiled. "So, why did you used to love me if I was such a jerk back then?" he asked.

I wanted to tell him that this wasn't a past-tense kind of situation. I still DID love him; there was no "was" here. I wanted to tell him that I don't believe that we choose who we love. Love, I felt, was a predeterminate fate.

"Even when I hated you, I loved you. There was always a strong bond between us. There would be extended periods of time where I just wanted nothing to do with you, and likely vice versa, but I couldn't leave you alone, and you couldn't let me go, either," I said.

"How serious was it?" he asked.

"It wasn't," I said. "It was ridiculous and immature. We were codependent. There were scary-serious emotions, but there was no serious relationship. We just never took that leap. That was the problem. It was game after game. I never really knew how you felt, and you always made me feel like a silly girl for wishing you'd love me," I said, sadly. "But I regret not telling you how I felt," I added.

He sat there for a minute, as though contemplating my words.

"Why didn't I tell you? I'm sure I loved you?" He said it like it was a question.

"I don't know why you didn't; but I also don't know if you did really love me," I answered. "We just couldn't escape one another. We were an intricate part of each other, somehow. Sometimes I loved you more than myself; sometimes I even loved you like you were an extension of myself. It was crazy love. I doubt it was healthy. There was a lot of ego involved on both sides. Neither one of us wanted the other to be happy with someone else, even if we couldn't make it work with one another. But, I don't feel like we ever really tried our best to make it work between us. We never took it seriously, we never really tried. We let it slip on by, and now it's too late," I said, and my voice cracked.

He brushed my hair out of my face and put his hands on my cheeks.

"It isn't too late," he said.

"But it is. You don't remember me, or our history. You're kind of like a different person," I explained.

He looked like he had been slapped in the face.

"You don't love me?" he asked.

My heart melted. Of course I did.

"I do," I whispered, "You're just not *my* Jared," I said, as though this explained everything. "This feels very new to me," I added.

"It's ALL new to me," he said. "But I can be him," he added, hurriedly.

I felt a rush of emotions. I was sad that Old Jared truly seemed to be no more. But, I felt hopeful about this relationship with New Jared.

It all seemed very melodramatic, but I leaned in, and we kissed. It was just as passionate, sweet, tender, and sexy as our kiss the other night by the fire. If anything, it was better. He caressed my hair, and every feeling I'd ever had towards him came rushing towards me at once. I wanted to cry tears of joy, of frustration, of release. This was simultaneously the man I always wanted and a strange, newfound lover. This was Jared and this was not Jared. It was like I was winning and losing at the same game, but the pure, overwhelming emotion of it all was breathtaking. I let myself revel in the moment. I was drunk with love.

Jared stopped kissing me, rather abruptly. I was taken aback.

Bewildered, I asked, "What's wrong?"

He looked at me for a moment, studying my face. "Hold on," he said.

He stood up and walked over to near where Pippa lay. He bent down and picked something up. I couldn't make out what exactly he was doing.

He approached me with his hand behind his back, and, crouching in front of me on one knee, presented me with a ring fashioned out of a flower.

My mind went blank. What was he doing?

"Marry me," he said.

I just stared at him, my gaped mouth opening and closing, mimicking the fish I'd caught.

Finally, I burst into tearful, hyena-like laughter.

He looked baffled.

"What?" he said, angrily.

When I finally caught my breath, I let all of the thoughts and over-analyzing slip out of my mind. I listened to my heart and said, "yes."

I was fully aware of how insane it seemed – and how inappropriate it was, given our circumstances. It was corny, and ridiculous, and didn't seem to gel with our given situation but ... why not? We'd learned – and were constantly reminded – that life was short. I, for one, would continually grasp for any shard of good in these dismal days.

He scooped me up and swirled me around with joy. It was such a moment of pure happiness, of sheer oblivion, and of reckless abandon. It was silly and illogical, but it was the most romantic experience of my life, no matter how asinine it did seem.

"Should we consummate our marriage?" I asked, greedily, only half-serious.

"Ooh la la," was his response. "Well, we're not married yet..." he joked. "Wait, was I saving myself for marriage?" he asked.

That set me off into another fit of laughter. "YOU?!?" I shrieked between bursts of belly laughter. Jared being anything close to pure was a hysterical notion. A riot.

He gazed at me, lovingly, and began tickling me.

Oh, how I hated being tickled.

"Jared, stop! STOP!" I yelled. I got the hiccups from the laughing and the crying and the tickling, which led to Pippa licking me with concern.

I silently wished I'd had my own paparazzo following me around, documenting my life. That moment was one I'd love to capture for all eternity: me wearing my floral engagement ring, Jared tickling me with such an amorous look in his eyes, and Pippa licking my face as I howled with laughter. That moment, in this dismal, dire new world, was the happiest I had ever been, bar none.

My handsome Jared shooed Pippa away and leaned into me with a ferocious kiss. This kiss was more intense than the previous one. This time, it was full of pure lust, pure desire, and pure need. It was him taking what was his. I was his fiancée. His Shelby.

He said, "I'll be gentle."

And, casting my anxieties aside, I let myself melt wholly into him.

Chapter 19

Jared was no amateur when it came to romancing the ladies. He was a god in the bedroom, from what I remembered. The layers of clothing made things a bit difficult, as he tried to unbutton, unzip, remove. I began to feel self-conscious, after who knows how many days of no showering, no toothpaste, and no deodorant. Thinking of it made me cringe, but I loved this man, and I needed him. If it didn't bother him, it wouldn't bother me.

Just as things were getting hot and heavy, a voice interrupted us.

"Guys! We're waiting for you to eat. It's going to be dark soon," Paulie called. We heard him, but didn't see him, and hurriedly disengaged from our entanglement, hastily reassembling ourselves and getting our wits about us.

Paulie appeared, slowly coming towards us out of the woods. If he'd seen what was going on, he didn't make any indication of it, though I knew I had to be absolutely beet red.

Jared seemed pretty perturbed but showed no indication of feeling at all awkward. He took my hand and helped me up.

"Coming!" he yelled, and we grabbed Pippa and headed towards Paulie.

"How was your day?" Paulie asked us, giving me a sidelong glance.

"Great!" I said, perhaps a bit too giddily. I didn't want to share the news just yet. It felt special and sacred; this secret between Jared and I. Now I had not one, not two, but three secrets: one with Eugene, one with Paulie, and one with Jared.

"I caught a fish!" I told him.

"I've heard," Paulie replied.

"And..." Jared encouraged, slowly.

"And, I really learned a lot on our walk! Thanks, Paulie!" I said.

Jared looked confused – and dare I say, hurt? – but, I mouthed, "later" to him, and that seemed to satisfy him.

On the walk back, I couldn't help but to think of what had almost occurred – and what was going to occur. We almost made love – sober – and for real. There's a first time for everything, I guess. We were going to be married, or, as close to officially married as we could be without a justice of the peace, priest, marriage license, or wedding. My insides were on fire; my brain felt like mush. This time, there were butterflies – not bats – flapping around in my tummy. I was on cloud nine, and Pippa sensed my happiness as she walked alongside me, tail wagging and eyes smiling.

Mrs. Jared Ketchum. Shelby Ketchum. Shelby Weiss-Ketchum.

I'd practiced all of these signatures on my notebooks in college, sometimes adding a little scrawly heart here and there. I'd said the names out loud in front of my mirror when we used to play bride-and-groom in elementary school; and in my early twenties, I'd even kept a notebook with our future kids' names: we'd have twin girls named Layla and Lola, and a boy named

Max. I thought about what kind of house we'd have, if we'd have a dog or not, and what our careers would be.

I'd had it all planned out for as long as I could remember: dusty rose bridesmaids' dresses, me in a couture ball gown style wedding dress, as princessy as can be, and him in an all-white tux, with white hydrangeas everywhere. We would have a harp play at our church wedding, and our reception would include a guest list that was the crème de la crème, a who's-who of New York, at a swanky hotel, perhaps the Four Seasons. It would be in Page Six, and for all the right reasons. I'd dreamt of my Dad walking me down the aisle, and my Mom tearfully lending me her treasured diamonds on my big day. I knew that one day, Mrs. Ketchum would take me under her wing, show me how to cook her favorite recipes, and envisioned her and my mom splitting babysitting duties. It was going to be hard with mine and Jared's bustling careers, but we would make it. We'd have it all: the American Dream.

Snap back to reality.

I glanced down at the flower ring on my finger and sighed. I wasn't going to have my dream wedding, or my dream life, but I had my dream man, and, really, what was more important in one's life than love? TRUE love? This was it, and I was living it. The daisy ring was better than the rock Ezra had gotten for me when we were engaged. The daisy ring fit me — not because of the size, but because it was from Jared. My love. My heart. MY Jared.

I wished that I could share the news with Tamra, with Daphne and Davis, with my parents. I also wished that I could share it with Owen. Oh, Owen would have been so happy for me. At least I could tell Eugene the big news! I couldn't wait, but, I still wanted to savor the moment privately with Jared for awhile. As we headed back to camp, we held hands, and I lay my head on his shoulder as best I could while we walked.

It was bliss. Somehow, in this new day and age, I'd found bliss. I glanced up to the heavens, and said a silent "thank you," to God. After all, this had to mean someone was watching out for me.

I knew that, in the grand scheme of things, it meant nothing. It was ridiculous. I knew it was not a real proposal and that we wouldn't really be married. I knew that we had way bigger things to worry about; there were far more important things that demanded our focus. But, it was a much-needed, quite-welcomed distraction. I didn't think anyone could blame me for wanting that. Yet, again, I questioned myself and my choices. Were my feelings sound? Rational? Justified? Was I losing it? And who got to decide which feelings were of value, or not?

We got back to the camp, and I could smell the fish cooking. Two fish – one being rather puny – wasn't a lot for eight people and a dog, but we made do with what we had. Like always, we would make it work. We also split a can of Spam and some of the grasses and berries that Paulie had left over from our walk earlier that day. We shared water out of a canteen and chatted about our day around the fire as we ate.

I was going to spill the beans – but just not yet. I wanted to wait. So, we discussed my yoga and meditation and I encourage them to do it with me the following morning. They all agreed, except for Neil. (Go figure.)

We talked about fishing, and chatted idly about the weather. Jared asked the guys if any more transmissions had come through on the radio.

"That's it!" Neil exclaimed. It was unlike him to speak, let alone speak with excitement, so we all turned to look at him.

"What, Neil?" Ted inquired.

"Jared sounds familiar. It's because I heard him on the radio," Neil said.

"Doubt it," Jared grumbled. I could tell he was annoyed. He really hated Neil for some reason.

"No," Neil insisted. "You were one of those guys talking with Thomas, weren't you?"

"Yeah," Jared said. "I told you, I used to camp with him!" he said, exasperated. "I don't know what you're trying to say, buddy," Jared said with a shrug, looking genuinely wounded.

"That's right," said Eugene. "Thomas wasn't always a bad guy," he said. "He helped Jared when he was first coming to," Eugene explained, defending Jared.

Jared was right. Neil seemed off. In fact, in addition to having a proverbial bug up his ass, Neil seemed unstable. Questionable. It made me worry, but I decided to push the thought aside and lighten the mood.

"I have a secret!" I said.

Eugene went pale and looked startled. He stared at me, disbelieving, and with pleading eyes. I gave an almost-imperceptible shake of my head, saying, no, it isn't what you think. Eugene caught my drift and immediately looked relieved.

"Well… Jared and I are getting married!" I exclaimed. I sounded like such a girl, and I knew that they'd think it was silly, but I didn't care. For the first time in a long time, I was genuinely, unbelievably happy – or, as happy as I could have been given the cancer and the apocalypse and my newfound status and whatnot. In this day and age, relative happiness was better than no happiness at all.

I held up my daisy ring and showed it to the men.

A round of applause and cheers broke out, including everyone but Neil, who sat, sullenly glaring at the rest of us. "What a grumpy Gus," I thought.

"So, when's the big day?" Garbo said, trying his best to sound like a girl, but failing horribly.

"I don't know!" I said with a laugh. "I have to find a dress first," I joked.

"Well we have to have a wedding," said Eugene with a smile. He was quiet this evening, and seemed pensive, but I was glad that he was joining in the fun.

"Let's set a date!" Paulie said.

"Tomorrow," said Jared.

"Tomorrow, it is." Paulie said with a nod.

I felt gleeful. Who knew that such happiness could exist in such awful circumstances? I never would have believed it myself.

"I just hope my ring doesn't fall apart," I said sadly. "I want to keep it forever!" I said.

"I'll make you a new ring every day for the rest of our lives," Jared said. "After all, I'm going to keep *you* forever!" he said.

"We have all the time in the world," I added. It was becoming a new catchphrase.

Jared leaned in and kissed me, and some of the boys made teasing, "oooooh!" and "awwww!" noises – but I didn't mind. This was paradise – fun in a time when fun was scarce. It felt nice to forget the world for a bit; it felt freeing to become lighthearted again, even if just for a moment.

"We do have to have a serious talk, though, you two," Paulie said. He nodded towards the bunker. "Let's go down and have a chat. Eugene, you too," he said. "And Pippa of course," he added.

We followed Paulie into the lair. I was curious as to why the others weren't invited, but I figured it must have to do with our getting married.

"I didn't tell the boys yet," Paulie started, "because I feel like this is more important for you, Shelby, and now, you, too, Jared," he said.

I suddenly felt uneasy. "What?" I asked, bluntly.

"Neil and I have been following the radios closely. The truth is, we have had some correspondence, I just wasn't ready to share it with you earlier. I had to really think about how I wanted to proceed with this. I feel, though, that it is now our responsibility to watch out for Shelby, especially now, and, well..." he said, taking a deep breath before continuing. "There could be a boat coming," he said.

"What?" I asked. "A boat? To where?"

"Europe," he said. "I don't have specifics."

"Who is it?" Jared asked.

"A rescue group from Europe. But don't get your hopes up too high yet. They are limited with how many folks they can take. Also, the last boat that was to come in from the Caribbean – some fellow preppers – never showed. Not sure what happened. The boat is small. They were going to take just a few of us. I know Garbo has relatives over there, so I'd let him go. I was going to send along Eugene and Shelby, and the rest of us wait for the next one, but now I don't know what to do because, well, with you two getting hitched and all ..." Paulie said.

"So all 3 of us can't go? What about Pippa?" I asked.

"I doubt they'll let you bring the dog. I don't know. But yes, I can't let Garbo down. His half-sister has a home in England. They seem to be doing okay there, for now, and with all things considered. So you three need to decide who's going. It isn't my choice, and I'm not trying to make this hard but ..." Paulie said.

"...But you're being kind in even letting any of us go. You guys have been waiting and just getting by for a long time, too," Eugene said. "The answer is obvious," he continued, as I burst into tears.

How could I leave Eugene behind? And why couldn't we ALL go?

CHAPTER 20

For about five minutes straight, I just bawled. How could I have just been so happy, and now be racked with such sadness? Logically, I knew that Eugene was not going to make it much longer anyway, given his age, so it probably made sense for Jared and I to go, and start our new life together. After all, we were going to be husband and wife soon, and I couldn't bear to leave Jared behind. I'd almost lost him once. I couldn't lose him again. Eugene understood.

And while the others didn't yet know, Paulie knew that, given the size of the trial group, that I was very likely one of the last woman left, and so, even though some of those guys probably deserved to go more, I, perhaps, needed it more than they did.

So, even though I understood the "why," I didn't understand the "how." How would I be able to do this? It was so unfair to all of them, and yet, I was grateful for this opportunity. I was torn between what the old me would do, and what the new me needed to do in the interest of self-preservation and survival. This internal struggle wasn't easy. None of this was easy. I suddenly felt silly for planning our faux nuptials.

It all became unbearable, not for the first time, and not for the last. The sobs I cried were sobs of guilt, of fear, of relief, gratitude, anxiety. They were overwhelmed sobs. Ugly sobs. Too-much-to-handle sobs. I could barely control my breathing or my thoughts. The lack of control scared me, yet, at the same time, exposing my raw self at my most vulnerable felt cathartic.

"Shelby, it will be okay," said Eugene, gently, rubbing my back.

"What about everyone else? And Eugene – I'll miss you! I'll worry!" I said.

"You're stronger than you know. And now you'll have Jared to take care of you," he said with a sad smile.

That was true. I took a ragged breath. "Okay." I said. "Okay, we can do this." I wasn't fully convinced. Something felt wrong – off, somehow. But then again, there was barely anything that ever felt normal or right, anymore – not besides Jared, at least.

"We can," Jared assured me.

"I want to take Pippa, though," I said. "I need to. Please."

I paused. "How do we know when to go?" I asked.

"Well, we don't. We essentially have to be ready to go at any time," Paulie said. "Based on the first failed attempt with the Caribbean boat, we'll maybe get about an hour notice, tops, and will have to head to the river then. We know when they're close as long as their signal can reach us okay. Weather may be a factor."

I was starting to feel anxious. This was real. I didn't even like going on cruises, how would I tame my anxiety while being stuck out at sea with strangers on a boat of God knows what size? And what if another storm hit? What if a rogue terrorist was on board somehow – weren't there MARF members and sympathizers all over the place? What if one of these new strangers attacked me, or raped me? I couldn't handle that again. I took deep breaths, trying to calm myself. Jared would be there, and, hopefully, Pippa, too. I didn't have many options if I wanted to escape Thomas, others who may be after me, and the desolation that had become the United States of America.

"It's okay, babe," Jared said, stroking my hair and planting a kiss on the top of my head. I squeezed his hand.

"Thank you, Paulie," I said. "You know I need this. As much as I don't want it, I need it, and I am so grateful to you." I leaned over and gave him a tight hug.

"Anything for our Queen," he said. I felt a pang. This man, who I had only known for such a very short period of time, was sacrificing a lot just to protect me. He could hop on that boat, or have one of his friends do so, and send them on their way to refuge, instead of offering it up to Jared and me. But I could tell that Paulie was genuinely concerned for me, especially given our recent speculations, and that he felt some kind of duty to keep me safe, and get me out of harm's way – perhaps in honor of his late wife, Courtney, who had shared a journey similar to mine – even if that meant getting me out of the United States. I truly appreciated it, and I told him as much.

"No problem," he said. "You need it more than I do. I'll survive; we'll survive. We can wait. We're prepared for this – it's what we do, remember?"

"Let me go break it to the boys," he said.

With that, I readied myself for sleep, snuggling between Jared, Eugene, and Pippa. We were a little family, and I needed to savor it while we were still all together.

Chapter 21

I had no dreams that night, and I awoke bright and early. I felt restless, and I sensed that my time with my new friends – and Eugene – would not be much longer. I was, however, anxious to celebrate my fake little wedding. It was a bright spot in a miserable world. I needed to cling to any brightness that could be mustered.

As it were, Neil was the only person awake when I got up that morning. I decided to kill him with kindness.

"Hello, Neil!" I said, cheerfully.

"Hey," he replied flatly. "Congrats," he said. I didn't know if it was in regards to marrying Jared, or my getting out of there, and I couldn't quite sense if he was being snarky or genuine, so I replied with an equally neutral,

"thanks."

"What are you doing?" I asked, trying to make conversation.

"Roasting almonds," he said.

"Cool," I answered, not knowing how to proceed with him. "So, what did you do ... you know ... before?" I asked, still trying to be nice.

"I ran one website for survivalists and preppers; and another for conspiracy theorists. Toyed around with blogging and photography, too," he said. "And I built model airplanes. Collected antiques and comic books. You wouldn't be interested," he finished quickly as though he suddenly realized he was having an actual conversation with a real-life human, and it scared him. "I like guns, too," he added. "And radios. I like listening. You never know what or who you'll encounter." Again, he looked nervous to be chatting casually with me in this fashion, and abruptly clammed up.

A chill went down my spine. I didn't know what to make of this guy. I knew quiet people and peculiar people and people who were interested in antiques, and computers, and guns. I knew lots of people who, on the surface, were a lot like Neil. It wasn't anything to do with his hobbies or his job or his appearance or ... anything. It was just HIM. His essence. Something about him was just off-putting to me. He looked so frail, so weak, so doughy, and so harmless, yet, at the same time, so very dodgy. He looked like he had a lot of secrets – secrets that you would most likely never want to know. It creeped me out a bit.

"That's neat," I said, even though I felt somehow oddly intimidated by him. "I was an aspiring screenwriter," I said. "By the way, I love comic book and superhero movies, so we have that in common! Jared used to want to own a comic book store; you guys should chat!" I said, way too enthusiastically. Ugh. I wanted to gag. I was trying way too hard with this guy.

"I suppose," he answered flatly, but I thought I detected a smile trying to peek out at the corner of his mouth. Maybe he wasn't so bad.

"Going to try yoga with us?" I asked.

He stared at me, disbelieving. "Um, no," he said. "You know, Shelby..." he started, and then just trailed off.

"Yeah?" I asked.

He looked at me warily.

"Nothing, never mind," was his response.

Okay, then.

With that, I stopped trying to make conversation. I just sat there, studying him thoughtfully. I wondered if he had friends. He wasn't the most likable person. He had pretty eyes, though. They were a clear, crisp, beautiful blue color, that I had rarely seen in real life. I could appreciate them. Maybe, at one time, before all of this, they had life in them. Warmth.

He looked like the scraggly beard belonged on him. His looked artsy, somehow. On some of these other guys, the beards just looked like what they usually were: itchy, nappy, unwanted scruff due to a lack of grooming. Ted had a beard that matched him. Neil's was the same. It kind of fit. I could picture him frequenting low-key coffee shops, but never talking to anyone; eating breakfasts at old-fashioned diners, always alone, perhaps with a newspaper, but usually with a laptop. Maybe he had a huge following online. I was really trying to find some positives with this guy. Maybe not everybody had them.

"Good morning, sunshine!" said a friendly voice. It was Garbo.

"Ready for our Euro-trip?" he asked excitedly.

It felt uncomfortable to discuss it in front of Neil, who shifted awkwardly as soon as Garbo said it.

"Um, yeah. I don't want to get my hopes up, though. More importantly; are you ready for YOGA? And my wedding?" I asked.

Calling it a wedding seemed positively ridiculous, but what else were we to call it?

"Both!" Garbo said excitedly. "I'm waking up the rest of those tools. I'm ready to get my yogi on!" he said.

I admired his enthusiasm. Out of the entire group, he's the one who I could most picture doing yoga, anyway.

A little while later, the men came trudging up out of the bunker, sleepily, groggily, some more chipper than others.

"Last call," I said to Neil, expecting him to explode on me.

"Fine," he said, and crankily fell in line with the other men.

If I were Snow White and these guys were my Dwarfs, he would most definitely be Grumpy.

I felt slightly victorious and gave myself a mental pat on the back. "Good morning, fellas!" I said, "and good morning, fiancé!" I said, blowing an obnoxiously exaggerated kiss at Jared. A couple of the guys groaned, with eye rolls added for good measure. I had to make myself a mental note to chill out with the cutesy, even if most of it was in jest. They were nice for even allowing me this marriage delusion, when most of them probably harbored some ill feelings towards me, given the boat situation.

"Let's begin!" I said, as I let the guys through a series of simple yoga poses and stretches called sun salutations. At first, there was a lot of grumbling and harrumphing, but towards the end of the yoga session, there was a lot less complaining, and, from what I could tell, a lot more relaxing. I took a peek back at my yoga protégées and found that some of them were doing rather well. Even the ones who were awkward (Paulie, Neil, Ted) seemed to be at ease and enjoying themselves.

"Now, we sit, and meditate," I said. "Focus on your breathing, and clear your minds," I instructed.

I thought about what we would have looked like to an outside spectator. We probably seemed like a cult — this small, mismatched group of people who lived in bunkers, did yoga en masse in the morning, and who sang around the fire at night. I was growing to like my little cult, though, and wondered if going to Europe was the right solution for me. Perhaps, Jared and I could stay here, and start a family here. It would be great – we'd be amongst friends. Our children would have an instant family, and a tiny community where they could grow up and be protected, provided for, and safe. They'd surely learn a lot from this crew. I doubted, though, that I could even have kids. And I doubted that it mattered, because I felt it in my bones that I wouldn't live long enough to see it through. Nonetheless, I felt like I was on to something with my new idea.

"Paulie, Eugene, Jared, meeting," I said.

I pulled them aside and explained my idea.

"Let's stay here. We don't need to go to Europe. You guys can protect us! We can have kids here! I can do my apparently destined part and help repopulate America … IN America! We'll all be together and it will be wonderful. Why didn't we think of this before?" I said, breathlessly. "Why complicate it? We're safe, you said it before. I can get used to this lifestyle. It's not so bad."

"We don't know who is after you, and once it catches on that you're the only woman left, we could be talking military presence, government involvement, or who knows what. You could be taken from us. We don't know how much of our government is operational, if at all, or who could be taking over. It may seem peaceful here but you saw what it has become out there. It's scary.

If the higher-ups find out there's one woman left, you'll be a most sought-after prize. And we don't know who knows what at this point. They could put a bounty on you, or take you prisoner and try to harvest your eggs, or use your womb to pump out baby after baby. They could be hunting you to use for medical research – or they could keep you as a lab rat to find the antidote to the chemical weapon that MARF, or whoever, has used on us. It's dangerous for you Shelby. But not just you. To be honest, Shelby, I don't want to put the others in danger, either. And if people out there know what we know about your existence, it could prove how valuable you are – " Paulie explained, and then stopped.

Ah. It sunk in. Paulie was trying to help me, but he was also trying to get rid of me. My alleged holy grail status, if you want to call it that, was too much of a burden for them. It put others in danger, too. My heart grew heavy. He was right. They didn't ask for me. They didn't owe it to me to protect my future offspring and me. Plus, if there were people hunting me, I'd be doing myself, Jared, and my future child a disservice if I stayed. I'd be better off in Europe where I could just blend in with other women, who I'd assumed were alive and well. But how could I turn my back on my nation if I could help them – or the world? I had two things to my advantage: I may be able to bear children, and I most likely had something in my blood that was immune to the latest deadly weapon to be used against America. Again I was torn: should I offer myself up as a sacrifice, or play the good little girl and go into hiding like everyone wanted me to? It was the conundrum of the greater good versus self-preservation, and I just wasn't equipped to make decisions of that magnitude.

"Okay," I said glumly. "Just an idea," I said. "I'm just going to miss everyone, and, quite frankly, it's scary. I also just don't know what I should do. Morally, I mean."

"Wait – what do you mean, 'what we know about her existence,' Paulie? How is she valuable to these guys?

Just to be a baby-factory?" Jared asked, exasperated. He and Eugene looked at me.

I sighed, "It just felt too ... heavy ... to discuss yesterday in the midst of everything..." I didn't know how to continue, to tell Eugene and Jared that I'd kept this secret from them.

Paulie chimed in, "We think we know why and how Shelby survived. Well, kind of."

"And?" Jared snarked, probing for answers. Patience was never his forte.

"Paulie's wife Courtney also survived the blast. So did another woman named Sahel and a few others that we know of. Well, we know that Courtney and Sahel were in the same clinical trial as me. They both had genetic breast cancer. We figured that perhaps whatever was in the medicine – or maybe even something in our genes – made us unsusceptible to the chemical attack, in the same way that men seemed to have been unaffected. So, in essence, I could be a baby-maker, and, my genetic code, or perhaps, the medicine in my blood, if it's still in there, could be a line of defense for future bio-attacks like this one, I guess," I explained. "If they had a way to research it, or do anything with it, but I mean, they – they don't..." I stammered, and trailed off. I was kind of rambling, but it was a lot to explain and sounded like pure science-fiction.

How was this real life? I myself didn't even fully understand it, and I was living it.

"Thanks for sharing that with your future husband, Shel. Kind of key information, no?" Jared growled.

"Listen, Jared, there's a lot of shit you haven't shared with me over the years! That was a big piece of information for me to digest – that the disease I loathed could have, in some twisted way, saved me.

I don't even know if that's good or bad, but I'm here, aren't I? If you were me, wouldn't you be wondering why that may be? I had to wrap my head around it. I wasn't ready to absorb it all! I am still not ready!" I said, on the verge of tears, and fighting the wobble in my voice.

Eugene laid a hand on mine. "I understand, Shelby. We all have secrets," he said with a friendly wink.

We sat silently for a moment. Suddenly, Eugene gasped. It alarmed me.

"What, Eugene, are you okay?" I asked with concern.

"Yes, yes. Shelby, on the count of three, tell me where you had your infusions done. Not your doctor's name but rather the hospital that administered the clinical trials," he said.

I was baffled but decided to oblige.

"1, 2, 3..." Eugene counted.

At 3, Eugene and I both said "Brookside."

I just stared at him. "Brookside Memorial Hospital & Wellness Center ... Dr. Bellagio..." I was confused. "Why? And how did you know?"

"There was a hospital bracelet in the Bible," Eugene said. "I saw it, pressed neatly between the pages, near the verse about hope, but I never mentioned it to Owen, because it was none of my business, and he seemed heartbroken enough. I figured, why re-hash what was likely a bad memory. I noticed the hospital logo, but didn't want to be nosy, and put it in another section of the book. I had never glanced at the name, or date, or any of that. I thought maybe it had to do with their fertility issues that he had mentioned to us. I don't know. When Owen passed away, though, I just assumed it was his bracelet, and that he'd had some underlying health problem that he was keeping from us," he said.

It took me a moment for it to click.

"Marta survived the chemical bomb!" I said. "Marta was in my same trial!"

I was flabbergasted. "There were two morning sessions. I just...that's crazy. Too coincidental! It can't be..." I said.

"Shelby, anything can be. From what you'd told us, it was probably the only place in the country, perhaps the world, doing that specific trial. They would probably take locals first, out of convenience," he said, "In fact, from working at the university, and volunteering at the university medical center, I know that they usually do try to keep it local," he said. "Within a few hours drive from the hospital or cancer center."

"But, Owen never mentioned it!" I protested. "It's just too far-fetched to be true. Owen would have mentioned it," I repeated. "He would have told us. I mean, I'm in a breast cancer trial, his wife's in a breast cancer trial, wouldn't that be cause for conversation?"

"Shelby, you never wanted to discuss your cancer very much. Plus, everyone has secrets," Eugene replied, in a tone that was both gentle and stern.

"But, Owen?" I asked.

"No, honey. Marta. Maybe she didn't want her husband to know," he answered. "Maybe Marta was the one with a secret."

It took me a minute to absorb that. How could you not be completely honest with your partner, especially your husband of so many years? Perhaps, she was trying to spare him the pain. Maybe, like all of these people were trying to protect me, she was trying to protect Owen. And in a way, I understood. She could have been protecting herself, too. Maybe she worried he would leave her, or look at her differently – as a patient instead of a person. Being sick made you feel worthless, in a way. What was pristine became flawed. Having breast cancer felt like a part of your womanhood was compromised. I no longer felt sexy and I wonder if Marta felt the same. Maybe she didn't want Owen to face the heartache, but maybe she didn't want him to view her as any less than the beautiful woman whom he had adored for many years, either. I could respect that. It all seemed a bit farfetched, but everything was farfetched in this strange new existence, including existence itself.

"Paulie, what do you think?" I asked.

He shrugged. "Anything can happen. Look at where we are. Look at what's went on. It seems strange, but, having a few connections to some women in a clinical trial doesn't seem so out there when you consider everything we've all been through. It does seem odd, but, maybe those women are watching from above and are on your side. Marta led you to Owen. Courtney led you to me. The Lord works in mysterious ways and I believe those ladies are angels. Listen, Shel, I don't know that it's true, there may still be other women out there that we don't know, that could prove our theory wrong," he said. "We don't know that it is just you, but it sure seems that way, so the reasoning behind it doesn't really matter, does it? You still need to be protected."

He had a point. It didn't matter if we were right about Marta, or the drug trial, or anything, really.

"It doesn't matter. Whatever happened, happened. What matters now, though, is that we keep you safe," Jared said, barely masking the urgency in his voice.

Eugene added, "We know it's all overwhelming, and a lot to take in. We know that it is all very scary, sweetie."

It was scary. It was hard enough adjusting to life here, where people spoke my language and were from my general area, let along, adjusting to life in a brand new country. It would be amazing, though, to get back to a normal life, and normal civilization. Plus, we'd have a nest egg if Eugene's bank did indeed grant me access.

"I will miss you," I whispered. "I will miss it here."

"We'll miss you, too," Eugene said, sincerely.

The rest of the day trudged on. I tried to put the conversation out of my mind and focused on my makeshift wedding. Jared was likely still irritated that I'd hid the Courtney-connection and drug trial theory from him, but, knowing him as I did, he'd get over it. I let him stew. It's not as though he'd never kept a secret from me before, anyway.

We dug out the old disposable camera we had, and took some photos of the four of us: me and Jared, Eugene and Pippa, as well as pictures of our new friends, saving some for the big "wedding." I couldn't wait to find somewhere in Europe to develop the photos, if these kinds of cameras were even able to be developed anymore.

"What are you wearing for your wedding?" Dustin asked.

"Umm…this?" I said, giggling.

"Here," he said, handing me a beautiful bouquet. "And some flowers to pin in your hair!"

"And here," Ted said, handing me an almost-pristine white blanket, to serve as a skirt or a shawl, I presumed.

My eyes warmed with tears. "Thank you! You guys are so sweet," I said. I felt like Snow White, or Dorothy from the Wizard of Oz — a beautiful heroine with an assortment of men fawning over her and doting on her and protecting her from evil. Unlike Dorothy, I'd never get back to home, but, like Snow White, I did have my Prince Charming, and, I hoped, a happy ending.

"Look, Jared!" I showed him what our new friends had done for me, genuinely in awe of their thoughtfulness.

"How nice," he said, giving me a quick kiss. "Let's get this over with," he said, jokingly.

"Oh, how romantic!" I said.

I asked Eugene to "walk me down the aisle" and wanted Pippa to walk with me, too. I put one flower in her collar and held her rope in my hand along with the bouquet.

We had Garbo "officiate" while Paulie played some semblance of the wedding march. Everyone sat respectfully, even Neil, and I dare say I saw a tear gleaming in Dustin's eye.

We were in such a depressing time, and, thus, I believe that our quasi-wedding ceremony was something that inspired everyone. It gave them hope, at least, it gave me hope. It was a breath of fresh air to be celebrating instead of mourning.

Garbo gave us an almost-accurate, marriage ceremony, and, when it came time to exchange vows, we had agreed to just wing it.

"I, Shelby Weiss, take you, Jared Ketchum, to be my not-so-lawfully-but-definitely-spiritually wedded husband, from this day forward, until, forever. We played house as kids, we played games as young adults, but in the face of tragedy, we've come together to play the most important roles of our lives: husband and wife. I can't wait to be yours, finally, and to love you, always," I said, trying not to cry. "We have all the time in the world," I added, only breaking Jared's gaze for a moment to glance at Eugene, who looked on, proudly.

"I, Jared Ketchum, take you, Shelby Weiss, to be my wife. While I can't remember most of our lives together up until this point, I will remember every second of every day from this point forward. I'm keeping you forever. You light up this dismal world. I can't wait to love you, and I can't wait for you to be the mother of my child. Here's to starting a new chapter together, far from here," Jared said.

He kissed me.

"I didn't say you could kiss your bride," Garbo said, "But, I now pronounce you husband and wife. NOW you can kiss her, man!" he joked.

The rest of the guys applauded as Pippa jumped at our legs and barked. There was no real rings, no real officiate, and, well, no real wedding, but it was ours, and our love was real, and that was all that mattered. It was so far from perfect, and yet, so perfect at the same time.

My wedding with Ezra would have been perfect. It would have been much prettier, and much more extravagant, and my marriage to him would have been good enough. It would have been fine. Expected. Comfortable. But this? This was better than expected. Despite our circumstances, it was better than just being fine. I was married to Jared, after all this time. Jared, who broke my heart so many times, without ever knowing it, and yet, still remained my ideal. My standard. The love against which I'd measured all other loves – and finally, it was mine. I was holding it in my hands, and I was never going to let it go.

We gathered around the fire for our "reception," and we all split a few bottles of beer. (In addition to their stockpile of water, beer was something else they'd prepared to have on hand. My kind of preppers!)

We were all talking, and laughing, and enjoying ourselves. I noticed that Neil wasn't around, and figured he was being a party pooper down in the bunker, which neither offended nor surprised me. However, I felt like I maybe got through to him earlier in the day, so I decided to go take a look and try to get him to join the party.

As I stood, I made out a figure in the darkness, heading towards us.

"Oh, there you are!" I called. It was Neil. "Come join us," I said, motioning him to come on over and have a seat.

As he moved closer, I saw a glint of silver as the fire reflected off of the object he held in his hand.

I gasped.

It was a gun … and it was pointed right at Jared.

CHAPTER 22

Without thinking, I did what any love-crazed, wannabe-Superwoman would do. I immediately lunged in front of Jared, just as Neil pulled the trigger.

The bang was deafening, and then, the pain in my arm was blinding. My senses started to betray me. I looked into Jared's eyes, stunned. I wasn't able to speak.

If I thought I'd been hurt before, I'd thought wrong. This was pain like I'd never felt. It hurt so badly it almost went numb, but, unluckily for me, it didn't. It teetered right on the edge of excruciation. I couldn't cry. I couldn't scream. I just gasped. Was I finally dying?

Action sprung to life all around me. The laughter turned into panic. The celebration turned into a state of emergency. Paulie ran to get the First Aid supplies. Jared held me, barking orders at everyone. Ted and Garbo tackled Neil. Dustin was frozen in headlights, but had enough sense to hold Pippa back, despite her whimpering and whining. Eugene flew to my side, comforting me and Jared. Everything was one big blur.

I believed I was approaching a state of shock. I was traumatized and the stress of the situation brought back other flashes of memory. I remembered the storm, I remembered running. I remembered an explosion. I remembered being hit over the head. I remembered awaking to Owen. I remembered the other time, awaking to Jared. I remembered being raped. Owen dying.

I felt sensations and heard sounds. Were they my own screams? Were they just fragments of memory in my imagination? I didn't know what was real and what wasn't.

As Paulie tried to stop the bleeding and get me cleaned up, I fought to stay conscious. I prayed to God that, if this was it, he let Jared, Eugene, and Pippa know how much I loved them. That was all I could think of: if I was going to die, I needed those around me to know how much I cared. It was the only legacy I wanted to leave: my love.

I wanted God to let Paulie know how grateful I was. I wanted the men to find happiness. (Well, except for Neil...) Oh, God, the pain. *"Please, God, just take me now,"* I thought, as I had, many times before. And like many times before, I had meant it. Heaven had to be better than this life.

I tried to focus on Jared. His face reflected the sheer terror that I'm sure was on my own. He stroked my hair, "You saved my life, baby girl. You saved my life!" he said. His eyes were wild, and dark. Emotions swam in those chocolate pools: anger, sadness, awe, panic, mania, love.

"You're a hero," Eugene echoed. "A real idiot, but a hero," he joked.

"Stay with us, sweetie," Jared added. "Oh, God, please stay with us!" he said.

I felt calmness wash over me with his words: I saved Jared's life. Maybe that was my purpose in this world: to save Jared. Maybe THAT is why I was spared: to save a life. I'd always had this bond to him, this strong connection that made me want to love him, and to look after him. Maybe I was his angel on earth.

I closed my eyes, and drifted away.

Chapter 23

Blackness surrounded me. I was getting used to blackness.

"Am I dead?" I mumbled.

"What a stupid question," I thought.

There was no reply.

I was cold.

"Guys?" I tried to yell, but my mouth felt parched. My throat was dry. I wasn't certain if I was talking, or breathing, or alive.

So, this was it. Death was a vast nothingness. There were no fluffy clouds, rainbows, or angels with golden trumpets. And where were my loved ones who had gone before me, waiting to greet me?

Where was God? Shouldn't he be on a throne? Or behind some glorious gates, at least? I wanted a spectacle: Jesus, Mary, lambs, and cherubs. Flowers and gold. Glitter and sunlight.

Peace. I longed for peace, both within and externally. I wanted peace to truly be with us.

"Shel?" I heard a voice. Maybe that was God. I truly hoped he was as forgiving as they say. I was many things, but perfect wasn't one of them – and I wasn't self-righteous enough to pretend that I was. I wondered how my judgement would go, but I felt prepared.

"Shelby!" the voice sounded excited, incredulous.

I jolted. I must have been in a deep slumber. I was alive. I was awake. Damn it.

I looked around, and saw a bunch of concerned faces staring down at me.

"H-hello," I said, equal parts baffled, disappointed, and relieved.

"Don't try to move, hun," Jared said.

"Stay put," said Paulie.

"Welcome back," said Eugene.

"What.." I started to sit up, and then screeched in pain. "We told you not to move!" Garbo chided.

"We knocked you out cold with a whiskey-painkiller combo. Paulie 's got you all cleaned up: disinfected, bandaged up. He stopped the bleeding. A real saint, that one," Eugene shared. I could tell that he was fighting back tears.

"The pain, though, I can't take away. I wish I could," Paulie said. "I am so, so, so sorry. I don't know what got into Neil. He's been known to have emotional issues. He had some kind of beef with Jared, we don't know why. We think the news of you two and Garbo setting off to Europe really set him over the edge. That and the attention you guys were getting. We knew he was kind of a weirdo, but never expected him to be such a wildcard, or to have violent tendencies," Paulie explained.

"I should have known!" I said, chastising myself. "Yesterday morning, he told me he liked guns. It was eerie," I said.

The guys laughed. "What?" I asked.

"Yesterday? You were out cold. You've been in and out of sleep for a few days now," Ted explained.

"Not your fault about Neil," Paulie said. "No worries at all. I should better screen the company we keep," he added. "Don't any of you guys try nothin' funny," he said, looking around at his friends. I knew the others were trustworthy. There was a true love and a true camaraderie there. Anyone could see that.

"Shelby, we're going to let you reacclimatize yourself, we need you awake, though. We are so glad you're up. We didn't want you to miss out and we didn't want to have to send you off without proper goodbyes. We got the call over the radio ... boat will be here in a few hours. We have to get ready to move, now, just in case they're early," Jared said, giving me a light peck on the forehead.

"Oh my gosh. Really?" I said. I was in no shape to be traveling, but, it was now or never.

"We've already packed up your things, but we're going to have to get you to the river," Paulie said.

"We'll all go together to send the three of you off," Eugene said.

I started to cry. They let me.

"Okay," I said, gathering myself. "Okay."

We began walking – me, hobbling, and leaning on Jared – but, mostly walking. Painfully, tenderly, walking. I'd sure been through the ringer.

"Wait!" I said, "where is Neil?" I asked.

"We took care of it," Eugene said. "End of discussion," he said, giving me a pointed look.

I kept my mouth shut. I didn't want to get into an argument with Eugene before I had to say goodbye, and I also wasn't sure if I wanted to know the gory details. Jared could tell me, someday.

"Do you need help?" Jared asked. I couldn't carry my own belongings, so Jared had most of our stuff, and I didn't to burden him, so I pretended that I was okay to keep moving.

"I'm fine," I said. We marched on.

About halfway through our journey, kindhearted Ted tenderly lifted me up, and carried me the rest of the way. It was a sweet gesture, and, lucky for him, I was a frail little package these days. A light little bird.

We finally got to the destination, and sat around talking until the boat arrived.

"How do you know they're coming?" Jared asked.

"We don't. We waited last time and the boat never came. I'm hoping this time is different," Paulie said. "Last word I received is that they're en route."

"Is Pippa coming?" I asked, hoping with all of my heart that the answer was yes.

"I don't know," said Paulie, honestly.

"I wanted to thank all of you. For welcoming us. For giving me a wedding. For teaching me to fish. For taking care of me after the shooting. Just thank you for taking us in, showing us the ropes, and being good friends. I will miss you all," I said.

"I agree," Jared said. "What she said!"

Everyone laughed, apprehensively. I was nervous for what lie ahead and sad to leave them behind, but I was also giddy with the realization that I was married to Jared.

Just then, we heard an unfamiliar cough. We turned around and there, by our bags, he stood: Thomas. With the Neil-drama, and the wedding, and the boat, and the clinical trial revelation, I'd all but forgotten about public enemy number one.

Adrenaline kicked in. I felt Jared slide something cool and hard into my hands. A gun! I swore I heard Paulie say, "Shelby, wait!" but I ignored his warning.

All I was picturing was the rape. I was hearing the sounds. Smelling the scents. Feeling the pain, feeling the shame. I relived the terror. I thought about the stories of Thomas hunting me, how he talked about me like a prize, or a peace of meat. I thought about all of the hardships we'd all faced, all of the injustice. When I looked at Thomas, I saw not only my rapist and my would-be captor, but I also saw the face of Neil, pointing a gun at Jared. I saw the faceless shape of the terrorists who had done this to our nation, to our women, and our children. I saw every person who'd ever done me wrong, and every negative situation that had ever come my way. With each new thought, I became filled with fresh anger.

My finger was on the trigger, but, I just couldn't pull it. Jared whispered in my ear, "do it."

Before he could stop me, I lunged towards Thomas, whose hands were now in the air. He was talking, but I couldn't hear the words. I just looked at his dirty, filthy, grimy lips, the lips that gave me unwanted, sloppy, sickening kisses. I trembled with hatred, and suddenly shooting him seemed too easy. Too fair. Too impersonal. After all, he'd taken something personal from me. He'd violated my body and my humanity and my privacy. He robbed me of my dignity.

I fumbled around my waistline and pulled a knife out of my makeshift belt. I blocked out all sights and sounds surrounding me. Thomas was protesting but I didn't care. After all, when I was protesting, he didn't care. Before anyone could stop me, I stepped closer, and, in a fit of blind rage unlike any I'd ever felt before, slit his throat.

I killed my rapist. I killed our enemy.

You would have thought that exacting such justice would feel good, but instead, I started sobbing. My insides crumbled. I knew that God would hate me now. I hated me. I don't know how I was capable of murder, but then again, it had really happened: I had just taken a human life. I wasn't in my right frame of mind. I was shaking head-to-toe and the men were scurrying around me. Oddly, Paulie seemed fixated on helping Thomas, but it was too late. I'd never be in heaven with my loved ones, I was going to hell with the bad guys, and Karma was going to get me good with what time I'd have left on this earth. I was stunned by my own actions.

"I'm proud of you," Jared whispered. I couldn't speak. Jared held me close. This was not the happy goodbye I'd wanted.

Paulie and the other men looked shaken, but Eugene piped up.

"It's okay, Shelby. He hurt you. He would have hurt you again. You've been through a lot, and if I'd have had the opportunity, I'd have killed him, too," he said.

"Me, too. From what you've all told me, I'd also have taken the chance," Dustin added.

I couldn't believe what all had transpired. It was unreal, but, having their support made me feel better, and, I just hoped that I'd one day be forgiven for my actions. I had mixed emotions: relief, regret, empowerment, guilt. I didn't know which feelings were the right ones to feel.

"He hurt me," I said, through tears.

"We know," Paulie spoke up, "and, there may be others out there like him, which is why we have to get you on that boat, honey," he said.

"Survival of the fittest," Jared said with a smirk, adding, "that guy was an asshole."

"To say the least," I thought.

"It's okay, Shel," Garbo said, patting me on the back. His friendly smile lightened the somber mood, and we turned our backs on the gruesome scene. Paulie wiped the blood off the knife, rinsed it off in the water, and gave it back to me. He also brought our bags over, and I was glad, because, I was still in a state of shock and didn't want to see Thomas's dead body. I shuddered.

As Garbo said his goodbyes to his friends, I pulled Eugene aside. "I still have it," I whispered.

"Good," he said. "Keep it safe, and keep yourself safe!"

"Hey guys," I hollered, "you'd better take really good care of Eugene!" I said.

They all solemnly swore to do just that.

"Eugene, you've become like a father to me. A father, a grandfather, and a friend. I couldn't have made it this far without you. If Pippa has to get left behind, please care for her. And PLEASE care for yourself. You've got a lot of life left to live. I just wish you could live it with us," I said, sadly.

"Chin up, sweetie. You call me Mr. Interesting, just consider this a new chapter in my book: Mr. Interesting, Survivalist!" he said. "Plus, I'm looking forward to the day I get to reunite with my Adelaide," he said. I could tell that he meant it and, that while he was sad to see me go, that he was happy with the newfound group of friends he'd found in these men.

"I love you, Eugene," I said. "I'm sorry you had to see that," I added, referring to the Thomas fiasco.

"Love you, too, Sugar!" he replied. "And hush."

He turned to Jared. "You take care of her, Jared. She's precious cargo!" he said.

Jared smiled, "I know. Trust me, I know," he answered.

"Now, be careful you guys. We are getting Shelby out of immediate danger of being hunted here, and Thomas being gone was a good step but there are still so many unknowns and she needs to move, now. You guys, just be aware on this boat, and you be aware once you get to your destination. Always be aware; always be prepared. For anything and everything. Don't reveal too much. Don't trust too many. Remember things I've taught you. If everything is kosher and normal over there, try to integrate yourselves into the culture where ever you land. Change your names, get jobs, dye your hair, whatever. Don't let people know you're Americans, if at all possible. I wrote a list out for you guys; just some do's and don'ts and things to keep in mind, okay?" Paulie said, handing us a tiny notebook. He looked at me, "Don't let anyone fool you." It was a piece of advice that I resolved to remember.

"You guys got your knives, all your other stuff, and a spear?" Dustin asked.

"Yes," we answered. We all knew that I had my knife, that's for sure.

"You taking your fishing pole, too?" he asked me.

I hadn't thought of it. Maybe I should. It may come in handy to make myself useful on the boat.

"Packed it," Garbo said with a knowing smile.

"You thought of everything!" I gushed.

"But you won't be using that for a while, little lady," Paulie said, nodding towards my shoulder. Ouch. In the midst of the action, I'd almost forgotten that I'd been shot. I guess, as I believe in Karma, that I may have taken a life by killing Thomas, but, I also saved a life by saving Jared, so, maybe it all would be okay.

"Yeah, let's give it up for Shelby. Talk about heroics. Saving her little hubby-wubby! Getting the bad guy!" Dustin said, jokingly.

It wasn't really funny, but we all laughed. It hurt, but it, at the same time, felt wonderful.

"It's here!" Ted hollered. We saw a boat approaching in the distance. I felt both terrified and exhilarated. This was truly a moment that was bittersweet. I felt a lump form in my throat. That boat was hope. That boat was change. But that boat was also leaving behind the life to which I'd, against all odds, become accustomed to living.

I gave Eugene a long embrace, kissing him on the cheek. We both cried. There were no words to speak. I knew his heart, though, and he, mine.

I hugged each man, giving Paulie an extra-long hug. "Thanks again," I said under my breath, "for everything. Please watch out for Eugene," I said. "And, I'm sorry for the trouble I've caused."

"Shhh, kid. Shh.." was his reply, and he squeezed me gingerly, but firmly. I winced, but it was worth it. "Good luck," he added.

Jared and Garbo shook hands with the guys, both offering hugs to Eugene. I grabbed Pippa's rope – I was dead set on this dog coming with us! – and all the men said their goodbyes to her, too.

The boat docked and we hurriedly, but carefully, stepped aboard.

"No," the gentleman said, as I approached.

"Excuse me?" I asked, indignantly. I was, after all, Queen Shelby, didn't he know?

I turned to Paulie, panicked. "I thought you said this was all good to go?"

The man chimed in, "You are okay. The pup is a no," he said.

I felt like my heart was being ripped out. "No!" I shrieked, refusing to let go of the rope. Paulie met me and gently pried my fingers away from Pippa. I gave her one last kiss on the nose, nuzzling my face into her fur. "Thank you, I love you, be a good girl," I told her, even though my heart was breaking. Out of all of the horrors I'd witnessed, the deaths, and the disaster, this was almost the worst goodbye. Parting with Pippa, who had become my best friend, was almost the biggest tragedy of all.

I bawled as, moments later, the boat began to quickly pull away from the shore. The last remnants of my life were on that shore. One of my last sources of comfort were in that dog's brown eyes. I began hyperventilating as I saw Paulie, Eugene, and the others waving goodbye, the furry outline of Pippa growing smaller and smaller. I could hear her crying, shrieking barks. We had really bonded, and I felt so badly for her – she'd already lost Marta and Owen, I couldn't believe that she was going through this again. The poor dog, she couldn't have known what was going on. I felt slight comfort in the fact that Eugene and the guys would be there to care for her.

"Calm down," I told myself. "You're with Jared. You're starting a new life." I took a few deep breaths.

My eyes clouded with tears as I watched them fade away. Suddenly, I saw Pippa break free from her rope. She was too fast for the men to chase her, and she began swimming after the boat. She was a Corgi, though, with short little legs, not built for swimming.

"Sir!" I exclaimed. I didn't even know any of these people's names yet. "Pippa! Pippa!" I yelled.

"The dog! I have to get to her! She's coming after us!" I screamed hysterically.

Before he could answer me, I pushed past him and dove off the side of the boat, swimming towards Pippa. It was hard to swim in the multiple layers of clothing and with my wounded shoulder. The water was icy cold. I was in such pain. I realized I could drown. Panic set in but as Pippa approached me, I felt at peace with my decision. We doggie-paddled, as the boat reversed, throwing a life preserver down. Jared rescued Pippa first, and then, me, bringing his two soaking wet girls up onto deck. I'd never, in my life, been so grateful to him. I was a lucky girl.

"The captain isn't happy with you," Garbo said. "But, he knows the story. He knows what precious cargo you are – to me, and to the rest of the United States! They'll let you keep Pippa if you care for her and clean up after her."

I threw my arms around him. It hurt.

"Ow! Thank you, thank you, thank you!" I yelled excitedly.

He went out and yelled to the guys that Pippa and me were safe, and the boat pulled away, for good. We waved goodbye until we could wave no more.

As I dried off and settled into our journey to a new world, I snuggled against Jared.

Jared, Pippa, and me. A happy little family. It didn't hurt that we had a friend in Garbo, too, who was becoming chummy with the other guys on the boat. For now, I didn't want to socialize. I just wanted to rest. My arm hurt, I was cold, and, despite my contentment with Jared and Pippa, I was sad to be leaving Eugene and the others behind.

As we continued to sail along, I grew restless. Jared had fallen asleep, and I was in pain, but, grateful to be dry and warm and away from the atrocities that I'd been living as of late. I already missed Eugene and the others, but, I knew that I had to get away from there.

My tummy rumbled, and so I found my bag to see what rations were available to me. In the outside pocket, there was a note on green paper that simply said, "S."

I knew it was for me, and I didn't know who put it there, but, I recognized the stationary – I'd seen it with Neil's things. I, inexplicably, felt a chill go through me as I unfolded it.

Shelby;

You're probably on your way now, if you're reading this.

And I may or may not be dead. Thomas was only on a mission to protect you. This seemed to be the safest way to let you know. See, when I first met you I knew I'd recognized Jared's voice. I heard the men chatting on the radio days after the event.

Yes, Thomas wanted to capture you, but only to protect you and keep you safe from harm. He wanted to uphold you – to truly make you Queen Shelby. He may have had delusions, but he didn't want to harm you.

Jared did. Shelby, Jared remembers you. He knew who you were. His amnesia is a ploy. He kept saying he had to find you, to get you, and he knew you by name, before you met him. He kept saying you were his. He seemed to have a plan.

Shelby, I believe you're marrying your rapist. And I don't know his intentions. Be careful.

- Neil

I felt the bile rising up into my esophagus. This couldn't be true. Neil was deranged; even the other men thought he was a little off. What kind of sick joke was this?

I put my hand over my mouth. It couldn't be true, could it? I folded the note back up and stuck it into the bag. I wasn't sure what kind of sick bastard would do that to me, but, who knows where Neil's mind was. I mean – he tried to shoot Jared. He was the nerd stereotype in my movie. He was weird. The longer I thought about the distressing words on the green paper, the more infuriated I grew. How dare Neil accuse Jared of something so heinous? I shook me head and tried to brush off the chilling note, puzzled at what Neil's intentions could have possibly been. I laughed to myself, thinking, "maybe he was in love with me!" I, after all, had shown him kindness and perhaps his jealousy was why he shot Jared. As sick as it was, it made me feel, in some way, a bit flattered.

I ventured back over towards my husband, and gazed at him lovingly. The longer I stared, though, the more amorous I grew. The note was, undoubtedly, untrue. This was *Jared*, after all. Jared, of high school skip days, and childhood games of hide and seek, and nights of kissing and cuddling following nights of drinking. This was Jared who was obsessed with Halloween, and strip poker; who used to send me love notes in elementary school and buy me balloons on my birthdays; and who I used to do shots with in college. This was Jared whose dad was my dad's best friend, whose parents used to babysit me, who I'd sat behind at Easter mass. Jared who gave the best hugs. Jared.

With trepidation and confusion, I watched Jared sleep. I thought back to the first time I realized I was in love with him – REALLY in love with him. I was probably about 20 years old, and while I'd always had fleeting crushes on him here and there, there was one innocuous moment that summer that changed something within me for good. We were at a bonfire with a bunch of friends. It was summer, and there was a mix of us – both high school and college pals. A group of us had driven out to a farm, sleeping bags and coolers of beer in tow. We'd all spent the night around the fire, swapping stories, swigging drinks, and sharing cigarettes. The night was filled with lightening bugs and laughter, the sky was filled with stars, and the air was permeated by the exuberance of youth. Though Jared and I were separated for most of the night – and admittedly, both flirting with other people – there was a magnetic attraction between us unlike ever before. I'd catch him stealing glances at me from across the flames and I'd do the same. Pangs of jealousy ate at me as two beautiful blondes flanked him on either side.

I myself was on a self-imposed break from dating, but also had no trouble luring in the opposite sex. I'd always had a close and flirtatious relationship with Jared, but it was that night when I realized it may be more than that. The exact moment it happened was nothing exciting, but it was one that I'll never forget. Long after others had gone to sleep, a few of us shared a large blanket near the dying embers, gazing up at the stars. As the drunken rambling died down, our eyelids grew heavy. Before I dozed off, I realized that Jared was asleep with his head in my lap. I didn't dare move. I rarely had the opportunity to study him so carefully, to see him be so vulnerable and at peace. I remember thinking how beautiful he looked in that lighting. He wasn't putting on airs: he was who he was at his core. The moonlight bounced off his cheeks, and I noticed with brand-new eyes his soft skin, sharp jawline, full lips, and long, droopy lashes. I noticed the stubble on his chin, and the way his mouth parted subtly as he breathed. He was a boy on the verge of becoming a man, and I wondered why I'd wasted so much time on others, when he was there all along.

As the fire burned and my 20-year-old heart fluttered, I had wanted to lay down with him, but I didn't dare disturb the moment. So, I just watched him. At one point, he stirred and looked up at me through heavy-lidded eyes, murmuring, "I love you." I don't think he knew what he was saying, much less who he was saying it to, but it didn't matter: those words were branded on my heart forever, and they would permanently change me. I'm not sure what precisely made me fall for Jared that night – was it those words he mumbled in a waking dream? Was it the alcohol, the physical contact, or the giddiness of summer? I'll never know. But even in this moment as I watched him sleep, I caught a glimpse of the boy who caused me to fall and never recover. He stirred, and I snapped back to our nightmarish reality as a part of me still wondered if he'd meant what he had said on that bonfire-lit evening so many years ago.

"What are you thinking?" Jared asked me.

"Just about everything," I answered. "You," I added with a smile.

"You know what I'm thinking?" he asked.

"What?" I answered.

"I'm thinking about loving you forever. I'm thinking about snuggling you, and nuzzling you, and kissing your neck, your shoulder, your nose, your lips, your ears, your feet, and every last part of you," he said, sexily.

"Jared!" I said with mock chastity.

"What can I say," he said, "a girl who will take a bullet for you is pretty damn hot."

I sighed and let myself melt into his kiss. It was exquisite. Every part of me tingled with anticipation.

Jared began to gently peel off my clothes, layer by layer, gingerly, tenderly, much as he had begun to by the river bank, before we were so rudely interrupted. It felt like an eternity; he was taking it slow, for sure.

"You're so beautiful," he murmured.

"Even with the stench? And the stubble?" I joked.

"Especially with the stench and the stubble," he said, and suddenly stopped removing my clothes. "Give me a little striptease," he said.

I obliged.

As I got down to my panties, Jared said the seemingly-innocuous phrase that would change everything forever:

"Aw, yeah, let me see that sexy little heart tattoo," he murmured appreciatively.

I froze. Panic set in, but I hid it. So I mustered a smile while trying to continue to be sexy for my new husband and lifelong love. I had been telling myself that we were sailing towards a horizon of nothing but hope, that we were beginning a new life and a new family together. But in that moment – I knew.

Jared had never seen, or known about, my heart tattoo. I had gotten it for Ezra, and Jared – neither Old Jared nor New Jared, would have ever had the opportunity to see it except ... that night.

Neil was right. I was about to make love to my rapist.

And now we had all the time in the world to spend together.

I forced a sultry smile, wiggling my hips ever so subtly, but the unsettling feeling in my stomach wouldn't rest, and my brain was working in overtime.

How was I supposed to act in this situation? What should I do? Was this what Battered Woman Syndrome was like? Or was I going crazy; just plain losing it?

Who in their right mind would continue on with this lovemaking charade knowing this new information? Was I punishing myself for something?

Again, the lines of right and wrong were blurred in my head. I questioned my mental status: Was I mixing up the tattoo timeline? Or had Jared, in fact, seen it at some point? Was I wrong about this? I hoped I was wrong.

Thoughts kept trickling through my brain: Jared's amnesia, Pippa's initial reaction to him, his remembering my last name – had I ever told him that? He had that memory eating dog food when we were kids – if he had amnesia, how did he remember those things? Perhaps I'd had these doubts all along, but was in denial, not wanting to suspect my love of these horrible things. How quickly Prince Charming was plummeting off of his platform...

I triple-checked my memory, just to make sure. Did I have the heart tattoo at any point when we'd hooked up? NO. I got it for Ezra in a desperate attempt to spice up our relationship. I never cheated on Ezra. The next time I saw Jared was during his scuffle with Owen. So, did he see it when...? Oh, God. He couldn't have *raped* me. I was feeling sicker by the second. He did. There was no way he'd have known about it, otherwise. Eugene was the one who'd helped me to get dressed again after the incident. Not Jared. If anyone saw my tattoo, it was Eugene ... and maybe, my rapist. Could Eugene have mentioned the tattoo to Jared? Or, was Jared the bad guy all along?

I thought about his mood swings, and his irritability, his history of possessiveness, his encouraging me to shoot Thomas, him saying he was proud that I'd done it.

"No," I thought, and inwardly, I was violently shaking my head like a whirling dervish, as though the thoughts and the truth would come tumbling out, falling into the waters never to be seen again.

As I continued to go through the motions for Jared, I tried my hardest to remember the night of the rape. It was Thomas, I knew that. But did I? I didn't actually see my rapist, nor did Eugene. Only Jared claimed to. I heard him, though, right? I thought long and hard, but all I could remember were angry whispers. Angry whispers that could have been anyone. Angry whispers that were Jared.

I thought of Thomas in those seconds before I killed him. I realized I didn't know the gruff stranger at all. He seemed calm, mild-mannered, and, actually, rather harmless. I shuddered. I'd done it in such a personal fashion, too, and with such conviction. But what was I basing my convictions on? I felt tormented. I didn't kill an innocent man; I couldn't have. Thomas was after me. He was a threat! He was dangerous. *He* was the bad guy.

I replayed the murder in my mind. Thomas was on the shorter side, only a few inches taller than me; Jared was over 6 feet tall, and in excellent physical shape. How couldn't he have overtaken Thomas the night of the rape, unless Thomas had a gun? If Thomas had a gun, why wasn't he using that to restrain me during the rape, and why wouldn't he have used to defend himself, as I had walked towards him, wielding a knife and a gun and a determination to kill?

"Oh, God," I whispered. I felt excessively unsettled, both in my stomach and in my mind.

"What's that?" Jared said, winking.

"Oh, God," I repeated, more sensually. I was in survival-mode. I didn't know how dangerous he was. I had to play nice for the moment. "I want you," I continued, for added effect. It was crazy on my part, but I felt a breakdown coming on, and I also couldn't deny that my body wanted what my heart now didn't. My world was now one of constant conflict: save myself or save humanity? Love Jared or hate Jared?

Inside, I kept analyzing. I kept telling myself that I knew Thomas was dangerous, but really, what solid reasoning did I have? Other than the initial scuffle with Owen, and my ending-of-his-life, most of my intel on Thomas had either directly or indirectly come from Jared.

This was so like me – to be blinded to reality because of Jared. It was a pattern that I'd succumbed to my entire life. As much as I fought against being some clueless-woman stereotype, maybe I was. Was I being blinded by love? Blinded by Jared?

And maybe, just maybe, Eugene had a feeling about Jared all along. Maybe that's why he didn't want me sharing the money or letting him know about it. But why wouldn't he share those fears with me?

I stared at Jared's gorgeous face and flawless body, as he looked on, admiring me. He really was a paragon of physical perfection. His eyes were appreciative with heavy lids and a lusty glow. He gave me a victorious, boyish grin.

"Come and get me then, babe," he murmured, and as his hand brushed my cheek, I felt a chill – was it the wind, or the realization that I was about to make love to my husband, the rapist?

At that moment, I sprinted to the edge of the boat and threw up over the side, into the waters that I wished were taking me back to camp, or washing me away, to another time and place.

As I wiped the bitter barf from my lips, I turned around nervously to face my husband.

The vomit may have been nerves, and could have been written off as your standard bout of seasickness, I suppose. The alternative was that it may have been due to the realization of what I now knew to be true: I killed an innocent man. I was still in danger. I was married to my rapist, and, well, I just might be carrying his child. That was another possibility that I'd have to consider. After all, I was that holy grail, that sacred vessel, and the only logical explanation for what he'd done to me was to impregnate me. I'd never been seasick before – it'd explain the vomiting.

Panic began to consume me, but I had to keep my cool. I had always wanted a baby, especially one with Jared, but, not like this. How could Jared do something like this to me? I thought about a time in my early 20's when I was in a bad relationship that, at times, verged on violent. I remember the times that Jared would tell the guy off, and, on other occasions how he'd get in the face of anyone at the bar or club who would mess with me. Often, all it took was a glance from him. He was mild-mannered and on the quieter side, but, he had an intimidation in his eyes when he wanted to, not to mention a physically daunting build. He was my protector, so he couldn't be the enemy, too. I knew that he was, but, a part of me couldn't bear to acknowledge it.

I wondered if I was just, finally, going crazy. I'd always had a propensity for the dramatic, fretting about things that weren't there, creating situations in my mind – it's what made me a good writer and a crappy girlfriend. So, I did my best to fight my suspicions. He could have, maybe, seen the heart tattoo another time. Maybe I'd mentioned it, maybe he'd caught a peek of it when I was going to the bathroom – I usually did it in private, away from the guys, of course, but maybe he'd stumbled upon me one time without my knowledge. I assured myself that this was a viable possibility. If not, he had tattoos, and so did I, and we'd had so much time to do nothing but talk, and it wasn't as though I'd archived every single conversation in my mind. It could have gotten brought up.

For now, I couldn't let Jared know what I was thinking. I had to put my feelers out – I had to try to figure out why Jared would do this to me. I couldn't let him sense my fear or my distrust. I had to act normal, and continue on, until I could figure out what this meant, and what to do. I told myself it was because I was an open-minded, fair, individual, and was giving him a chance – benefit of the doubt, innocent 'til proven guilty, the whole nine. Really, though, it was out of fear. I didn't want to let him know that I knew. I figured that it had to be smarter to just be normal, and play along – for now. Maybe another part of me, still, just didn't want to believe. Maybe, just maybe, I was happier living in denial.

"Honeymoon's over," I thought. I knew that this would have to be that Oscar-worthy performance that I'd often daydreamt about.

I batted my eyelashes at him, "Sorry," I said shyly, rubbing my stomach, as if to explain that I was queasy. "Sea-sick, I suppose," I said.

He looked disappointed – I ruined the moment. Though he'd done it (me) before, he had yet to seal the deal with his new wife.

"That'll happen," came a booming voice from behind me. I looked at Jared and mouthed, "sorry," even though I certainly wasn't.

"Garbo! Hey, there," I said. I was so relieved to see him. Jared looked none too thrilled, naturally, but, we were in close quarters and would most certainly be stuck with one another, for awhile. Alone time, thankfully to me, would be sparse.

Pippa trotted over to Garbo, sniffing his feet, inspecting the floor of the boat. As he reached down to pat her, his jovial expression changed.

"Are you okay?" he asked.

"We're good," Jared replied.

"I was talking to Shelby," Garbo said, quickly adding, "but I'm glad you're well, too, man."

"I'm just a little nauseated," I replied.

Garbo looked concerned. "You look pale. You've been through so much. You need sleep. You've been through too much," he said again, sadly, and almost imperceptibly shaking his head. "Are you resting your shoulder?" he asked, "and everything?" he added awkwardly, and I suppose he was thinking about the cancer, for which there was nothing I could do.

"Trying to," I said. "I think I'm just driving myself crazy now that I have some time to think," I added with a laugh.

Maybe that's all this was – me letting my mind get in the way, or some kind of self-sabotage. It wouldn't be the first time that my own thoughts were debilitating to me. Neil's note was just setting off a chain of anxious thoughts. For as long as I could recall, any time that things were going well for me, I'd stress over when it was going to end. My therapist called it, "waiting for the other shoe to drop." I had spent so much time surviving, on the run, worrying, fighting, and now I was in a much better place, and married to the literal man of my dreams, on my way to safety.

Maybe my worry over Neil's note and Jared's role in all of this was just my mind kicking into high gear, mentally preparing me for the worst. I'd read once that dreams serve the same function, that they allow you to play out the most weird, extreme, sometimes scary or ridiculous scenarios so that, if these things were to happen in real life, you'd be prepared for them and have at least some kind of experience to draw on. I idly wondered if that was true. If so, no dream had prepared me for any of this, aside from being with Jared, but, everything I had gone through was so much stranger than fiction, and I don't know that any dream could ever have prepared me for it all, in whole or even in part.

It made me feel better, the consideration that I was just being crazy. The tattoo comment could have a gazillion explanations, and the option that it was just me making a mountain out of a molehill was more comforting than envisioning Jared as a liar, a rapist, or as anything less than my knight in shining armor and the leading man in the story of my life. I knew he wasn't perfect, but he wasn't a bad person. In my opinion, he just wasn't capable of the sheer horror of which he was being accused.

Garbo looked concerned, while Jared just sat with his mouth in a flat line, undoubtedly wishing that Garbo was anywhere else but with us. I wondered, briefly, what Jared's end game was, if he was, in fact the proverbial bad guy: impregnate me that night, and then what? I'd eventually figure out, timing-wise, that the child was the rapist's – so if I thought that rapist was Thomas, how would Jared have benefitted? See, it just didn't make sense. Right?

"Just take care of yourself. You need rest, girlie, and your body needs to heal," Garbo said.

"He's right," Jared added, looking concerned. Was it real concern, or faux?

I felt my stomach drop. A voice in the back of my mind was telling me that Jared was uneasy because I was carrying his legacy – hence the concern.

"Shelby, you aren't looking so swift, just lay down," Garbo said. Jared nodded in agreement. I hated being taken care of all the time, treated like a fragile piece of my grandmother's china, but, I knew that I needed it. I needed to sleep, and to block out this life – any respite I had from it was now much-needed and quite-welcomed.

Chapter 24

I dreamt of Pippa, babies, and blood. I had one dream where I watched myself get raped, over, and over, and each time the man's face became clear, it was different: Thomas, then Jared, then Thomas, then Jared. I saw myself slit Thomas's throat, only to realize that I'd accidentally killed 4-year-Old Jared instead. I awoke, out of breath. My hair was sweaty, and matted to my face. Again, my stomach lurched, but I refused to vomit, as though it would somehow make my fears come true, as if by letting go of that bile that I'd also be heaving away my happy little fairy tale ending. I wished sleep would wash over me once again. In sleep, nightmares were only that. It hurt too badly for this all to be my actual reality.

It was pitch black. I couldn't see anything or anyone, but I felt Jared laying next to me, and heard the light snore of Pippa's snooze, which was, somehow, comforting. The boat rocked and swayed, and as the water ebbed and flowed, so did my emotions. I felt myself slipping away. Gone was empowered me; Queen Shelby was no more. I now felt like a fearful child lost in the mall, or hidden behind her bedroom door as she hears her parents fighting in the living room. I pulled my legs to my chest, wrapping my arms around my knees and curling into a little ball, like I used to do any time I had a childhood nightmare. This was, after all, a nightmare. Everything. All of it.

It didn't seem real, but at the same time, my life before also felt like a fantasy. I wished it were a movie that I could pop in and watch at any time. I longed to see the documentary of me. I wanted so badly to see the faces of my relatives, my colleagues, my friends from home, and even Owen and Eugene and Paulie and the others. I missed practical strangers from my life before all of this: the lady who worked at my favorite bagel shop, the teenage dog-walker who'd jaunt past our apartment every day with 6 or 7 dogs on an assortment of colorful leashes, the mailman. I missed going places, and knowing where I was going. The most boring details of my life were fading into a black abyss; the minutiae were in danger of turning into sepia-toned memories that would be lost, but never found. I wanted to remember what my quilt felt like. I wanted to hold the handle of my favorite coffee mug. I wanted to drive a car, to ride a subway, to visit the library, to go to the mall. I wanted a hairbrush, toilet paper, mouthwash, floss. I wanted food, even the food that is bad for me. Give me candy, give me kale. I didn't care. I missed it all. I wanted to read, to write, to think, to chat casually. Nothing was casual anymore – everything was dire, urgent, necessary.

I thought about how empowered and positive I'd felt, trudging along with the guys, heading to Paulie's camp. I was optimistic, I was in control, and now, here I was, teetering on the edge of deep depression and ultimate submission, when I was supposed to be safe and happy, and on my way to a brave new world.

I needed to meditate. I closed my eyes as tears began to leak out of the corners. I took some deep breaths to get myself centered. I tried to practice progressive relaxation, focusing individually on each body part from the tips of my toes to the roots of my hair. It helped just a little bit, but then, I'd take any morsel of relaxation that I could get. I longed to feel whole. My being at its core now felt like a fragmented mess; my mind was in no better shape.

The more present I allowed myself to become, the more the pain set in. I noticed the dull ache in my heavy breasts. I noticed the stiffness in my back and neck, the pain in my shoulder that was still healing, my sore throat, and my dry skin. The pain, at least, reminded me that I was here. This was real, and I was alive, for better or for worse.

When I had gotten the cancer diagnosis, I felt like my world would just end right then. Every night I'd go to bed, fearing never to wake up again. Everything felt urgent to me, because my days felt numbered. Time felt more finite than it ever had before. I stopped dating because, let's face it, who wants to date the sick girl? I didn't want to snag an awesome guy and then go ahead and die on him. I couldn't do that to someone.

My first ray of hope came when I got into the clinical trial. Now, a part of me wishes I hadn't been accepted. That part of me wished — now, without any morsel of a doubt — that I'd just died along with everyone else. There was no proof that it is what saved (or condemned) me, but it seems likely that it played a role, at the very least. It was working, or seemed to be, according to my doctors, but, we never got to complete the trial, and I wondered if my body was just chock-full of tumors, spreading like wildfire, ravaging my bones and my tissues and my organs. A part of me hoped so. Jared didn't seem like Jared to me, now that his essence was more than muddled with suspicion. Other than Pippa, he was all I'd really had to live for, and, the more I thought about it, we didn't even know what we were truly sailing towards. It could be worse than the life we'd left behind.

What was worse, I wondered: having to live with cancer and not doing the trial, thus risking illness and death, or having done the trial and living this life I had now? I sighed. I didn't have the answers to anything, let alone to a question like that one – and honestly, it didn't even matter at this point. What was done was done.

I let myself drift off to sleep again – there wasn't much else I could do, and shortly, I awoke with a gasp. Jared was on top of me – and for how long I'd waited for this, and how I'd missed it, I froze up in terror, because now, now it was all different.

"Hey, you!" he drawled.

"Hi," I whispered, hoping that my slightly trembling voice didn't give away my trepidation.

I decided once again to (blindly, dumbly,) play nice. I momentarily blocked the night of the rape and my new realizations out of my head. I gave myself permission to just go with it, justifying it by thinking: "I need to play along to survive." I rationalized what I knew wasn't rational, and I allowed myself to melt into the chocolate pools of his eyes, to caress his statuesque shoulders, to kiss his sensuous lips, and told myself to forget about all of my worries and fears. To forget that he raped me. Probably.

I let myself enjoy it – I needed this. I needed the release, I needed the passion. I'd missed it, I'd missed him. The ecstasy was in stark contrast to the hell we'd been living, and for a moment, I didn't care what Jared had done to me or what he could possibly be plotting moving forward — I just wanted him, and us, and this, even though I knew it was wrong. Dead wrong.

As we collapsed into an exhausted heap, the terror sank back in. I felt conflicted. I was disgusted with myself, because I knew it — I knew it in my bones. It *was* Jared that raped me, that any excuses were moot and any reasoning was not reasonable at all.

I sat Indian-style for a few minutes, silently. I felt paralyzed. Jared occasionally landed a butterfly kiss on my shoulder, and I, like a used-up prostitute, just let him. I was defeated. I'd just made love to my rapist, and I'd enjoyed it. It was dark and twisted. I was dark and twisted.

I began trembling. "What's wrong?" Jared asked.

Not knowing how to answer, I lied. "Nothing, I'm just chilly." (*"And quite possibly having a mental break,"* I added silently to myself.)

He hugged me tight. My Jekyll and my Hyde. My kryptonite. I didn't know what to do. It wasn't a "let bygones be bygones" situation, not by any means. No one in their right mind would think that way: but at this point, after everything, was I in my right mind? I wasn't even sure anymore. Plus, I didn't know how to move forward without ignoring what I knew. I had to play nice, at least until we were on European ground and I was off this godforsaken boat. Then, and only then, could I escape this man-of-my-dreams-turned-man-of-my-nightmares.

I pondered my options. Was feigning ignorance the only option? I wasn't sure. I could tell Garbo, but how would I ever do it without Jared finding out or overhearing? He never let me out of his sight. I could just end it all, and make it look like an accident or like my sickness overpowered me. Suicide is the most selfish act a person can commit, this it true, but is it, in extreme cases such as this, the best alternative? Let's face it: I'd thought of it a number of times since awakening in the bank ruins on that fateful day.

I wished that I'd had a crystal ball. I didn't know what God – or whoever – wanted from me. I wished that I could see what Europe would hold for us. I pictured it as a civilization just like America was before the hell we'd endured. I pictured just waltzing back into a normal life, but, I also realistically knew that wasn't what I should expect, because it was not likely. I figured I could talk to the rescuers. They weren't friendly, and were none too pleased with me after the Pippa escapade, but, we'd been on the boat long enough that I felt like it would be okay to strike up a chat.

"I'll be back," I told Jared, as I stood.

His eyes narrowed. "What are you doing?" he asked, suspiciously.

I wasn't a good liar, and couldn't think of one quickly enough.

"Going to chat with the men," I said.

He was on his feet in a matter of seconds. "I'll come with you," he said authoritatively.

Ugh. Why didn't that surprise me? In the past, I would have found it to be endearing, like he was an eager little puppy-dog following my every footstep. Now, it just infuriated me.

I walked up the steps and found the captain. It was him and three other guys on board. I cleared my throat. "Ahem. Hi, guys," I said, trying to force cheerfulness that just wasn't wanting to emit itself. True cheerfulness was now obsolete.

They all glanced at me and uttered not a peep. "Tough crowd!" I joked. Nothing.

"So, where are we going?" I asked.

It took a few pauses before someone answered me. One guy – lanky as could be – must have taken pity on me, because he saw fit to answer.

"Guernsey," he replied. I stared blankly.

"Near St. Peter's Port," he added, as though that were in any way helpful to me.

"England," the captain chimed in, exasperated.

"Oh, okay, okay," I said. "Thanks. What are your names?" I asked.

I suppose they could tell that I wouldn't relent, so, they begrudgingly introduced themselves.

"I'm John," said the captain. "That's Randall, Phil, and Kearn," he said, gesturing towards the other guys.

The captain had some kind of accent that I couldn't place – maybe Irish, maybe Scottish, maybe some kind of hybrid? He had a robust pot-belly but was thin everywhere else, with an elongated nose and sunken-in eyes. Randall, who spoke in cockney, looked like, in his heyday, that he could have belonged to a boy band of some sort, Phil was the lanky guy, and Kearn spoke with an Island accent – Trinidad, Tobago, Barbados? – and had skin the color of a rich dark chocolate, with enthusiastic eyes. He seemed trustworthy, and Phil seemed okay, but Randall barely uttered a word, and the captain was as grumpy as could be.

"Can you tell me about it?" I asked, timidly.

"It isn't like it used to be," Kearn said. (Oh, I loved his accent!) "The U.K. had a few attacks, too, but nothing like you guys, for whatever reason." he added. "Plus, not as bad of weather."

Oh. My spirit was crushed. I was hoping for my movie-version of Europe. (Didn't I at least deserve that much, after all I'd been through?)

"Same thing, women and kids gone?" Jared asked.

"Nah, just a rash of car bombings and riots, and lots of vague threats from MARF." Phil said. "It'd been going on for a while, even before the 'States got hit," he said, raising an eyebrow.

Oh. I couldn't imagine proper old England looking like that. The Middle East, yes. Africa, yes. But the home of Princess Di and Buckingham Palace and afternoon teatime? No. I wanted royal weddings and scones and Oxford Street shopping and Kate Middleton, not more ashes and more dust and more death and more destruction. I began to wonder how skewed my worldview was before all of this, and how I could not know that this type of stuff was going on in the world around me, before it essentially wiped out the United States? Ah, the good old American way – ethnocentricity at its very finest.

"Will we be safe?" I asked.

They all turned to look at me, "We hope. As fellow preppers we want to help people stay safe, and we know that in America, the situation is more dire. But, we've just found that…" Randall said, trailing off and taking a breath.

"That they're hoarding women now," Phil finished.

Jared's face clouded over with anger. I felt faint.

"What?" Garbo said, as he walked over to join the conversation.

"What?" I repeated, breathlessly.

"We didn't know. Just found out. They just started it. Women are still alive, but they're afraid of the same kind of attack in Europe," Phil explained. "They're starting to keep women in underground bunkers, trying to find a way to preserve them and the kiddos in case of a similar chemical attack on the Brits," he said.

My mind stopped functioning. I had no words. Was I leaving a bad situation to sail straight into an even worse one? I missed the camp. I missed the cave. I missed Brooklyn. A kennel of women didn't sound appealing to me in the least. Why couldn't this world just come to its miserable end, already?

"They're doing it to keep women safe," Garbo said, trying to be reassuring, but, as hard as he tried, it wasn't very convincing at all.

"Who…who is doing all of this? I mean, who attacked us?" I asked.

"MARF," Randall, Kearn, Phil, and John said in unison. It wasn't the first time I'd heard of them, but I wasn't more than vaguely familiar.

"MARF?" Jared spat out, like it had a bad taste in his mouth.

"The multi-national association of righteous fellowship. They have an agenda. They've been under surveillance for years but they're comprised mostly of traitors and moles, a few people here and there from all over the world. No central hub, virtually no buzz or intel. Impossible to pin down, it seems. Extremely powerful," John explained, glumly. "They've got friends in high places. They hate Westernized culture, modern progress, and so on. Basically, they seem to hate everything and everyone. Most of all, they seem to love power more than they could hate anything else. Their agenda is simple: power. Domination."

"Ohhhh, yeah, I think I maybe heard about them," I said.

"You 'think' you maybe heard about them?" Phil laughed. "You Americans," he said, and only then did I detect a mild British accent in his speak.

I guess I never did pay much attention to the news, unless it was directly affecting me. I supposed that this mentality was more common than not in the United States and may be, perhaps, a reason why we were becoming so very hated in this world, and a part of the reason why what happened, happened. I hated to acknowledge it, but, it could possibly be why no one was bothering to come look for survivors after the storm and the blasts.

"Thank you guys for coming to rescue us," I said. "I know that most people don't even want to bother with Americans anymore," I added.

"Don't flatter yourself too much," Grumpy John said. "We have a pact as preppers to help others like ourselves who are survivors in need, plus, we're mostly doing it for Garbo here."

"John knows my sis," Garbo explained.

"*You* are pretty important to the American people," John said, casting a glance my way.

I remained silent.

"If the U.S. wants to sustain their population without foreigners coming in to overtake the country, well, they're going to have to do something. Doesn't seem there are many women of childbearing years, if any, left over there," he added. "I'm surprised they're letting you go," he said, and something about his words sounded ominous to me.

The fact of the matter is that our government would most likely NOT be letting me go if they knew that I was still alive. I somehow knew it in my gut to be true, and so, maybe going to a potential woman-farm in the U.K. was a better option for me.

We sat silently.

John continued, "Whoever gets you knocked up, kiddo, is gonna be a real hero for your nation," he said. "The giver of life," he said sarcastically. I shuddered. Jared's eyes gleamed, not amorously but triumphantly. The gleam hit me like a punch to the gut.

"Thank you," I said. "If you'll excuse me…"

I couldn't sit there and be discussed like a product or a prize any more. I was certainly damned if I do, damned if I don't, in this hellish situation. I once again mildly wondered if I already was in hell or some kind of purgatory, and then recognized that I was again creating a delusion.

Sigh.

What if I was already pregnant, from the rape? I sensed that I was. I touched my belly tenderly, and for a second, pretended it was the way I'd always pictured it to be. How it was supposed to be. A warm, loving sensation cascaded over me, and for a second, I felt that peace and calmness, that "glow" that pregnant women always exude.

Jared sat down next to me, and must have seen me in my moment of maternal bliss. I quickly moved my hand, but it was too late. He looked flustered for a minute, and I knew it was because he, at that moment, knew that I knew.

I was already pregnant, and not from an hour ago… but from THAT NIGHT.

We just stared at each other. His expression almost looked as though he was daring me to say something about it. I felt like a prisoner, because, I knew I couldn't. Not yet. I had to stay on his good side for now, and, what if he became my only ally in Europe? Could I forgive what he had done to me? I remembered how much he hurt me. I was afraid that night, thinking that my rapist was going to kill me, as he tore up my insides and beat me to a pulp, and a part of me was hoping he would just finish the job and do me in. Could I forgive that? Could we start over, a happy little family, like I'd always dreamt?

I had so many questions: why would he do it? He had to have known that I would have given myself to him willingly, so the blindfold and the violence and the restraint wasn't necessary. It wasn't rational. Why would he pin it on someone else, if he was trying to get me pregnant – didn't he want his legacy to be his crowning moment? Didn't he want that glory? He had to have been in an unusual, unstable state of mind at the time. (Were any of us in a right state of mind anymore?) He wasn't thinking clearly. He wasn't himself. He couldn't have been. Old Jared would not have ever done such a thing to me. None of it made any sense.

I knew that I was making excuses for him. He couldn't take back the things he'd done, and there was no "reason" behind his actions that would be reasonable or justifiable. I should never allow him to get away with it. This was how people got stuck in those ruts: abusive relationships, bad marriages, dead-end jobs. This was how people scarred themselves mentally and emotionally for life. This was trauma, a trauma that I would re-live forever. To just accept it and allow it wasn't healthy. What I was doing was fucked up. Maybe I was the one who wasn't in their right mind. It wasn't normal or reasonable to just "go with the flow" after what Jared had done to me. I knew it. He surely knew it. But he knew, too, that, at least for now, he had the power.

He knew that when it came to me, he'd always had the power. All along, my notion of a strong and independent post-feminist woman was a farce. A lie. Because this one man had always controlled me, and now, potentially always would – unless I did something about it.

And I'd get even with him. I'd make him regret not just that night but his entire existence. But for now – for now I'd continue playing my Oscar-worthy role: happy wife. If only.

I swallowed my anger and hatred and love and confusion, and smiled my conflicted prisoner's smile at him, while holding out my hand. He grabbed it, looking at me curiously, and gave it a squeeze. I saw relief in his eyes and thought, *"Yes, I deserve at least a nomination for this role."* I could see what he was thinking: that he was wrong about my knowing what he had done, that he was misreading the situation.

I smiled at him, inwardly plotting and planning. I would escape him. I'd make it to Switzerland and make a new life for myself. If I was pregnant, then the kid would come with me. We'd move somewhere desolate, rural, far away from big cities and big media and big politics. We'd flee from Jared. We'd flee this life. I didn't know how I'd do it, or how my baby and I would survive, but, I would figure it out. I had to. I just had to escape Jared, and get to Switzerland, somehow, and I'd do whatever I could to start my new life – our new life – without him. I'd make a new identity for myself, but it just had to wait, for now. I knew that, somewhere within my body lie a possible antidote to this new kind of weapon and that I could save thousands or millions of lives. Old Shelby would have sacrificed herself in a heartbeat, or at least would have wrestled with the decision. To save the world, or not to save the world? Old Shelby would have let the government vampires suck her blood for a cure and would have opened her womb to become the esteemed mother of a nation. New Shelby, though, couldn't bear the pressure, and had very little empathy left to give anyone. It was every scarce woman for herself. Everyone else would have their opinions about whatever decision I would make but only God could truly judge me. I had my reasons to make the choices I was going to make.

I looked out over the horizon and tried to release my worries to the wind. I wasn't sure how most people would behave in this awkward, unfathomable situation. I didn't know how a supposedly strong and empowered female was supposed to act when facing everything that I was facing from malignancy to surviving an apocalypse to being hunted to murder to carrying my rapist's baby and marrying said rapist. I didn't know how I was supposed to act, think, or feel, with the continuation of the American people and perhaps all of the world's women in my dainty little hands. Was my just up and leaving America behind a selfish act? Should I care? What did I owe anyone? I didn't know how I would get on in Europe. Would I be prey there, too, or would I be able to escape and become a nobody? For the first time in my life, I longed to be a nobody: a nameless, faceless nobody. I didn't want to be a celebrity or a supermodel or a famous writer. I didn't want to be Shelby Weiss. I didn't want the pressure, the stress, or the responsibility that came with being me. I didn't know how my future was going to look, or how people expected it to look. I only knew that I would figure out what to do, and how to make Jared pay, but not right now.

Right now, I'd let my delusional fairy tale continue. I'd allow myself to pretend he was still Old Jared, the Jared I'd spent my life loving. Just for a little while. He'd get his. I'd make sure of it. I leaned my head on his shoulder. I just had to keep up the façade, for now. I wasn't sure that it was the right choice, but I was too mentally drained to decide otherwise.

Chapter 25

I awoke with a start, and it took me a moment to regain my bearings. I was cold, and it was windy. A Transatlantic boat trip was never on my bucket list, and now I could see why. It certainly wasn't a smooth ride. I looked at Garbo and Jared, both nearby, and out cold. I wondered how they could possibly be asleep, and while I was pleased that Garbo was getting some rest, I detested how peaceful Jared looked as he slept. He didn't deserve serenity. He wasn't entitled to that after what he'd done to me.

I became filled with rage and abruptly had a change of heart. My rolling over and being nicey-nicey, the doting wife, the perfect lover – it was not acceptable. What he had done to me was not acceptable. I had to get a plan together, and fast. I decided to take my chances in speaking with Captain Grumpy. Slowly, I stood, and for a second I was reminded of my first time standing in the bank: wobbly. I steadied myself and quietly tiptoed up to speak to the Captain.

"How much longer do we have?" I asked with trepidation.

He harrumphed, and I gathered that he was not pleased with my presence.

"Couple days," he said. I'd felt like we'd already been sailing forever, and it was hard to believe that just three days had passed. All I did was sleep, and think, and rest, and sleep, and think, and rest, with occasional bouts of conversation and food.

Ahh, the food. It was nothing exquisite like I was used to eating in Manhattan, but, it somehow tasted better than anything I'd ever dined upon before. I remembered the first morsel of food I'd had, on the first day on the boat. After burnt mice and old Spam, plants from the woods and spoonfuls of Crisco, a turkey sandwich with tomato and fried egg, and a glass of cow's milk tasted like heaven. At that point, I would have eaten anything they'd put in front of me. When they opened a bag of potato chips, I practically orgasmed. To say that they were mouth-watering was the understatement of the century: and the commercials were right – there was no way I would be able to eat just one.

Variety wasn't the spice of life on this boat, though – survival was – and so, our meals were easy, convenient, and simple: hard-boiled eggs, coffee, toast, lunchmeat, nuts, and potatoes. We used a small portable grill to cook our food, to warm our coffee, and, sometimes, to warm our hands. It wasn't luxury, but it was life, and it was my only option. I missed the most simple pleasures of life before: fingernail clippers, running water, body lotion, and hair salons. I missed heat and computers, music and microwaves. My heart ached and I wasn't certain if it was out of hunger, sadness, or longing, or perhaps a combination of the three.

As if reading my mind, Captain Grumpy said, "Come closer," accompanied by a quick and crotchety hand gesture.

"Yes?" I inquired cautiously.

"We have soap, toothpaste, and a comb. We are using these things sparingly, rationing our supplies. The men didn't want me to tell you about it because women use up all that stuff, but you can use a bit," he said, begrudgingly.

So Captain Grumpy had a soft spot! I ignored his sexist remark and gave him an unwelcome hug.

"God you need it," he said, holding his nose, and, despite his straight face, I thought I saw a twinkle of humor in his steely gray eyes. "Just a LITTLE BIT," he reaffirmed.

"Thank you so much!" I said, enthusiastically.

He directed me to the sparse washing area, that I hadn't noticed up until that point. I really had been in my own world since boarding the ship, and it was no wonder, considering everything I'd had on my mind, and all that I'd been through.

I didn't have a toothbrush, of course, but my index finger would have to do. I rinsed it with water and then squeezed a small dollop of toothpaste onto it, and rubbed the glorious minty-fresh paste on my sore gums and grimy teeth. It was heavenly, and I took my good ol' time, enjoying this most basic indulgence.

Up next was the comb. It was discolored and missing some teeth, and barely made its way through my tangled, dirty, knotted and windblown hair, but, it was better than using my fingers. I was once again meticulously dragging on the simple action of (rather unsuccessfully) combing my hair, for now, it was a symbol of pure opulence, in my mind, and in this new existence. I took a second to give myself a scalp massage. It felt glorious and almost forbidden. I sighed with contentment.

Next, I picked up the bar of soap and just inhaled. I breathed the fresh, clean scent in, slowly, lavishing my attention on the fragrance. I don't know if it was from hormones or exhaustion, but the smell brought me to tears. The smell of clean soap reminded me of childhood, of purity, of home. It reminded me of life before – a kind of life that I may never have again. The idea of cleaning my body was also overwhelming. I didn't know where to start, but at that moment, I was so very grateful for the surprisingly kind captain.

I dipped a rag in a bucket of water, and wiped my legs, arms, stomach, breasts, face, neck, ears, and feet, along with my most intimate areas. I didn't want to remove my clothes and so bathing was a challenge, but a welcome one. After wiping my body down with the cold water, I rubbed the soapy bar against my skin, enjoying both the scent and the sensation. I closed my eyes, and allowed myself to envision the soap wiping off the negativity: Jared, and my confliction, and my fears and my worries and my cancer and my crazy and all of the gray.

Suddenly, I felt a hand grasp my wrist. My eyes flung open and there he stood.

"Jared!" I yelped.

"What do you think you're doing?" he barked, never letting go of my wrist.

I squirmed to try to break free of his grasp. I had to admit, it hurt.

"Washing myself!" I exclaimed. "God," I muttered under my breath.

"What was that?" he asked. There was a darkness in his eyes that I wasn't familiar with.

"Jared, so what, the captain offered me the toiletries and I gladly took him up on the offer," I replied, with a smart-ass tone in my voice.

"Don't do that. You don't know what he wants. People expect things. You don't know what he's planning. What were you going to do, let these guys see you naked?" he asked.

"Do I look naked?" I sniped.

"Jesus, Shelby..." he started, stopping abruptly.

He took a deep breath as if to calm himself, and dropped my hand. He plastered a (fake) smile on his face. What a psychopath.

"I'm sorry. Let me help," he said. I cringed. Regardless of what I'd let happen, I didn't want this man touching me anymore.

"No. I'm already done," I said, and pushed past him.

Add "ruining my one small moment of zen" to the list of things that he'd done to infuriate me.

"You don't understand, Shelby!" Jared said, "I can't risk it! No one else can have you," he said. I could tell that he was trying to keep his voice calm and level, but I could sense the anger and desperation seeping through.

Now it was my turn to be angry. I was keeping my feelings bottled up for far too long.

"That's a decision that I get to make, Jared. It isn't for YOU to decide. I am an adult, and I am my own woman, and you can't control me!" I hissed.

"You are my WIFE, Shelby! You are mine," he gnarled.

"I am no one's. I am my own person. I may have married you but I don't...belong...to you. I am not a possession!" My voice was getting louder, and more heated. I could feel my cheeks flushing.

"You are really making me angry," he said, speaking in an ominously quiet cadence.

I shuddered, and then, my demeanor grew steely. Ice cold.

"I think we both know that if ANYONE has a right to be angry here, it's me," I said with a glare.

Jared stood, looking at me with a stunned look on his face. I couldn't read his emotions. I also couldn't tell if I was making a mistake in letting him in on the fact that I knew he had raped me.

To cover my tracks, I added flippantly, "You aren't the one who the whole world seems to be after."

He looked relieved. "Oh, my Shelby. I'll take care of you, doll," he said, and grabbed my hand.

I think he wanted it to seem like a romantic gesture but it seemed too harsh, too protective, too grabby. I played along even though, at this moment, I now hated him with every ounce of my being.

What was I going to do?

CHAPTER 26

Pippa lay her head against my leg as I sat cross-legged on the floor of the boat. Jared and Garbo were casually chatting, and I, as per usual, was daydreaming, lost in my own thoughts and anxieties.

I liked to think I was a tough girl. Flawed, but tough. In my own narrative, I was Lara Croft, or Katniss, or Wonder Woman. I was Angelina Jolie or Halle Barry – a strong, fierce female, both beautiful and strong, both sexy and empowered. When I did my yoga I felt like an earth goddess, and when I was running, I felt like an Olympic athlete. But, now in reality, I was a small, frail girl. I had always been neurotic and girly, and usually better in my mind than I was in real life. I often wondered if I had narcissistic personality disorder (or some other undiagnosed mental illness,) because in my head I was more of a superstar bad-ass than I was in my real life. I often treaded on self-righteousness. I guess I was like a movie that looked good on paper, but, didn't quite pan out on the big screen. I had all of the parts to be a hit, but I was often falling short. I was not a box office sensation. I was a flop, and I never felt more like it than I did right now, stuck on a boat with Jared, feeling broken of spirit and soul. My body was beginning to break down, too. I absentmindedly wondered how much longer I could go on.

I was a flop.

I didn't even notice that I had begun to cry. Garbo looked alarmed, "What's wrong, Shel?" he asked. Jared's face mirrored his concern.

"Nothing," I said. "I'm fine." I wiped the tears away, inwardly chastising myself for being so obviously not the strong woman I wanted to be. It was just too hard – all of it.

My thoughts rained down on me, delivering blow after crushing blow. I suddenly wanted my mommy – very much so. I longed to be lost in that place of lovely denial, of beautiful disillusionment, where Jared was still my perfect Prince Charming, and where having a baby would be a beautiful miracle and where there was nothing ahead of us but hope.

I also longed to be dead. I had cancer. I was supposed to die. Why didn't I? Why wasn't I off in some beautiful someplace – Heaven, if you will – with the ones I loved? With the people I'd lived for? Why wasn't I at peace in that someplace, instead of living this hell?

Hell. My faith was shaky at best and I'd often formed my own breed of Christianity, where Heaven existed but Hell was a myth, where living a good life made up for tithing to the church and attending every week, but what if I was wrong? If this life wasn't hell, then hell surely awaited me.

I thought long and hard about what I'd done to deserve this. I had plenty of wrongdoings, shortcomings, mistakes, and sins, in my life before all of this. I'd cheated on an ex-boyfriend, once. I had a couple of unpaid parking tickets and unpaid bills. I was known to skip school when I was younger, and once lied about having a famous cousin. I went through a promiscuous phrase and a shoplifting spell and I liked to drink and I used to smoke. I probably, on occasion, cursed when

I shouldn't have, or disrespected my parents, or told a little white lie to my boss. There were times that, at church, I would let the collection basket go by because I was saving up for a designer handbag or my half of the rent. I'd made fun of someone's shoes, maybe more than once. Were those things worthy of this hell? I thought the cancer was a punishment of sorts – this was even worse!

All of my thoughts kept cycling – a constant replay of questions and an endless stream of anxiety and confusion. If I was being punished for the bad parts of my life, then what would become of the good?

What about fostering animals, buying McDonald's for homeless veterans on my way home from work, donating blood, giving to charities? What about when I tutored kids for free, or volunteered at the library, or organized a food drive? What about the times I did go to church, and youth group, and Bible study? Were all of those things meaningless because I wasn't perfect?

But who was perfect, really? Who deserved to get into Heaven? Judging by the people I'd known, no one was really good enough for Heaven or bad enough for Hell. It seemed as though we were all on the same playing field, in my mind – and now, the only person who really "deserved" this hell we were living was Jared, it seemed. Pippa certainly didn't deserve it. Garbo, neither. So where did I fit into all of this? I sighed.

"Do you guys think we're already dead, and this is like, purgatory? Or hell?" I asked, immediately regretting the decision to pose the silly question out loud.

Jared looked at me disdainfully and snorted. What a pleasant husband I had.

"I've thought of that," said Garbo, "but I can't think of one thing I'd done so bad to deserve it."

"So you guys think this is all as terrible as I do?" I asked.

"What a stupid question, Shelby. We all do!" Jared interjected, not bothering to conceal his eye roll.

"Excuse me?" I fumed.

"Hey now, is the honeymoon over?" Garbo joked. He came over and flung an arm around my shoulders, giving me a squeeze, as Jared glowered at us.

"I think we're all here for a reason, and just 'cuz I was prepared doesn't make it any easier," Garbo said. "We'll figure it out," he added, and as if to punctuate his thought, Pippa let out an adorable little yip.

"I'm just glad to have you guys," I said, smiling at Pippa and Garbo, and outright ignoring Jared who was ignorantly beaming at my statement.

"Well, we should be getting there soon," Garbo said. "Any plans yet, guys?" he asked Jared and me.

"No, we – " I started, but Jared cut me off.

"We'll keep Shelby on the down low, probably have to find disguises, and get work somewhere, maybe travel to the countryside. We'll have to get rid of the dog somewhere, too, I guess," Jared said.

"What the fuck, Jared? Are you CRAZY?" I exclaimed. "No, no, we are NOT getting rid of Pippa, what the fuck is your problem?" I yelled. "We didn't discuss this! Get rid of Pippa? I'll get rid of YOU!"

He looked quite taken aback at my explosion, but there was no way that, after all of this, I was getting rid of Pippa, my loving confidante and trusted companion.

"Okay, okay, geez, we'll have to talk about it," he said with a placating tone in his voice. I was still glaring at him. "It's fine, we'll figure it out, it's okay," he said, trying to be soothing but mostly just pissing me off.

"Shall I leave you two alone?" Garbo asked, looking uncomfortable.

"Yes," Jared said, at the same time that I said, "No."

Garbo stood there awkwardly. We all stared at one another.

"I'm going to take a nap," I announced, to break the silence.

My stomach was in knots and I wasn't sure if it was out of anger at Jared's suggestion (or just his presence in general), if it was out of anxiety and anticipation about life on "the other side," as I'd begun to think of it, or, if it was, as I suspected, the baby that I was almost certain was inhabiting my belly.

I snuggled up next to Pippa and curled into a ball. As each wave rocked the boat I envisioned waves of peace washing over me until I drifted off into another dreamless sleep.

I awoke to nothing. It was pitch black, and silent. I glanced around. Jared was snoring, and Pippa was sound asleep, too. The rocking of the boat coupled with not being able to see anything all around us was triggering panic within my body. I was trying to calm myself, but I felt the familiar signs settling in: rapid heart rate, shallow breathing, hot flashes, shakiness, nausea, cold sweats. I was having a panic attack, and it was one of the worst I'd ever felt. It was all-consuming, and I actually began to pray that it wasn't a panic attack at all. I began to pray that it was death, finally coming to take me far away from here, to that someplace else where I'd so longed to be.

"Please just take me away, God," I whispered out loud.

I didn't know what exactly came over me but the physical sensations got worse. As the panic became more grueling, I began to wonder if this was it, if I was finally going crazy.

"God please take care of Pippa, and please just take me away from here," I whispered, again, out loud but quietly enough as to not wake Jared.

I looked at out where the horizon should be, still seeing black nothingness. That was my future. Nothing. A sea of black unknowns. I began to hyperventilate. The cool, salty mist burned my eyes and parched my lips. Thoughts raced through my mind: being stuck with Jared, forever. Being farmed like a dog at a puppy mill. Being held captive. Being hunted, forever. The loss. The loneliness. The uncertainty. Leaving my friends behind. Possibly being the only American woman left on earth, and, who knew what the future held. What if MARF launched the same attack in Europe? What if I was the only woman in the world? What if this baby was only the first of many? Would they line up to rape and pillage me, to impregnate me? Would I be mothering a nation, a species?

I gave a quick thought to the baby that was likely inside of me. I didn't think I loved it. I didn't even think of it as a person. I should have hated it. It didn't belong there. It wasn't conceived out of love. That baby was half evil. I vomited. I couldn't breathe. This had to end. "It's too much," I said in a panicky whisper. I quickly stroked Pippa and gave her a kiss on the snout, and then I ran to the edge of the boat and jumped into the black nothingness, praying that my soul and the soul of that innocent babe would be saved.

And then there was nothing.

Chapter 27

I awoke to Garbo holding me in his arms. It was still dark, and we were swimming towards the boat as I choked on the water and sputtered and shivered. I saw the men peering down at the waters, concernedly.

"It'll be okay, Shelby, you fell," Garbo said between ragged breaths.

The men threw a life raft down.

"I didn't fall," I said weakly. "Garbo, I want to die!"

"What? You are talking nonsense, Shelby. It may be shock. Let's get you back on the boat," he said as we made it closer to the boat. "You're lucky I spotted you," he said.

Pippa barked. My heart broke at the thought of my selfishly leaving her behind. "Pippa," I whispered, mustering a smile.

"Can you help me kick, Shelby? It's okay if you can't, but can you try?" Garbo asked me.

I felt bad for the guy. "Yes, I can try," I said, and together, we swam towards the boat.

When I got on board, all of the men were very attentive and concerned – even Jared was sweet, but, then again, he had to keep up the charade, now didn't he?

When I looked at his beautiful face, loving as it appeared, though, I wondered if I was being paranoid, after all. Was Jared really my rapist? I didn't even know what thoughts of mine were real anymore.

"Oh my God," I thought to myself. *"I'm going crazy."* It wasn't the first or the last time I'd think it.

I thought about the full magnitude of what just happened. I'd had a panic attack, and I'd tried to kill myself. I literally attempted suicide. It was against everything I believed in, but tempting me all the time.

I felt like I was being swallowed by a sea monster. I was living a nightmare. What if Jared was harmless and I was the crazy one? I didn't quite know what was real and what was my imagination any more.

Maybe I was the crazy woman in the attic. A hysterical heroine from a Victorian novel. I was not Katniss, I was not Lara Croft. I was insane.

"Oh, God," I said out loud. I thought of the baby. I glanced down at my stomach and that's when I saw it. Blood.

There was blood everywhere – all over the crotch of my pants, as though my pelvic region were falling out.

"Oh, God," I repeated. My vocabulary suddenly seemed very limited.

I looked at Jared, and he looked at me, as white as a sheet and as pale as a ghost, with coal eyes and angry eyebrows.

I furrowed my brow and acted confused, "I – I don't know what's happening," I said. It was an understatement, for sure. I had no idea what was happening with my life anymore.

"Shelby, why would you do this to me?" Jared asked, and, I swear, I heard a crack in his voice. It was dark on the ship but I was willing to bet that there were tears forming in his eyes.

"Am I that bad?" he whispered, and skulked away.

I began to cry. What if I was wrong about Jared this whole time? What if I just tried to kill myself to escape a man who loved me more than words? The man I'd loved my whole life? Did I just cause a miscarriage? Kill an innocent baby with my selfish, thoughtless act? Who was I?

"Shelby, what is this?" Garbo asked, with concern.

"I think it's just my period," I lied. "I'm so embarrassed," I said.

Another lie. Embarrassment was the least of what I was feeling at that moment.

The other men, after finding out that I was going to be fine, went their separate ways. Garbo stayed nearby.

"Shelby, honestly, what's wrong?" he asked. I knew that I could trust him.

"Garbo, I'm afraid of Jared," I said. "I think he's who raped me. I think he got me pregnant and I think I just lost his baby," I said. "Now I'm really scared," I added.

"No offense, but you sound crazy right now. That dude loves you more than life. No way he raped you. That was Thomas, Shelby. Are you okay?" he asked.

"I don't know," I said, honestly.

"Man, I hate to tell you this, Shelby, but I think you're having some kind of breakdown," he replied.

My mouth was fixed in a straight line, my eyes had lost any sign of life. There was no way he'd believe me about Jared.

"You're right," I said, forcing a woeful smile.

"You need sleep," he said. It was a phrase I was so sick of hearing. "You've been through so much." Another one.

"I jumped, Garbo," I said. "I just wanted to give up," I added.

I could barely make out his face but I could tell that he looked sad. He shook his head slightly.

"Girl, that's no way to talk," he said. "I think you need to go see your husband, and go get some good sleep," he said, rubbing my shoulder. "Are you okay to walk?" he asked.

"I'm not sure," I said, and it was the truth. My body felt shaky, drained, and absolutely spent. He walked me over to our area so that I could speak with Jared, and Pippa followed suit.

Garbo gave me a peck on the cheek, "Goodnight, Shelby. I'm glad you're okay," he said.

When Garbo went up on deck, Jared turned to face me. The lantern's shadows played upon his face, his face that was as exceptionally handsome as ever.

I stared at him, trying to interpret his forlorn expression. I saw sadness. I saw defeat. I saw pain, confusion, and dismay. I saw anger. I imagine that my face was mirroring his own, and that all the things I'd felt were also brought to life by my features.

"You jumped, right?" Jared asked me.

In that moment, looking at him, hearing his tone of voice, I really began to second-guess myself. This man cared. This man loved me. This man was hurt. Could I have been wrong?

"I'm sorry," I said. I left it at that, I didn't feel that I needed to explain any further.

"Why, Shelby? After everything, why?" he asked me, and began to cry.

Oh, shit. This was Old Jared that I was seeing. This was the boy I'd grown up with, and the man I'd grown to love. My heart was falling into pieces.

"It's not you…" I began. I realized how cliché that sounded. "It wasn't you. It's just me and this life. Jared,

I am afraid and mad and I think I'm going insane," I said, and it was the first thing I'd said to him in a few days that wasn't a lie.

"Why would you do this? We can face anything together," he said, grabbing my hand, and my tears joined his own.

"I'm sorry," I said, and, in that moment, I truly meant it.

"There was a baby?" he asked, gently.

"You know there was," I said, unable to mask the scorn that crept back into my sentiment.

"What? Shelby? How would I know that?" he said, appearing truly baffled, and I did remember that he was a good actor. As was the trend lately, my feelings were mixed. I chided myself. I should know better than to fall for his charms and his brown puppy-dog eyes, especially after what he'd done to me.

"Yeah, I guess now you can't be Mr. Awesome who helped to repopulate America, huh? You always wanted to be a super hero and my spawn would be your chance, right?" I said, hotly.

"Excuse me?" Jared said, and I was the darkness creep back into those brown puppy-dog eyes.

"You heard me," I said, my voice icy and full of razorblades.

"I always knew it, but now it's confirmed. You're fucking crazy. I don't know what you're thinking," he said, "and yeah, to be able to have a baby and start a family with you, that WOULD make me feel like a super hero, regardless of the circumstances," he said.

"Just shut up! We both know the truth, for once in your damn life, own up to it! Be a man! You always make excuses and expect the whole world to bend at your will, well, guess what, Garbo is right, the honeymoon is over, you selfish bastard." I said.

"I don't know what you're rambling about woman, but you are certifiable right now. Legit crazy. You fucking killed our baby, if there even was one. You tried to kill yourself, days after we got married. I just don't get you. Honestly. I'm not giving up on us, though," he said.

"Like I told you, I never will," he added, and grabbing my arms, he brought me in for a passionate kiss.

I fought it, at first, but he wouldn't let me go, and I sobbed and sobbed, through this beautiful-ugly kiss. I let my thoughts float away as the rain began to soak us, washing away the blood and despair and leaving me as confused as ever as I intermittently mumbled, "I hate you," and "I love you," thus summing up the predicament that was my life.

I thought back to the first day of the after, being cold, alone, and in a dark, unfamiliar place. I'd felt weak and disoriented and confused. I felt the same way in that moment with Jared. I wanted to believe that he was innocent, and a part of me hoped that maybe, just maybe, it was all in my head — that Jared was still the Jared of my dreams and not the man of my nightmares. However, at the same time, I feared that very notion: could I be that...crazy? That paranoid? That untrusting and unstable? I didn't know which was worse: Jared being my Prince Charming and me losing hold of my sanity, or, Jared being the "bad guy."

I considered what I'd have the heroine do, at this point, if I were writing a movie script. Most of the women in the screenplays I'd written were stronger than this, they wouldn't have even let the situation get this far if they'd suspected such terrible things about their lover. Would my lead character be playing sleuth, trying to get to the bottom of why she was raped in the first place? Or would she be the tough chick I'd always liked, putting the man in his place with an immediate confrontation? Of course, she could also be the weepy, willowy wallflower, letting Jared walk all over her, making excuses, and living in a happy state of denial. While I didn't want to be that fragile woman, I also wasn't sure that I fit in any of the other categories, and it left an acidy taste in my mouth.

Not only did I not know who Jared was anymore, I'd lost myself somewhere along the way, too. I wondered if the real me had died along with all of the others who'd lost their lives. Maybe I was only a shell of my former self; maybe my substance had washed away in the hurricane; maybe my credibility had suffered the same awful fate that so many men, women, and children in America had suffered. I was dead inside, and any remnant of life or happiness had been killed once I realized what I thought I'd realized about my Jared.

His beard was scraping and burning against my skin, and his scent was repugnant, but I needed his embrace and his kisses more than ever. I had to cling on to any sense of familiarity – any sense of the old me – that I could. While I wasn't ready to forgive him for raping me, I also wasn't ready to let him go. I didn't care how damaged that made me, or how wrong it was in theory. Sometimes, what's right in one moment is wrong in the next, and vice versa – and in this moment, I set all rationale aside, because I needed Jared.

"Why did you do it, Shelby?" he whispered between kisses, and I could feel tears streaming down his face. "I have always loved you," he said. "Why would you try to leave me? Why would you ... our child..." he trailed off, as his voice cracked.

A man that raped me, that hated me enough to rape me, wouldn't have been this torn apart, would he?

I kissed him back even harder, murmuring, "I don't know, I don't know! Why did YOU do it, Jared?"

He pulled back from me, with his eyes narrowed.

"Shelby ... I don't know what you think you know about me, but you're wrong," he said, levelly. He put his hand on my forehead, and then softly caressed my cheek. "Are you okay?" he asked.

I didn't know how to respond. I stared him in the face for a long time and glumly replied, "I loved you for so long. I just want you to know that," I said.

"Shelby, you're worrying me," he said. "You're scaring me."

"You're scaring ME! What do you WANT from me? Why would you put us in this position?" I shrieked, and began uncontrollably sobbing once again.

He tried to lay a hand on my back and I swatted it away. Pippa began to bark with concern and Garbo came back to check on us, concerned with what all the commotion was about.

"I just want to be alone," I said calmly, between sobs, before he or Jared could speak.

I closed my eyes in despair. It would have been so much easier if my plan had worked. I'd be gone, away from this boat, away from this world. Pippa nuzzled up against me and I was again wracked with guilt. How could I have nearly left her behind, to fend in this cruel world without me?

I truly didn't know who I had become. I wasn't sure I wanted to get to know the new Shelby, any more.

I heard Garbo and Jared speaking in hushed tones in the background but chose to block out the muted conversation. I let the waves sing their lullaby to me as I rocked with the ebb and the flow of the waters, and I let myself sleep, for our new lives were almost near.

CHAPTER 28

I awoke alone, cold, and disoriented.

Oh. This time, I wasn't alone. I peered up into the faces of the men who were staring down at me, urging me to awaken.

"We're here. We have to get you off the boat casually, without being sighted," said Captain Grumpy.

My mouth was dry and my eyes were swollen. I felt messy. My limbs felt heavy and my abdomen ached. I didn't feel like moving, but I knew that this was my chance. Hope lived on those shores and I needed to cling to that in order to survive.

We were careful to "gruff me up" a bit. I tucked my hair into a hat, dressed in layers to hide my shape (despite it looking more skeletal and less curvy as of late), and smudged pen and dirt on my face.

The man huddled around me as we exited the boat. I held what little belongings I still had in one hand, Pippa's rope in the other. Jared stayed close. He was careful not to hold my hand or place an arm around me, and I could tell that it was killing him. The Captain had lent me a pair of sunglasses, and, thankfully the morning was bright, albeit a bit on the chilly side.

The boat dock was unremarkable. A British boat dock didn't look any different from the ones back home. The weather was cool, gray, and muddled. The air felt thick with a fog, and somewhere, in the distance, a bell faintly tolled.

I scanned the scene. I didn't see any other women, and most people hanging around were going about their own business.

We were instructed to look for Garbo's brother-in-law in an older-model green sedan. As we waited, we said our quick goodbyes and bids of gratitude to Captain Grumpy and his crew.

"Thank you so much for everything," I said. "Pretend I'm giving each one of you a big hug," I added. Despite my struggles, I was quite grateful that they'd gone so out of their way to help us. I knew not to hug them, as to not draw attention to myself. Plus, I wasn't sure about how it was in Europe, but hugging wasn't a stereotypically manly act back home. I was trying to tame my more feminine mannerisms, at least until I was safe and sound, and out of danger of being hoarded or harvested.

As we stayed in our little cluster, they each quipped quick reminders:

"You'll need to cut and dye your hair."

"Find a way to get new identification."

"Obtain a gun whenever you can."

"Get out of the U.K."

A man sauntered up to us, with a little boy in tow. It was the first child I'd seen in ages, and my heart sank. He was a beautiful, glowing example of youthful innocence. I fought back tears. I still hadn't fully acknowledged that I was pregnant, nor had I fully mourned the loss. The reality of it took my breath away. The kid tipped his hat towards us, as his father shook hands with the Captain.

"How's it going with you all?" he asked.

"Good, good" the guys replied. I kept my mouth shut.

"How's everything here?" the Captain inquired.

"Sucky," the boy answered, as his dad shushed him.

"I'm afraid it's getting worse. MARF is going overboard with the threats. We don't know what to expect. For now my Elaine and Millie are safe, but they've both had friends and acquaintances taken into custody," the man replied.

I stepped on Jared's foot, as if to let him know to keep the man talking. He, of course, didn't get my clue, but Garbo was smart enough to continue the discussion.

"Where to? Why?" Garbo asked.

The man eyed him up suspiciously, but seemed to relax once Garbo added, "I'm visiting my half-sister and am concerned for her and my niece."

"The government is taking them into protective bunkers – sort of a quarantine if you will – but we've heard in some parts that the women are being forced to ... procreate ..." he said, with a slight nod towards his son as though to explain his lack of detail.

Inwardly, I gasped. "How awful," I thought. They were going to hoard babies, too. It was like a puppy mill.

"America's done," the man continued. "I suppose you all know that," he said with a raised eyebrow. I tried to keep my eyes focused downward. "Seeing what was done over there and hearing the threats that have been made to us, it's been a real nightmare," he said. "The end times are near," he added.

I shuddered. I'd felt like I'd already been living the end times for some time now. I couldn't imagine a hell worse than what I'd left behind – but the reality here also sounded pretty terrible.

The men continued to discuss the situation and I continued to survey the scene, quietly. England was still a lot more normal and lively than the skeleton of America that we had left behind. While a gloom hung in the air, I liked to see people in cars, people talking, people working. It seemed a little more alive than what I'd left behind. I felt relief wash over me. For the first time in a while I felt more alive, too. I took a deep breath and let the crisp air embrace me. I needed it.

Just then, we saw the car pull up. We gathered our things and nodded goodbye. I hoped that those guys knew how very much I'd appreciated their help, and I thought I saw the Captain wink as he tipped his hat goodbye.

Garbo hopped in the passenger's side, as Jared, Pippa, and I crowded in the back seat of the car.

"Guys, this is my brother-in-law Proudlock," he said to us, as Jared replied "Hello." I wasn't sure if Proudlock knew of my real identity so I faked a cough instead of producing an awkward silence.

"How's Deana?" Garbo asked, inquiring on his sister.

"She's fine, but we're worried. The state of things is bad. We're thinking of getting out of here at some point, Garb, so I hope you'll be able to join us. Where are your friends going? We can't risk having them stay with us, too," he said, matter-of-factly.

Jared bristled, but, I wasn't offended at all. I understood that, in this new world, we all had to look out for number one. Garbo caught our eyes in the rearview mirror and shrugged apologetically.

"Is there a motel you can drop them at?" he asked. "Or a hostel of some sort, maybe a little remote?"

"Sure," Proudlock said. "There's a small joint on our way, it's on the outskirts, used to crash there during my time at university," he said, and I could tell by his smirk that he'd had some fond – and likely wild – memories of the place. I smiled and looked down at my lap. I missed fun. I missed wild and free memories. I missed college and high school and innocence. I missed being carefree.

As we drove, I thought about my options. I had to stick with Jared at least initially. I wouldn't be very good on my own, navigating this new country and I was still ill from what had gone on the day before. As much as I didn't want to need him, I did. I wasn't good at geography, and I had no idea how to get to Switzerland from England. I truly wasn't even certain of the direction, or what it was near. I'd still held on to Eugene's key, though – somehow. Thankfully, I didn't lose it in my jump. I chided myself for not thinking that one through. Truth be told, I hadn't prepared myself for survival in that moment. The key was the literal key to my future. I'd hoped that the bank would be easy to find once I'd arrived. But how was I going to get there with no money? How would I stay safe? How would I escape Jared?

As usual, I had more questions than answers. This wasn't a new phenomenon for me. I'd always wanted to know the who, what, where, when, why, and how of everything, immediately. The inability to simply Google search any question that popped into my always-worrying brain just heightened my curiosity and exacerbated my need to know.

Soon we pulled up to a rustic looking bed-and-breakfast on an old dirt road. Somehow, it was not what I'd expected. In my mind we were going to be living the outlaw life – seedy motels and the like. This place looked rather decent, particularly given my standards as of late. Proudlock turned in his seat and looked at us sincerely, "Good luck. This place doesn't require ID," he added.

Ah, so maybe he DID know. Not wanting to take chances, I just nodded. Jared offered up a handshake and said, "Thanks, man."

Garbo exited the car with us, telling Proudlock to hang on while he walked us in to the lobby. Before entering the building, we said our goodbyes.

"Garbo, I'm going to miss you so much," I said, giving him a big hug, quickly wiping away tears. Bidding adieu to Garbo was hitting me harder than I'd expected. I saw the same emotion reflected in his face. "Thank you for everything, seriously. You are a wonderful person and I wish you nothing but the best. Really gonna miss you. Please find me someday, when things are normal – we can have a beer!" I added.

Jared looked jealous, but I ignored his sour puss. Garbo squeezed me back, "I'll miss you too, Shelby. YOU take care of yourself, for real girl!" Giving me another hug, he quickly whispered, "Be careful," into my ear, and, for some reason, his tone seemed urgent and pleading, and sent a shudder down my spine. Garbo wouldn't leave me here alone with Jared if I was in REAL danger, would he?

"Thanks, Garb," Jared said, quickly pulling Garbo in for a half-hug and patting him on the back. "I'll take care of Shelby," he added.

"Shelby can take care of herself," he said, winking at us, but, as he bent to pet Pippa, he looked up at me with an intense look.

"Any chance I can just come with you guys?" I said, half-joking.

"What the hell, Shelby, am I that bad?" Jared said, exasperated. He tried to sound like he was joking, but I knew he wasn't. He was irritated at my remark.

"No, I'm so sorry, it's too risky guys," Garbo replied. "Well, I'm off, good luck, I'll miss y'all..." and he quickly planted a friendly kiss on my cheek, then turned and walked towards the green Ford. I silently begged him to turn around and rescue me, but, then again, I didn't want to put him in any danger. Keeping Garbo safe was the least I could do, and I didn't want the consequences of any decisions I'd make from here on out to affect him in any way.

He and Proudlock watched as we entered the building and waited a couple of minutes before driving off. I felt like a piece of my heart was going with them. I'd really grown to care about Garbo and it seemed that every new friend I would make these days would eventually just become a stranger once again. Or die. It broke my heart.

"Shelby, don't talk, let me do all the talking, you're going to carry all of our stuff," he said, handing me his bag.

"Gee, thanks," I replied, and he rolled his eyes.

Ah, marriage.

He rang the bell at the desk and a pale round fellow with an apathetic gaze checked us in.

"My friend here is going to start taking our stuff into the room and unpacking while I check us in," Jared said. "Can we have the key?" he asked.

Doughboy didn't even cast one glance my way, and tossed me a beat up room key on a dingy cat keychain. I let Jared check us in, and headed towards our room, 101A.

As I struggled to unlock the door, I had an alarming revelation: Jared had money! How else would we be staying here?

When he knocked on the door, I let him linger out there for a second. As I stared at him through the peephole, I considered what the hell I was doing, letting this man who was now a practical stranger – who I basically knew nothing about – into my life and now my room. He pounded again. "Let me in!" he hollered. I sighed, and opened the door.

As he closed it behind him, I ripped into him. "You have MONEY? How in the world do you have money? When were you going to tell me? What were you planning on doing with it? How come I didn't know that?" I spat out, in one breath.

"Calm down, Shelby," he said. "Paulie sent us with some cash, I wasn't supposed to tell anyone."

I narrowed my eyes at him and sighed. I had no clue whether or not I should trust him, but, where ever the money came from, it had gotten us a bed for the first time in God knows how long, and so, I was okay with it. Besides, I had my own secrets.

The room was small, unkempt, and old-fashioned. It reeked of stale cigarette smoke, floozy perfume, and cheap booze. The curtains looked like they hadn't been washed in decades, but the bed looked cozy and inviting, except for the person who I would have to share it with.

After inhaling a bowl of water, Pippa found a spot by the register and curled up, snoring happily.

"Well," I said. "Okay. What now?" I asked.

He opened his bag, and pulled out scissors, bleach, and a bottle of vodka. My mouth fell open.

"Where did you get all of THIS?" I asked. I grew fearful. What else did he have in there? What was he planning?

"Bargained with the Captain," he said. "Drop it," he added.

I felt like a prisoner or a kidnappee. Was this a hostage situation? I couldn't be sure. The tension in the air was stifling.

"Let's drink," he suggested. "And do your hair," he added.

"Jared, did you steal this stuff?" I asked, taking a sip of the vodka.

"So what if I did, we'll never see those guys again," he responded, grabbing the bottle back off of me.

"No! Jared! No. What has happened to you? They were good to us!" I asked.

He gave me a boyish grin accompanied by a shrug and a swig.

"What do you mean?" he asked, but his unrelenting and all-consuming charm wouldn't work on me this time.

"You. You aren't the same," I said.

"We've established that," he said.

"No, I don't mean because of your alleged amnesia," I said, rolling my eyes, "I mean just you as a person. Your morals. You never would have stolen from people who were trying to help you, never," I said. "And you never would have…" I trailed off just as he interjected,

"What? What Shelby? I never would have what? And what do you mean, alleged?"

"Give me that," I said, grabbing the vodka and hoping to change the subject.

"Here," he said, thrusting the bottle at me.

"What about you, angel?" he said with a sneer, watching me chug my liquid courage.

"What about me?" I said in a syrupy-sweet, sugar-laced tone, swirling the vodka around the bottle, teasing him both with it and with me, as I licked my lips slowly, intentionally.

"You're bad," he said, his eyes gleaming, and his lids growing heavy. I knew that lusty look – but I wouldn't cave to it, not this time.

"You are," I said firmly.

He sauntered closer to me, in between sips. "You're sick, you know that?" he said. "Twisted." I laughed, wildly.

"What's so funny?" he asked. "I kinda dig it," he added with a little smirk.

"You. You're funny. I am not the sick one," I iterated flippantly, practically spitting the words at him.

His face grew dark. "Okay, Little Miss Mindfuck. Little Miss Cancer," he said.

The words were like a knife through my chest. I'd all but forgotten about the diagnosis that saved/ruined my life, and to hear him throw it at me like an insult was like salt in a wound.

"Oh, you love the attention. Poor little Shelby. Ya know, you think you're perfect," he continued, "you always have. News flash: you're not." His condescending, snarling tone ripped me apart in spite of myself.

"Ouch, Jared," I said. Even though I, at this point, despised him, his words stung nonetheless.

"You're lucky you're the last American woman alive – and you even fuck that up," he said.

"What?" I sputtered. "What do you mean?" I grabbed the bottle angrily and took a long drink. Jared was really asking for it. Our tolerance was low these days, and we were both getting tipsy, which was probably not good.

"You think we ever would have gotten 'married' in normal circumstances? That's what you always wished, huh? That's what you'd tell your little annoying girlfriends and write in your stupid journals?" he said.

His tone was mocking, and the way he used air quotes when he sarcastically said "married," cut like a knife.

"Don't look so deflated," he said. "You know this is just a business arrangement," he added with a wink. It was a punch to the gut, and I had no air left within me.

Speechlessness is foreign to me, yet, there I was, staring at Jared, with gaping mouth and wide, confused eyes that betrayed my tough-girl act and fully displayed my flood of hurt.

He put the lid back on the bottle and tossed it onto the bed.

"Aww, c'mon," he said, as he drunkenly hugged me. I tried to resist.

"Get off of me," I said. "What do you mean, business arrangement?" I asked.

"Oh, come on, you fucked it up for me on purpose, no?" he asked.

"The baby?" I whispered.

"The baby?" he mocked me. "Yes. Your selfish actions cost us our kid, which cost me a lot," he said. "You know there was a bounty on you, right? Money & power will make us all do some crazy shit..."

"Fuck you," I said. I didn't know how else to answer.

"I was never pregnant anyway," I lied. "I told you all, it was my period," I said.

"No, see, it wasn't. You haven't gotten your period since right before your rape, have you?" he asked, stroking my hair.

It sent chills through my body – and not the good kind. I needed to hear him admit it.

"Jared, if I was pregnant, it had to have been Thomas's, I'm sorry. It just couldn't have been yours, I was having symptoms before we ever ... consummated our marriage …" I said, waiting for him to confirm my suspicions so I could justify my behavior.

"We both know it wasn't Thomas's baby. We both know it wasn't Thomas," he said. I froze. Why was he admitting this?

I swallowed hard. It was both what I needed to hear and what I had dreaded all along. I had a choice. I could get hysterical, or I could play the naïve woman. I could forgive him and just move forward. I had to do what I needed to do in order to survive.

"I guess you're right, I could have gotten pregnant after the rape," I said, playing dumb. Before he could correct me, I added, "Let's try again?"

"What?" he asked, looking incredulous at my seeming stupidity.

"Well, you're being an asshole right now because you're exhausted and you've been drinking. You're not making any sense, but I know you love me, and so if I'm going to have a baby, I want it to be yours. God forbid someone finds me and takes me back to the U.S. or someone captures me here – I'd just rather my child be yours," I said. "I still love you, Jared," I added – and for the first time in my entire life, I didn't mean it.

I straddled him before he could respond, and things got hot and heavy pretty quickly. Once I stripped down, carefully hiding Eugene's key in the process, he flipped me on my back and hovered over top of me.

"I don't understand you," he said.

"I never understood you," I replied.

As Jared made hate-love to me, I reached my arm down over the side of the bed and felt his bag on the floor. I navigated my fingertips, quickly finding the scissors, and, just as Jared was about to give in to his passion, I forcefully jammed them into his back.

His eyes grew wide and he screamed out in a mix of pleasure and pain, immediately collapsing on top of me and squeezing his hands around my throat.

I fought it, but at the same time, a part of me welcomed death. Jared was not the man I'd spent my whole life loving and my future seemed bleak. But, if I was going to die, it wasn't going to be at his hands. He'd done enough. In one final thrust of strength I was able to pull the scissors out of his back and push them into his neck.

His grip loosened and his eyes grew wide.

I began to cry heaving sobs, and kissed him on the lips as he took his last breaths. "I am sorry. I did love you," I said. "So much."

"Me too," were his last words, but, I didn't believe him.

I cried for what seemed like hours, but was likely only moments, looking at the lifeless body of my prince, laying in a pool of his own blood. He was dead by my hands. My body was wrecked, the sobs were uncontrollable as I recounted all that had happened in the past couple of days, the past couple of weeks, and the past couple of months. I shook all over, feeling relief and regret. What had I done? Who had I become? I lay next to Jared for a bit, at one point even throwing my arm across his chest, imagining our life of love just one last time.

I envied Jared, as he lay there, no breaths, and no burdens. My saving grace was Pippa, licking my tears and innocently wagging her stubby tail. She was hope. I was free of the baggage that was Jared and now I had a chance to truly start anew. I felt badly about the many things she'd witnessed. But we had a new life to start together. First, I had to keep Pippa away from Jared's corpse. Then, I had to wipe the crime scene.

I knew I had to act fast, though. I watched enough movies and read enough books to know, at least generally, what to do in a situation like this. As I washed his blood off of the scissors, I wondered if I could be considered a serial killer at this point. First Thomas, now Jared. Did two murders a serial killer make? Which heroine was I now? What kind of movie had my life turned into? I said a quick prayer of forgiveness, and said a final goodbye to Jared and my old life. I was prepared for the next chapter and could only wonder what that would entail.

I had no time to ponder. I took the scissors to my long, thinning hair and cut it as short as I could, crying the whole time. Goodbye, hair. Goodbye, Shelby. I then dumped the bleach on my head which burned and stung like crazy; the scent made Pippa whine.

"Shh, girl," I said.

I left the bleach on my scalp for a few moments, until I saw my hair go from brunette to brassy orange to white-blonde. I wondered what to do with Jared's body. Pippa kept trying to investigate and I knew she was going to get rambunctious – we'd have to move as soon as it was dark. After all, she was an animal, and a malnourished one, at that. I struggled to keep her away from Jared while focusing on the other tasks at hand. I couldn't let her cave into her instincts. I couldn't allow her to devour him. He may have deserved that fate, but I had to at least preserve Pippa's goodness, decency, and dignity. She deserved that.

I took a quick shower, the first one in forever. I wished I could enjoy it more, but I couldn't risk the wasted time. I was feeling surprisingly in control. I finished the very last micro-swig of vodka and went through mine and Jared's bags. I had half a sandwich that I shared with Pippa. I found the rest of Jared's money which equaled out to $105. I could work with that. I shoved it in my back pocket once I dressed myself and put the scissors, his knife, and a box of raisins from his bag into my own. In his bag, I also found a map.

"Thank God," I muttered, to no one in particular.

I no longer cared where or how Jared got the money or the vodka or the map. I needed to survive.

The thought of surviving reminded me of the night by the fire, singing along with Eugene and Owen (and Jared before Jared was a monster) and that happy memory suddenly seemed like so long ago. I smiled a smile laced with sadness, and said yet another a little prayer, asking God to forgive me for my actions, to keep Eugene safe, to say hello to Owen and my family and friends up in Heaven, and, for some reason, to have mercy on Jared's soul. I also asked him to keep Pippa and I safe and out of harm's way. I needed to figure out how to get to Switzerland and from what I could tell, it wouldn't be easy, but it seemed that I could take a train. I was bound and determined to do it. This was my new future.

I waited until the wee hours of the night, and left no trace of my presence in the room. After I'd rinsed the bleach from my hair, I'd used the rest of the bottle to disinfect and to wipe away my fingerprints and DNA. Jared's clothes were soaked in the bathtub with water and bleach. I let Pippa have a sip of water and took a deep breath. I then I carefully set fire to the sheets with matches that were left behind in the nightstand drawer. I couldn't believe that for the first time, I was literally and figuratively leaving Jared behind.

I had no idea how long it would take us to get to the rail station or what we may encounter on the way – but I was a brave new girl, and this was a brave new world. I wasn't going to let uncertainty or my fear of the unknown get the best of me. I'd gotten this far.

"Let's go girl," I whispered, and, before closing the door on him for good, said, "Goodbye, Jared." I blew a kiss, and then changed my mind and gave him the finger.

I tiptoed off of the property and then began to run north towards the rail station. My eyes were adjusting to the dark, but I thought I saw a figure leaning up against the car in the distance.

"Great," I thought. "We're caught." It seemed unlikely that the man hadn't seen me, and so hiding wasn't an option. Should I run the other way? I wasn't sure.

As I got closer, I saw that the car was a shade of green and that the figure was – was it? Yes! It was! – "Garbo!" I whispered, excitedly.

I picked up Pippa and began to run towards him.

"Garbo!" I said.

"Hurry up," he said. "Get in," and he threw my bag into the car, ushering us in.

"Garbo, what are you doing? How did you know?" I asked.

"Shelby, we all had suspicions of Jared for a while. When you told me that you tried to kill yourself on the boat, I knew something was very wrong, and I didn't like the way he acted around you," he said. "I – I also went through your stuff when you were asleep the other night, after I rescued you," he said, embarrassed. "Shelby, I saw the note from Neil."

I gasped. "Oh, Garbo! You knew!"

"I knew. But I didn't know how to tell you because after that, Jared was by your side every second. I explained to Proudlock that I had to come help you, and he understood, I was just hoping that when I saw you leave that place that you were alone – well, you and Pippa," he said. "I knew you could take care of yourself, at least temporarily" he added. "You're one tough lady."

"I..." I began, not knowing what to say. A part of me was mad that the had let me go to begin with, or that he hadn't come sooner, but most of all, I was just grateful that he came at all.

"We don't have to talk about it. I'm just going to get you out of here," he said, squeezing my hand.

"Good," I said.

I began to cry, silently, tears of joy, and gratitude, and remorse, and exhuastion. I was shocked and shaken by what I'd done and questions remained when it came to matters of my sanity. I looked at the smoke in the rearview mirror and felt a shudder through my body.

"Thank you, thank you, thank you," I said, and I meant it.

"Music?" he asked.

"Oh my gosh, yes!" I replied enthusiastically. It was amazing how much one could miss the little details of life – music, for example.

He cranked up some Radiohead and I watched the night sky as we drove towards the train station, finally feeling whole and leaving the past behind.

Chapter 29

Garbo handed me $500, cash. I gasped.

"Garbo, I can't..." I said.

"Shelby, you have to," he said with a gentle smile.

"Also, here's my niece's old fake ID," he said, handing me an ID of a blonde woman named Barbara Marie Dhali.

"So, may name could be Barbie Dhali?" I asked, making the first joke I'd made in a long time.

He laughed, "I'm glad to see you this full of light after...everything," he said.

"So I can use this?" I asked.

"For now," he said. "It was the fake my niece used before she turned 21. She could get into bars and buy liquor, but I wouldn't try to get a home loan or anything like that," he said with a laugh.

I felt nervous.

"I'm scared," I said. "I don't know what to do."

"Barbie, I assume you're going to Switzerland for a reason," he said. I gave an almost imperceptible nod. "Do your business, and find a place far off in the countryside. Stay disconnected. Life will be lonely for a while. Just stay on the down-low until stuff blows over – if stuff blows over. And look at it this way – anything will seem better than what we'd left behind."

He had a point. In fact, a country home, with just Pippa and me, sounded like heaven. Ignoring the world. Just us two.

"Wait – Pippa?" I said, suddenly alarmed. How would I take her on the train?

"Ah – hold on," he said, and popped the trunk.

"Madame," he said, bowing to Pippa and placing a dog carrier in front of her, which she sniffed and examined excitedly.

"You've thought of everything," I said. "You're my angel," I added, and gave him a hug.

"One more thing," he added, and popped open the glove compartment, placing a small pistol in my hand.

"This was my sister's. Semi-automatic pocket pistol. We always kid her about it because of how tiny it is, and the pink stripe on it, but it'll get the job done. It's loaded, be sure to keep the safety on, and I put a pack of bullets in your bag. Do not shoot yourself," he added with a smile. "Seriously, Barbie Dhali. Please."

"No worries, Garbo. Seriously, thank you so much, you are great. Are you sure you don't want to come along?" I asked.

He looked sad. "I can't. Not yet. I have to help Proudlock protect my girls," he said, referring to his half-sister and niece. "It's just where I belong," he said. "But I'll visit!" he added.

I knew he wouldn't.

"You won't know where to find me," I said.

"Once this all blows over, I won't ever stop looking," he replied, and suddenly, a wave of regret washed over me. Why couldn't I have spent my life loving a man like Garbo?

"You'd better get going," he continued. "Get your ticket and get out of here ASAP. This train goes to Zurich. It'll take a good 7 hours or so. While you're on the train, figure out where in Switzerland you're heading towards. If you need to, once you get to Zurich, you can get the next train to Zug. Again, just be safe and stay on the DL until you're settled into a place far away from civilization," he said. "You don't need an ID for this rail, don't draw attention to yourself, try to act like a guy, keep your face covered like you're asleep. Don't talk to anyone. Keep Pippa's crate on the seat next to you and mind your own. In Switzerland, the situation isn't nearly as bad. There's barely any situation to speak of, save for some threats. They're pretty chill. You can be a girl there. Haha. They're neutral and they stay out of everything," he added, half-joking. "P.S., Shel, I mean, Barb, learn some German."

I was terrified, but I couldn't let him see it. Now was the time for me to truly be my own heroine. I put on a brave face and said, "Wow, thanks. Garbo, I really hope I see you again sometime."

"Me too," he said. I shuddered, recalling Jared's identical last words, but, looking at Garbo, I realized that the past was in the past and my future was comparatively bright.

He gave me a hug goodbye, and, to his surprise, I planted a soft, sweet, friendly kiss right on his lips. "Thanks again," I said, and began to walk towards the ticketing counter.

"Hey," he called after me. "Try Appenzell," he hollered.

"Appenzell?" I repeated.

"Find a small, quiet place, outside of Appenzell," he said.

I smiled. "Okay," I said, waving goodbye to Garbo, and to my sordid existence.

"I'll wait for your visit!" I called out to him.

"Yup," he said, beaming. "Good luck!"

I bought the tickets for Pippa and myself, and boarded the train.

As we pulled away from the station some time later, I saw my problems getting smaller and farther away. My mind already felt more clear, more calm, and more sane. I could breathe again.

I didn't know what the future held for the rest of the world, or for the existence of America, or for women, but I somehow felt in my heart that I would be safe. I knew that it was wrong for me to run away and to keep to myself, but I felt as though it was my only option. Cancer or not, woman or not, murderer or not...I knew, with every ounce of my being that, somehow, some way, that I would be okay. I couldn't have said that even one day ago. I couldn't risk that on the off chance that I may possibly be some kind of antidote, or some kind of savior. The guilt would weigh on me forever, surely, and at some point, I might change my mind. But, for now, this is what I needed to do: I needed to take care of me.

A conflicted heroine, and her little dog, too. That was my character. A flawed badass with a soft spot. A sinful sometime-believer. A living, breathing contradiction.

I would forget the past, forget my sins, and forget the life to which I'd bid adieu. I would refresh my perspective, and focus my mind. I would rebuild myself, create a new identity, and dive in to a new future. I knew that there were no guarantees, and I knew that I'd still have a lot of struggles ahead. And maybe, maybe someday I'd be able to use what I'd discovered for good. But for now I'd be content on just doing me.

After all, I had all the time in the world.

Epilogue

"Barbara, visitor!" my secretary hollered at me over her tortoiseshell glasses.

Instead of tensing up with fear like I used to, the words brought with them an abundance of warmth. I practically sprinted to the door.

"Garbo!" I said, throwing my arms around my handsome friend. I had never, ever been so happy to see someone.

"Sh..Barbara!" he said, laughing at his near slip-up.

"It's about damn time," I said.

"I know, I know," he said, almost bashfully.

"Wer ist das, Fräulein?" my girls chorused curiously.

Garbo glanced at me, eyebrow raised.

"Studenten, das ist mein Freund, Garbo!" I announced, in choppy Swiss-German.

"Ooooh!" they all said, and I blushed.

"I may or may not have said you were my boyfriend," I explained.

"Accidentally," I quickly added, feeling a familiar blush spread across my cheeks.

"Friend, friend!" I yelled at the girls. "Barre!" I said, and they all sprinted to the ballet barre.

"Look at you," he said with a smile. "Teachin' ballet. Who would have thought it?"

"Oh, Garbo, I love it! I'm a new person," I said.

"Indeed," he said, looking me up and down, appreciatively.

Twelve long years had passed since our hell on earth. It simultaneously seemed like just yesterday but also like an eternity ago. Shelby Weiss seemed like a character in a movie, who I'd lived and loved but, as I'd matured, discarded.

Of course, there were times when my heart ached thinking about Davis and Daphne and Tamra; of my parents; of Eugene and Owen and Paulie and the guys; of all the tragedy we'd endured; and yes, I grew sad and angry when I thought of being raped, when I thought of my suicide attempt and my miscarriage, and when I recalled killing Thomas and Jared, but, overall, I finally felt like the strong and empowered women I'd so often written about. The haunting scars of the past lived deep within me but did not define me. Most importantly, I was happy. I felt free. I had faith. I wasn't living in my head so much. I was enjoying life and living in the present – something that, even before all that happened, I had rarely taken the time to do.

I wasn't a movie star or an Oscar-winning screenwriter, but, I was making a happy living and had a happy life here in a little town outside of Appenzell, Switzerland. I had a modest home, and a few friends, a fat cat, and Pippa was still alive and kickin' at 16 years old. (In fact, she was the "mascot" at our village dance studio!)

"How are you? You look great," he said.

"I feel great," I replied.

"Yeah? No cancer?" he asked.

"To be honest with you, I don't even know. I don't want to know. I've not seen any doctors since before that clinical trial, but, I haven't had any symptoms, and

I've been feeling fine. I've been taking lots of herbal supplements, drinking lots of tea, eating clean, and living a simple, quiet lifestyle. I'm happy. I feel good, and, whether it is still active or not, in some weird twisted way that cancer may have saved my life, and, I'm finally at a place now where I can appreciate that," I said. "Over twelve years since I was diagnosed, so, I'd say I'm doing something right!" I'd heard stories of people living with malignant tumors for years, and of people surpassing life expectancies and overcoming dire prognoses all the time. Now, I was one of those people, and I was content in my state of ignorant bliss when it came to my health.

"That's great. I'm so happy for you. I can't wait to catch up even more, but I'll let you get back to your class. Mind if I watch?" he asked.

"Not at all!" I said.

I often thought about the events that the world had seen in the past 12 years as I looked at the innocent faces of the girls in my class. They had all the time in the world in front of them, and many were so young that they didn't know about the uprising and the takedown of MARF, about that powerful country that was once called America, and the terrible things that happened to it. They didn't know what women had endured all throughout parts of the world, and didn't know how lucky they and their mothers and sisters were to be spared. They didn't know that, just a few months after settling in Appenzell, I anonymously donated samples of blood for research to help combat MARF's chemical warfare. They didn't understand how peace had come nor did they recognize that peace had ever left, but someday, they'd learn about it at school. I just prayed that they would never have to endure the hell that we'd been put through, but I asked God to give them the strength to endure it if they ever did.

I never shared my whole story with them. I told them that I'd moved here from a land far, far away. They thought I was a queen or a princess of some exotic place. I'd hear the young ones giggling about it and making up stories. I was glad that they didn't know the unstable anti-heroine that was Shelby Weiss. To them, I was a pretty lady with a funny accent who walked straight into their lives from a fairy tale. To them, I was special, or magic, someone famous or important. Though it was funny now, at one point in time, I kind of was. But now, I was average. I was normal. Ironically, "average and normal" was an existence that I used to bemoan. Now, I thank God for a normal life, every day, for at any given time, we don't know how many of those days we have left.

We may have had "all the time in the world," but now, finally, I was content to just … exist.

www.ingramcontent.com/pod-product-compliance
Lightning Source LLC
Chambersburg PA
CBHW022135170626
46807CB00005B/1946

* 9 7 8 0 6 9 2 6 7 4 0 4 8 *